THE SINGING BONES

A Novel of the Life and Times of Naturalist
Georg Wilhelm Steller

Stephen Spotte

Published by Open Books

Copyright © 2019 by Stephen Spotte

Interior design by Siva Ram Maganti

ISBN-13: 978-1948598224

For the northern fur seals and Steller's sea lions (*in perpetuum*), and the spectacled cormorants and Steller's sea cows (*in memoria*)

If every species constructs for itself a different world, which is the world?

N. Kathryn Hayles

Sunday the 10ᵀᴴ of March in the year 1709 holds a special place for me. On the morning of that day I was born dead. The stillborn child didn't twitch or take a breath. I speak of him in the third person because my spirit had departed, and I was nothing but mortal remains.

He was placed mute and motionless on a dressing table in his family's house in the free city of Windsheim, Franconia, 34 miles west of Nürnberg. While his mother lay in childbed weeping softly the rest of the family left the room to pray. The midwife, refusing to relinquish him to death's grip, stayed behind and burned sulfur beside his nose hoping to induce a cough. When that failed she wrapped his quiescent little body in hot blankets, changing them often as they cooled. After a couple of hours he emitted a loud squall and recovered completely. It was a miracle. The family, hearing his cry, rushed to the bedroom, where everyone wept and prayed, and his father raised his arms heavenward and shouted, "Praise be to God for His eternal mercy!"

My parents named me Georg Wilhelm Stöhler in honor of the burgomaster of Windsheim, my godfather. I was the family's second child of that name, an eponymous older brother having died in October 1706, just short of age 2 years.

The head of our household, born Johannes Jacob Stöhler in Nürnberg, was cantor at the gymnasium (Latin school) of the nearby Lutheran Church of St. Killian, where he also served as organist. Jacob Stöhler, the name he was known by, was a widower with a son, Maximilian Philipp Jacob, when he married my mother, Susanna Louysa Baumann from Würtemberg, a year after his first wife's death. The first wife's name had been Anna Regina, and she died at age 32. Maximilian was 15 when I was born and moved to Nürnberg to study music when I was age 4. He died in 1717, and I never really knew him.

Johann Augustin was my parents' first child and my full brother, born 3 March 1703, 6 years before me. We called him Augustin, and he was the only sibling I was close to and with whom I stayed in intermittent contact as an adult. Between our births came the first Georg Wilhelm (December 1704) and Johann Friedrich (December 1706). After me, at intervals of roughly 2 years, three sisters arrived followed by three more brothers. All of us survived childhood. The fact that Vater seemed unable to keep his hands off our mother nearly led to fucking himself out of a place at the dining table.

My family could be described as lower middle-class and obviously fecund, the social status and dignity accorded a cantor (his position allowed him to carry a sword) being incommensurate with such a meager salary in light of his many duties. In addition to cantor and church organist he instructed boys enrolled in the lower grades in various subjects.

Of Mutter I recall very little, except she was sturdy, somber, and harried, always pushing the hair out of her face. I often wondered why she didn't cut it or confine it under a scarf to make that movement unnecessary. I kept my opinion silent, of course. Ours was a raucous household. The only peace she probably found was while sleeping, and even then we must have disrupted and addled her dreams.

Vater flitted through our lives like a misplaced soul, skinny, frantic, head topped with a sandy mop of frizzy hair. He seemed always on the move and confused about the timing of his next task, whether tutoring the gymnasium boys or pumping the enormous organ in St. Killian's and transmitting praise to God through his favorite hymn, Luther's own composition, *Ein feste Burg ist unser Gott*. That God is a mighty fortress was perhaps his favorite metaphor, and it rang forever in my head like an irritating case of tinnitus.

At supper he fidgeted and jerked, not infrequently dropping his cutlery on the floor while waving it about emphasizing God's displeasure for grubby little sinners like us. At meals and during other family times when we gathered he prattled endlessly about faith, inculcating us to obey the Lord's Word in all matters and never utter His name in vain or we would certainly fry in Hell. From across the table Augustin would give me a sly look and raise his eyebrows almost imperceptibly, lips in a subtle smile. I couldn't look at him without laughing, so I concentrated on my plate, pretending to study its contents.

In the park on the day of my birth the last remnants of snow have melted, although a few patches cling stubbornly to shady places and overhangs in the rocky landscape. The weather is cold, wet, and unpleasant, but a few pedestrians nonetheless stroll along the cobblestone walk of the public park, bundled and hunched against a driving sleet still undecided whether to surrender to rain and accept spring.

Green is appearing everywhere: on the grassy berms and mossy boulders around the pond, in the scrolled violin-necks of ferns already ankle-high. A flock of resident greylag geese, semi-tame, has cropped the winter grass until it looks carefully mown. The geese eat nothing else, and no one feeds them. Rooks in their somber black plumage stalk the rooftops and call out in raspy voices. They now have company: colorful songbirds newly arrived from the south probe the tree bark for insects and scratch for worms in the softening earth.

At night the geese sleep restlessly, nervously, floating on the pond safe from foxes and other terrestrial predators including some humans who would gladly wring their necks and convert them into featherless Sunday dinners surrounded by onions and carrots and roasted slowly in wood-fired ovens. And why not? The park is public property. No one would protest if you, one of those casual strollers, wanted to capture a fat goose and take it home for supper. The geese recognize their status as prey and by means of internal calculations keep a certain distance. They honk as you approach and waddle down to the water. If you follow too close behind they break into an awkward, rolling run.

I remember the geese clearly and also Herr Krause, an old man with a bushy white moustache and yellow teeth. He sat on one of the benches facing the pond, smoking his pipe and watching, eyes magnified and vaguely disturbed behind his thick glasses. I would see him every morning on my way to school. Once he stopped me and patted the space on the bench beside him, indicating I should sit. When I did he said quietly, "Can you hear it, boy?"

"Hear what, sir?"

"Her bones," he said. "Last week she was barely humming, but today she's singing softly."

"Who, sir?" I said, straining to hear music.

"Nature. Spring is here, and her bones are singing."

"I hear birds singing," I said.

He looked directly at me, eyes serious and huge. "The birds are only some of it. You must tune your ears to pick up the full symphony. The appearance of birds and leaves are evidence of nature's flesh, but her bones are her strength and character. These are the trees, rocks, and earth, even the pond. Her bones are everywhere underground and above. They sleep quietly enough through winter, but awake in spring and regain flesh. You notice their presence as the ground thaws and the days lengthen. Then leaves and birds appear; insects are in the air. Rocks warm in the sun, and frogs bellow from the reeds. These are the sounds of transient flesh. To discern the timeless melody that underlies all this takes patience. Anyone can hear it by listening carefully, but few bother. Try and you'll find out. Now, get along to your lessons."

Childhood memories filtered through time's mist are notoriously unreliable, but as I recall Herr Krause turned and looked again at the scene before us, a placid pond imprisoned by rocky ledges. On its surface gliding geese disrupted and wrinkled one another's shadows, sending their fractured remnants scurrying outward. I wondered what Herr Krause was experiencing that I couldn't. I was rising to leave when suddenly the world turned strange, and I sat back down. Submerged in the bird twitters and new leaves stirred to faint shivers came a different sound, barely perceptible, close yet far away, an atonal blend of pitch and rhythm like a distant buzzing of bees, although not exactly. It was more a sensation than anything else. It descended from the sky and rose simultaneously out of the ground; it emerged from the trees and rocks and moved sinuously through the air as if seeking something. I absorbed it into myself, feeling it penetrate my bones and rush through the marrow until I tingled all over. I was at once euphoric and calm as if suddenly given a great gift. This could only be nature's singing bones resonating in synchrony with my own until our separate harmonies ceased to be discordant.

Every morning afterward I sat for a few minutes with Herr Krause on his bench. Neither of us ever spoke to the other again, each privately harboring a common secret. Then one day he wasn't there. I asked Vater, who said God's angels had come and taken him to Heaven. We would meet him in good time, but never again see him in the flesh. The soul, he reminded me, lives forever, but the flesh is mutable.

From then on I never stopped listening to the fugue of nature's immutable bones. I gave everything to describing her flesh in words that were always inadequate. In the vast, crescive silence of Siberian winters I could hear her rhythmic breathing beneath the tundra and deep in the dark earth of implacable forests. I felt her shuddering exhalations levitate at the feet of slumbering trees waiting for spring. Nature preparing to yawn and stretch, tuning her bones to the metronomic drip of melting ice, anticipating that singular morning when a gun-metal haze replaces perpetual night, and the world awakes.

I never understood how or why I can hear the singing bones when others hear nothing, or what drives me to examine every object in my path, urging me to note its intricacies, its color and form, to pause and listen to its unique melody. Perhaps what I feel is only the transient thrill of discovery reinforced by addictive waves of excitement, a sense of feeling lightheaded, as if at high altitude. Acting alone and without direction the hand reaches for the pen to quickly record observations before they evaporate from memory. Nothing about this "strange malady," as Augustin good-naturedly called it, ever changed, and I grew to adulthood still insatiably seeking the mysteries nature sometimes reveals on close examination. If this is an artifact of childhood, as some detractors have told me, then the child will never age.

Years later in one of his letters Augustin wrote that the park had disappeared, consumed by a creeping neighborhood of immigrants. Their language, he said, is incomprehensible, like the jabbering of unfamiliar birds. However, as the old German residents die and young ones take their places the immigrants seem to them increasingly less strange, almost as if they were becoming Germans. The offspring of both cultures now mingle and play together in the streets, and he wondered whether these children of our own race believe the immigrants have always been here.

And the park. . . yes, the park. Who recalls an empty space populated only by natural things? Very few. People are social creatures; they tend to remember buildings, shops, markets, churches, utilitarian artifacts of their own creation. Now, Augustin reported, even many of these have been replaced by other structures as fires and the changing times demanded. But what has disappeared permanently is what no one remembers: the space once containing benches and towering linden trees that cooled and humidified the hot, dry days of summer. The linden isn't only a superior shade tree, it symbolizes all things good about humanity. Who suspected such qualities as love and fertility, prosperity, loyalty, friendship, and kindness could be embodied in cellulose and lignin? Now the lindens and their silent wisdom are gone.

2

As a boy I slept in an iron bed decorated with twisted vines, some having attained a patina of rust giving them the illusion of life. The mattress stuffed with lumpy cotton and old rags sagged in places from lack of enough boards underneath to keep it suspended evenly in its frame. Augustin and Friedrich had their own beds in the same room. In winter the only heat was what rose meagerly from the first floor.

Our parents slept in the bedroom next to ours, and in the night we could hear Vater shouting, "Praise to God in Heaven!" as he ejaculated, followed by a series of hallelujahs of diminishing volume as his squirts attenuated to dribbles. Finally, the headboard stopped banging against the wall. After Augustin explained to me what was happening and that Vater wasn't just praying enthusiastically I pictured copulating dogs and squirrels and Mutti lying on her back with legs spread, silent and patient, waiting for Vater to finish and hoping the sum of his prayers had been expressed openly and he wasn't holding back an unspoken request for another child. She would have too many, and we would wring her dry.

Augustin was no taller than other boys his age, but he seemed so to me. He told he would be a doctor someday, perhaps a personal physician in service to a dowager princess or even the court in Berlin. He had big plans. Maybe I would be that too. I said I didn't want to serve anyone. I couldn't express the feeling it gave me, but a mix of frustration and anger. I said I wanted to be an explorer and a naturalist, to see new lands, new plants and animals no naturalist had seen before. He laughed. "That would be fine too, Georg Wilhelm. Now, the trousers of mine that Mutter gave you are still a little big, so try these instead.

I was close to your age when I last wore them." True to his dreams, Augustin trained in medicine and later served as court physician to several dukes and duchesses.

Augustin had the kindness and temperament to be a fine physician, and he had frequent occasions to practice on me during our youth. The local fields and forests contained mammals such as badgers, foxes, river otters, wild boars, even wildcats. These last resemble gray tabby housecats with fluffier tails. The nearby Schlossbach Municipal Forest was famous for its enormous colony of European gray herons. Of other birds most of the central European species were represented in the surrounding woods and fields, notably the capercailzie and blackcock. Then there was the Aisch River with its finny treasures. All presented opportunities to stalk nature and injure myself. I regularly fell from trees and slipped on rocks while attempting to catch crayfish and aquatic insect larvae in local streams. I occasionally cut myself while skinning birds and small mammals captured in homemade traps. And the thought of finding a new plant could send me rushing out the door to trip blindly on a cobblestone.

"It's unseemly for a man to cry," said Augustin while dressing a cut on my knee. I must have been eight or nine. "Except when praising God or grieving the death of a loved one. Women and children are permitted to weep, but not men."

"But I'm a child," I protested.

"No, Georg Wilhelm, you're a man in a child's body and crying a child's tears, a man who will someday do great things. Now dry your face. This salve will take away the sting. And you've muddied your good shoes. Vater won't be pleased. Don't worry, I'll clean them for you and polish the buckles." He looked at me and smiled.

"I was in a tree chasing a beetle, and when I reached for it I fell."

"Don't climb so high next time. Let the beetle go. There'll be others."

"Maybe not like this one."

Augustin rose to this feet and looked down at me sitting on the edge of my bed. "Oh-ho, a new species? How can you tell?"

"I can't, but I was going to take it to a museum and ask some professor there."

"And then what?"

"Maybe the professor will name it in honor of me, and then I'll be a famous naturalist." The implausibility of this notion made us both laugh.

My teachers at the gymnasium had no interest in natural history, leaving me to my own devices. Students and faculty spoke only Latin in the halls and classrooms, and a library copy of Dioscorides' *De materia medica* and a few minor Latin texts helped fuel my love of plants and show the order in their relationships, but my education in this area was entirely self-directed.

At age 20 I delivered an oral valediction, graduating from the gymnasium at the top of the class and immediately accepting a public scholarship to further my higher education. Vater, you see, was too poor to pay tuition. On Sunday, 25 September 1729, I left home for the University of Wittenberg and officially matriculated 5 days later. The intention was to study theology. I expected to be gone 2 years and return an ordained Lutheran preacher, but fate intervened and except for Augustin I never saw or heard from my family again.

Wittenberg was a noted center of Lutheranism, but I found the curriculum rife with bigotry and unpleasantly entrenched in a stony orthodoxy that left no space for disagreement or even discussion. I took advantage of opportunities to preach in the surrounding communities, but my sermons received poor marks from the professors, who expected a more positive projection of personal rectitude and dynamic proselytizing about Pietism, a recent offshoot of Lutheranism becoming fashionable at Wittenberg. This new creed held that being a devout Christian was inadequate; living a demonstrably pious life every waking hour was also necessary. I felt such an additional burden on a populace already squashed like insects under the heavy boot of Protestant guilt left too little time for other thoughtful pursuits. As a consequence I sensed my interest in theology evaporating, increasingly replaced by an innate fascination for the study of natural things. Although I accepted natural phenomena as God's works, I was nonetheless curious to learn how He enacted them. Surely there were physical causes within the purview of humankind to investigate and ultimately understand.

Disgruntled by religious studies I switched to philosophy, which is secular and emphasized logical reasoning, a necessary skill when assessing nature's puzzles objectively. As to natural history itself, Wittenberg offered few opportunities to acquire formal knowledge other than the *hortus medicus* (apothecary garden), where I often went alone to study the plants, notebook in hand. There was also an anatomical theater that was used intermittently. There I joined the medical students in their dissections of human cadavers when these became available, and we furthered our anatomical investigations when they weren't by dissecting and examining domestic and wild animals under guidance of the medical professors.

Augustin was a big influence in my life at this time. He had obtained his *doctor medicinae* degree, married, and was living comfortably and working in Köthen. I visited occasionally, and we discussed possible careers for me. He emphasized the advantages of becoming a physician. I liked studying medicine and wished to learn all I could about it, although I had no interest in becoming a practicing clinician. My aspiration was a professorship in botany at a prestigious university with opportunities to lecture and conduct research. I also had a desire to explore the natural histories of new lands and study strange peoples and their languages and cultures. To become a competent naturalist would require better training, an important part of which was preparing formal taxonomic descriptions accompanied by appropriate illustrations.

Since childhood I had wanted to draw natural objects and tried many times, but never demonstrated the aptitude. How rewarding to both describe in words and illustrate my future discoveries! I became inspired to try again after attending a modest display of drawings and paintings by Wittenberg art students. The makeshift gallery was a popular café near the campus where a few dozen unframed works had been pinned to the walls.

There were the usual vases of flowers and bowls of fruit, but among them was a startling painting of a North American skunk. The artist had presented his subject in a few simple strokes employing only black paint on white canvas. The animal was depicted walking aggressively toward the viewer, head down, short legs bowed to the side, its form and movement captured perfectly. The bushy tail, achieved in two strokes, curved away to the left. Another graceful line, not even finished, beautifully caught the curve of the back. The distinctive break where a white stripe extends longitudinally against the black fur was indicated by two simple lines. Head and ears were interrupted curves, mere hints of shape and form, the eyes just flicks of the brush. In place of redundant detail the artist had defined the essence of his subject by omission, framing empty spaces for the viewer's eye and mind to fill. The entire presentation was simple and elegant, so much so as to seem impossible, and in that exquisite simplicity, ineluctably true.

The work was unsigned and appeared to have been dashed off in a few minutes. I asked the name of the artist, but no one knew. The sketch had mysteriously appeared on the wall when those responsible for the exhibit were looking elsewhere. The other works were labored and unimaginative in comparison. *This* was an artist, convincingly showing nature's essence in less than a dozen brush strokes. The interpretation had been flawless. He was obviously a man who had deeply observed the natural world and penetrated its soul.

My goal became to write as this obscure genius wielded his brush. Naturalists, I was learning, deploy words like mathematicians use their numbers, with accuracy and precision: nothing wasted, nothing entered into the equation that isn't an integral component of the solution. Words are signs substituting for something tangible. They represent and therefore must be understood and interpreted in the same way by disparate readers. Mainly for this reason naturalists write descriptions in Latin, a universal language.

Inspired by that presentation of a skunk, I tried once again to draw. Back in my room I took pen in hand and pretended it was a brush and I was making a passable representation of what my eyes saw, but no matter how diligently I practiced the lines were never satisfactory facsimiles of the mental pictures I held. I would always require an illustrator. That iconic image pinned carelessly to a café wall would stay with me forever, resonating in memory like a persistent spirit.

I vowed that my written descriptions would never be vague or unintelligible. The number of words is immense, their possible combinations nearly infinite. In contrast, the number of words available to me, those I can snatch from the air at any moment and arrange into sentences, is limited. What I write in literary terms will always be ordinary because the naturalist seeks to shrink language and make it more exact, not expand it and stimulate the reader's imagination to soar. The language of the naturalist has to keep the reader grounded and focused; by necessity it must be commonplace, even boring. Transparency is the objective: you want the reader to see directly through your words to the object itself, undistracted by superfluous and misleading adjectives and metaphors intended to divert the eyes and mind from reality. Only straightforward declarative sentences composed of words having the same meaning to every naturalist can provide an unambiguous description. Lacking all capacity to draw, this would have to be my objective: to "paint" my future skunks using words like brush strokes, making them clean and bold, minimal, exact, and timeless.

3

My scholarship at Wittenberg ended on schedule, and it was time to explore studies with professors elsewhere who looked benevolently on the natural world and were less inclined to divert their gazes heavenward. I visited the universities of Leipzig, Jena, and Halle, all with fine reputations and any of them suitable. Halle was famous for its religious freedom and encouraging open discussion and debate. It was also where Augustin had obtained his medical degree. It's faculty seemed the most enlightened. Professor Friedrich Hoffmann, then age 70, lectured in botany there, and he remembered Augustin. He was one of the most famous and respected medical experts in Europe.

I matriculated at Halle in 1731 and soon came under Professor Hoffmann's favor and friendship. He fostered my growing interest in moving to a primitive land as yet unreached by Europe's intellectual frontier, but was too busy to mentor me directly, being pulled in many directions because of his fame and expertise. The botanical garden had been neglected for years, and again I was left to study plants on my own using books in the university library. To support myself I obtained an adjunct teaching position in the *Waisenhaus* (orphanage) for which the university had become famous. Benefits included tuition and the opportunity and freedom to attend any and all lectures and demonstrations.

My duties as an instructor at the *Waisenhaus* provided room and board, and for those who taught extra hours, beer and better meals. My performance, however, was meeting with growing criticism from the higher-highers in whose collective opinion my lessons were mediocre,

I was too severe with the boys and too quick to lose my temper, and my piety was becoming suspect.

My foremost interests—botany and zoology—were medical tools, not separate disciplines, botany because the drugs available were derived from plants, zoology because it augmented the study of human anatomy. But things were different at Halle, thanks to Dr. Johann Friedrich Cassebom, a professor of medicine and a superb and far-thinking anatomist who became among the first to approach at least zoology as a separate science, holding classes under the rubric "zootomical disquisition(s)" and giving demonstrations not just on human anatomy but that of other mammals too, along with birds, fishes, amphibians, even insects. These lessons later benefited me enormously when isolated in the Siberian wilderness equipped with only knife and notebook and confronted with dissecting and writing descriptions of animals and their anatomies that no naturalist before me had ever seen.

Professor Hoffmann recognized the University of Halle's need for a professor of botany to start a program emulating Professor Cassebom's aimed at broadening the education of physicians in training. Despite having accepted a faculty position at Halle, Professor Hoffmann had remained confidant and physician to King Friedrich Wilhelm the First and still retained his title as *Royal Leibmedicus*. From this lofty position he offered to petition on my behalf for a new botany professorship at Halle. It was widely known that King Friedrich Wilhelm maintained a keen interest in university matters and considered faculty appointments his personal privilege and responsibility.

The professor obviously had the king's ear. My prospects could not have been more promising, although with Friedrich Wilhelm nothing was ever certain. His eccentricities were famous, not just in Prussia but throughout Europe. Probably no contemporary ruler was less predictable.

Following Professor Hoffmann's advice, in August 1734 I traveled to the *Obercollegium medicum* in Berlin and sat for a qualifying examination in botany under the famed plant expert Dr. Michael Matthias Ludolf. A certificate of expertise granted by a naturalist of Dr. Ludolf's stature could be a large step toward the professorship I sought. I passed the examination with honors and attained the certificate. While awaiting the king's decision I began giving lectures in botany at Halle starting 1 May 1732. The medical students received them enthusiastically and put much-needed reichsthalers in my pocket.

The king, who had suffered throughout his life from porphyria, took a sudden downward spiral. His urine, Professor Hoffmann told me, was again purple when left to stand a while at room temperature. No doubt, the professor added slyly, a color befitting the royal status of His Highness. My appointment and all other matters on the professor's docket slipped into abeyance when he was ordered to Berlin to bleed and otherwise attend the king for what was to be 5 months.

Friedrich Wilhelm was a notably difficult man, not unlike Peter the Great whose name I was to hear often after emigrating to Russia. He and Peter had been political and military allies. Friedrich Wilhelm was the son of King Friedrich, and when he took the throne of Prussia in 1713 he became King Friedrich Wilhelm the First. He was eccentric, shrewd, and despised whatever his father had admired, including anything French. He even ordered criminals to be dressed in French fashions before hanging them. His inherited porphyria probably accounted for much of his erratic behavior, such as spontaneously attacking and beating anyone near him with his cane, including his children, whom he often chased in a rage in and out of rooms through the palace. Mostly he craved military power and to this end poured most of Prussia's resources into an army and the infrastructure necessary to maintain it, measures Peter endorsed and encouraged.

For a monarch Friedrich Wilhelm lived frugally. The exception was splurging on his hobby of collecting giants. His agents throughout Europe were always on the lookout for men taller than 6 feet, hiring them, buying them, even kidnapping them if they declined to join his special regiment of grenadiers. This hobby wasn't cheap: an Irishman standing 7 feet 2 inches had cost more than 6,000 English pounds. The king dressed his acquisitions in colorful military uniforms and divided them into two battalions of 600 each.

Wary of incurring too much expense, Friedrich Wilhelm decided to breed his own race of giants, forcing his grenadiers to marry tall women. The anxiety of waiting for their progeny to be born and mature was often paired with disappointment when they were girls, or boys who grew to ordinary height. He put out word that he would accept gifts of giants as a way of currying favor. Peter subsequently sent him 50 from Russia, delighted to have found a fellow monarch with a similar hobby: being himself a giant standing 6 feet 7 inches, Peter collected dwarfs.

When ill in bed from porphyria's ravages or simply despondent, Friedrich Wilhelm rallied by playing with his giant soldiers, which he never sent into actual battle for fear of them being wounded or killed. The combined battalions dressed in full regalia were ordered to march through his chambers led by towering Moors wearing robes and turbans and playing cymbals and trumpets. Following just behind them and walking upright was the regiment's mascot, a gigantic trained bear.

This was the man on whom my professional advancement depended, and despite Professor Hoffmann's influence his frugality extended to creating new professorships. Time passed without my petition coming before him. Hopes fading, it was time to consider other career choices. Remaining a student and eventually attaining a medical degree were not among them despite the security of permanent employment. I had no appetite for my brother's staid profession and bourgeois life, comfortable and predictable though it would be. In addition, faculty politics, first at Wittenberg and then Halle, had begun to sour any interest in academia. Professor Hoffmann's kind and patient mentoring, intermittent though it was, I viewed as an exception.

By and large, university faculty members are self-centered pricks, interested in little except their own prestige and advancement; the students' needs and interests are secondary. Surely this was a peculiarity of German universities. Such was my naïve thinking then. As I was to learn in Russia, political backstabbing and internal strife are inherently part of any institution or bureaucracy. At any rate, now was the right moment to seek a job overseas, to make a clean start and leave Europe behind. After 2 years at Wittenberg and 3 more at Halle I had not taken a degree in any subject despite having qualified in theology, medicine, and natural history. I was 25 and nearly destitute.

THE LURE OF FARAWAY places was difficult to ignore. Imagine a time when the world was too big, its enormity so frightening that the thought of venturing into its terrible void made strong men shiver; a time when Earth's limits were infinite, like Heaven and Hell, its resources inexhaustible. But that time was ending, as I found out later, and only because I became caught in the maelstrom. It happened so slowly, so cryptically that like everyone else I felt nothing at first, saw nothing, heard nothing, contained as I was in careless indolence and selfish pursuits.

While at Halle I read *Dampier's Voyages*, marveling at the author's succinct and pinpoint observations on natural history, a supreme accomplishment for someone without training in the subject. And Defoe's *Robinson Crusoe* became a sensation when published in German.

But probably most influential on anyone fascinated by improbable adventures was a novel in two volumes titled *Die Insel Felsenburg* authored by Johann Gottfried Schnabel, an orphan and formerly a student at the *Waisenhaus* where I presently taught. It told a tale of shipwreck on a deserted island where the castaways find a paradise, establish a colony, and discover a treasure. The text is detailed with a map of the island drawn to scale accompanied by notes on its topography, a genealogy of the founders and their progeny, and descriptions of the indigenous plants and animals. Monkeys were tamed and trained as domestic servants. The tale seemed so real that many readers thought it was true, but even among skeptics only the dullest could fail to be awed and stimulated. As I was to find out, being marooned on an uninhabited island isn't nearly so glamorous as fictional literature depicts.

In 1721 Peter the Great had declared himself Emperor of All the Russians. The country was barely the age of a normal lifespan. Here was a ruler who had no idea where his eastern boundaries lay, but he moved quickly to remedy this issue and many others. To achieve his objectives he needed personnel with education and skills, and the only place to find them was Europe. Starting that year Professor Hoffmann and Peter began working together identifying promising young men from various German universities and placing them in jobs at the Russia Academy of Science being founded at St. Petersburg.

For templates Peter was using the renowned academies and museums in Berlin and Paris, as recommended by his friend and mentor the great Gottfried Wilhelm von Leibniz. Peter the Great died before the Academy opened, although he had already begun staffing it. When it became apparent that Professor Hoffmann would be unable to provide me employment at Halle he mentioned the possibility of emigrating to Russia and perhaps gaining a position there. Few such opportunities for teaching and research were available in Germany, and the Russia Academy might offer an exciting career path. He agreed to write a letter of introduction and recommendation I could present to the proper authorities on arrival.

Excitement about Russia was palpable in the scientific world. The *wunderkind* Johann Georg Gmelin had passed through Halle in 1727 enroute to St. Petersburg to assume a newly created position as professor of chemistry. Just 18 and already a respected naturalist, Gmelin had matriculated at age 13, written a dissertation in chemistry, and later obtained a *doctor medicinae* degree.

This splashy event and Professor Hoffmann's words were all the encouragement I needed. He cautioned that although my interest lay in natural history I was most likely to obtain a position in something practical, like medicine, especially if hiring at the Academy had somehow become delayed. Having never been to St. Petersburg he had no notion of the culture and employment practices at the new Academy. He felt confident, however, that lack of a *doctor medicinae* degree would not be a handicap in distant and primitive Russia if I wished to practice medicine. Any European medical training was highly valued, and he predicted I would quickly find work in this area. He noted that I already possessed more medical training than most licensed physicians in Germany. Furthermore, he admitted, knowledge of medicine even in places like Halle and Berlin remained rudimentary. It's a fact, he said ruefully, that none of the "experts" actually knows much about anything.

The working of the human body and the diseases that plague us are indeed poorly understood. Knowing this, I beg the reader's patience and understanding when I later describe the suffering I witnessed in Russia and my feeble attempts to ameliorate it. In truth, physician and patient are equally helpless without God's benevolent intervention. The medical arts contain so little knowledge, yet present so much to know. Sad to say, even the most educated among us remain abysmally ignorant of nature's secrets, despite living in an age of enlightenment.

Both mammalian physiology and the origin of diseases—two crucial cornerstones of medicine—were a mystery in my student days and remain so today. How the living body functions is opaque to inquiry even at the most exalted centers of learning. The best a practicing physician can achieve is to try drawing the internal source of his diagnosis across the body's boundaries to the surface where it can be observed, treated, and monitored.

Galen taught that the human body and everything else in the world is composed of four elements: air, earth, fire, and water. They exist in humans in a blend of four bodily fluids, or "humors." These are blood, phlegm, yellow bile, and black bile. Everyone, even if healthy, has at least a slight excess of one, rendering his temperament sanguine, phlegmatic, choleric, or melancholy. In healthy persons the humors are more or less in balance, but this changes during illness when the excess of a particular humor rises as a vapor and collects in the brain. Alternatively, the patient might be deficient in a certain humor, requiring special treatments and medications to return him to stasis. A physician's task is to diagnose which of the four humors is the causative agent, based in part on the patient's attitude and sometimes appearance. If sanguine he appears happy, generous, and loving, and his skin has a rosy glow; if phlegmatic he seems quiescent and cowardly and exhibits a pale complexion. A choleric individual demonstrates anger, violence, and an argumentative temperament, indicating a surfeit of yellow bile. Someone who is melancholy from too much black bile seeks solitude, is slow-moving, and miserable.

The humors are also defined by perceived qualities of the four elements. Yellow bile (choler) is linked with fire, and like fire is hot and dry. Air, which is linked with blood, is hot and moist. Phlegm, linked with water, is cold and moist. Black bile, the melancholic fluid and linked with earth, is cold and dry.

What tools are available in the physician's toolkit? Purgatives to encourage the expulsion of gall and various excrements; application of plasters to draw internal vapors and humors to the surface for discharge through the skin and orifices; a theriac might be necessary to sweat out deeply submerged anger. Evil matter is believed to be expulsed during menstruation and nocturnal emissions, even via hemorrhoids when the golden vein in the anus starts to bleed. To calm an angry womb the attending physician might prescribe wine and beer.

Experts can only guess the identity and source of humankind's protean maladies by carefully observing the visible; alternatively, from studying various fluids and semi-solid excretory products. By these I mean urine, mucus, blood, sweat, phlegm, and feces. Hence the emphasis on diagnosing causative agents like bad air, vapors, and exhalations. Certain diseases can be deduced based on abnormal skin color or condition and the appearance of boils, swellings, and supperations. Some maladies are exceedingly difficult to diagnose because they remain entirely internal. For example, anger by a spouse during marital *congressus* is believed to trigger excruciating headaches caused by black humors rising as vapors into the brain.

Note that fluxes are the foundation of what we study, typically shifting from inside outward, never the disease itself. The term "flux" describes a plethora of conditions. For example, an inner flux can be the sensation of pain flowing through the body. Either this or something specific like a headache, tinnitus, loss of hearing or sight, a slow tongue that becomes tangled during speech. The outer flux is its visible expression manifested in suppurating sores, tearing eyes, peeling skin, pus-filled boils and abscesses, all signs that evil matter is being expelled. Excepting fatal wounds, any putative locus of disease remains invisible to human eyes. The best we physicians can achieve is to somehow sense its presence using deduction and interpretation of indirect evidence. Surely there are better ways, but they have yet to be revealed.

The blood is a universe of its own. Even the identity of sex revolves around blood, although somewhat paradoxically. Womanhood is defined by the rhythm of the female monthly discharge, not the blood itself. In the context of treatment, bloodletting is useful to draw off the surplus turned "impetuous" or that for various reasons has become *Geliefern* (stagnant). An incidence of fright, for example, might direct the blood inward, bringing on stagnation. Then bleeding breaks the logjam, metaphorically speaking, encouraging normal flow.

Physicians stumped by lack of reproducible diagnoses bleed their patients as a central but problematic cure for everything: usually any malady is reducible to bad or evil factors in the blood responsible for the accumulation of humors in excess. Patients, having been inculcated almost from birth to the utility of bleeding, often ask—even plead—to be bled, or in a fit of panic and ignorance bleed themselves, sometimes with fatal consequences if they faint and fail to stop the flow in time or open an artery instead of a vein.

The physician is frequently handicapped by a tendency of most patients to self-diagnose or accept the uninformed diagnoses of friends and relatives, discounting the wisdom of modern medicine. Often a physician is summoned only to confirm the utility of someone's home remedy. In my experience this is especially true with female patients, who by not allowing the male physician to examine their private parts present to him as mysterious and unrealized beings. This is sometimes the case with the unmarried woman who presents with stagnated menses and morning vomiting, convinced of harboring a growing abdominal tumor, later to tearfully admit her error when the "tumor" within begins to wriggle and kick.

Dissecting a body, whether human or animal, offers insight at the organismal level, displaying everything in stasis while revealing little about living functions. A cadaver on the dissecting table represents a machine at rest. Given little choice, European medical faculties emphasize anatomy; anything requiring a physiological explanation can elicit only conjecture at this time. We are just learning that pain is life's gate-keeper and not merely the soul's suffering, and that metaphors used to describe pain actually represent sensation elided into meaning.

Because the drugs used to treat diseases and wounds are derived from plants, no physician's education is complete without at least a rudimentary knowledge of botany, and the deeper this knowledge the better for the patients. Botanical skills are less important in large European cities, which support shops operated by certified apothecaries. There medicines and plasters are concocted to standards and prescribed to patients by their physicians from fresh and dried plant material. In rural areas—and in any Russian city, large or small—the physician is his own druggist, left to devise remedies from the meager stocks in his cabinets. Hospital apothecary gardens where botanists are employed to tend medicinal plants are still too rare everywhere.

THE WAR OF THE Polish Succession was just ending, and on 22 February 1734 the Russian Army laid siege to the city of Danzig. It lasted until 7 July, and in the interim the Russians suffered heavy casualties. Rumors flew that agents of Russia's military were combing Europe recruiting physicians, surgeons, and anyone with medical skills, perceived or real. Apply at army headquarters in Danzig. Can you wield a bone saw? Step over here. Medical training went by the wayside; not even reading and writing skills were required. Word circulated that unemployed butchers were applying to treat the wounded, as were farmers and former soldiers, even (so they said) a man hopping on one leg who claimed surgical expertise based entirely on having survived an amputation himself. Anyone with rudimentary medical training was certain to be hired, so desperate was the need. Professor Hoffmann had been right. Practicing medicine indeed seemed a good way of at least getting to Russia, considering I could not afford passage on a civilian vessel.

I sold most of my books and spare clothes and carrying only a few necessities traveled by foot and coach to Danzig via Stettin, where the rumors turned out to be true: I and the few other impecunious students of medicine seeking employment were pulled from the queue and hired on the spot. In autumn I was given charge of a group of soldier-patients returning by sea to St. Petersburg. After running aground in the Baltic and facing imminent shipwreck and death, God's miraculous hand refloated us by redirecting the gale, and we arrived safely at Kronstadt, the port of St. Petersburg, in late November.

Shipboard medical duties prevented the keeping of a journal, but I can relate a few retrospective observations. In addition to seasickness, for which there's no standard curative, most of my patients were tormented by the fluxes, both bloody and white. Many also suffered malnutrition and the scurvy, almost as if they had been the besieged instead of the besiegers. Others presented with fevers and suppurating wounds of different sorts that because of a shortage of medicines I could only clean and bandage. Gangrene was rampant, and during my rounds I frequently ordered the removal of limbs both gangrenous or at risk of becoming so.

After reflection I sometimes think that instantaneous death would have been kinder than the slow, agonizing demise most of these men eventually suffered from our beleaguered medical assistance. When summoning the so-called *Chirurgen* hired to perform these tasks I was forced to witness their barbarous incompetence. Without exception they were insensate louts, oblivious to the plangent screams and inattentive to the dullness or filth of their instruments. While witnessing one amputation I slipped into a rage, punching the attending "surgeon" in the face several times and taking charge of the bone saw myself. Only God's watchful eye kept me from throwing these worthless beings overboard with the limbs they severed and the bodies of the dead.

And so I arrived in Russia owning little but the salt-saturated clothes I wore, a few books and other meager possessions, and the few rubles earned as payment for nearly drowning in service to my newly adopted country. I also had acquired a new surname. In 1715 my family changed the spelling of ours from Stöhler to Stöller, which in my case made no difference. The Russian alphabet comprises 37 characters, none capable of expressing the pronunciation of Stöller. The best any native Russian could manage was Steller. I didn't care, and Steller I became.

In St. Petersburg I was befriended quickly by Theophan Prokopovitch, Archbishop of the Orthodox Church of Russia. We met in the Russia Academy's apothecary garden my first full day ashore when the Archbishop strolled past taking his customary exercise and stopped to speak in Russian with the German gardener I had just met and with whom I was conversing In our native tongue. After a cheery greeting and small talk the Archbishop invited me home with him for tea. I was still ignorant of the Russian language except for a few halting words and phrases acquired from my patients at Danzig and during the sea voyage, so we conversed in Latin, which we both spoke fluently. The Archbishop, as I was to learn, was kind and generous, erudite, and unbiased regarding my Lutheran background. In any case my presence in the country was legal, Peter the Great having banned only Jesuits and Jews.

Theophan was suffering greatly from calculi and offered room, board, and a small salary if I would serve as one of the resident physicians in his extensive household. He employed several, all of them Germans. He guaranteed plenty of time for botanizing in the surrounding area. Even more important, as archbishop overseeing all the Orthodox churches of Russia his connections were impeccable, and he promised access to resources of the Academy, located at Vasilij Ostrov. I accepted gratefully and thanked God for my good luck.

The Russia Academy of Science was new like everything in St. Petersburg, the marshes having been drained and the city founded only in 1703. Peter had viewed western science as the principal means of launching his country into a new era of enlightenment, and the Academy would sit at the epicenter of this bracing movement. My ultimate hope was to become part of it, a member in some capacity. Peter had died 28 January 1725, 9 years before I arrived. He was 53 and had ruled for 43 iron-fisted years. With his death the Academy might have died too, but Yekaterina (Catherine the First), his widow and designated successor to the throne, issued a *ukase* in December that same year officially establishing it. A huge stipend of 25,000 rubles was set aside for expenses, and continuing Peter's plan the facility would be staffed by the brightest minds (mostly young and German) recruited from Europe's finest universities.

The road ahead proved bumpy despite this auspicious start. Yekaterina died 6 May 1727 after ruling barely 2 years. She was succeeded by Peter's grandson through the lineage of his first marriage. Peter the Second was a minor and immediately became the center of a power struggle among his advisers. Within a year the royal court was moved to Moskva, its original seat, leaving the Academy forgotten and in chaos. It was already running a financial deficit. The staff members were embroiled in traditional academic bickering and outright power struggles, and the affiliated Russian *boyars* (noblemen), all laymen, were grappling with each other for power and prestige. Many in St. Petersburg society looked on the imported foreign intellectuals as arrogant parasites sapping the country's resources and performing no useful functions. What practical value could come from studying plants and animals, stones and stars? Of preserving and displaying artifacts and oddities from unknown lands before a mostly illiterate and indifferent public? Peter's minions were even erecting a special building for this purpose called a *kunstkammer* divided into what the Germans called *wunderkammers* (wonder-rooms) filled with many glass-fronted "cabinets of curiosities." The objects to be displayed were themselves exotic even to experts, the categories into which they fit only now becoming understood. In the view of many St. Petersburg *boyars* and fashionable women the whole undertaking had been a colossal waste of money, Peter the Great's grand delusion.

Just as the situation seemed it couldn't worsen, it did. Peter the Second died in Moskva 19 January 1730, following his grandfather to the grave almost 5 years to the day. He was succeeded by Anna Ivanovna, daughter of Ivan, Peter the Great's half-brother and early co-regent. She returned the court to St. Petersburg 2 years later in 1732, discovering the Academy now 30,000 rubles in debt and the staff paralyzed and demoralized from constant infighting. She seriously considered abolishing the institution and sending everyone back to Europe. Fortunately, her advisers talked her out of it, arguing that the looming Second Kamchatka Expedition presently on the drawing board was too important to scuttle. The Academy, they said, was integral to seeing the Expedition's objectives achieved. Just as critical was the public relations aspect: the Academy represented intellectual and cultural credibility, and its participation was necessary if Russia hoped to join the European enlightenment from which it had been excluded so long.

A year of intrigue and strife followed Anna's death on 17 October 1740 until Peter the Great's daughter Elizabeth grabbed the throne 9

November 1741. The Academy's situation then deteriorated further as the palace and the Russian bureaucracy, sometimes in concert, at other times in opposition, began usurping control. But by now the Expedition was well underway, and in the end its leaders would cover themselves in glory. Peter the Great would have been proud.

This brief history provides the disquieting context into which I again insert myself and my small role into the narrative. Nature to the uninitiated appears chaotic when in fact her components have been carefully ordered by God on High in patterns both symmetric and asymmetric. He sets them before us to decipher. We see them in the facets of mineral crystals, so perfectly repeated as to look manufactured. We notice them in the replicative spirals of nautilus shells, pine cones, cauliflower and lettuce heads, leaves on the stalks of many plants, and the carefully ordered arrangement and packing of seeds in floral heads. We see the Fibonacci sequence and the "golden ratio" repeated in the veins of leaves and in the number of sepals and petals of flowers and notice that primroses are among the relative few that deviate from this arrangement in having only four of each. To isolate nature's patterns we must observe carefully, and proper observation requires slowing her movements so they can be measured and described, thereby revealing how her parts fit together so seamlessly.

This is my one objective, my only purpose for God having placed me here. My existence is focused exclusively on describing the workings of nature and committing my discoveries to paper so others may learn from them and proceed beyond the point where my paltry contributions end.

On gaining introduction to the Academy through the Archbishop's good graces I immediately introduced myself to Dr. Johann Amman. A Swiss and just 2 years my senior but already a renowned botanist, he had been in his position only since July 1733. We became friends and were soon botanizing together in the surrounding countryside while struggling to learn the Russian language and understand the culture. It was on his recommendation that I was later admitted to the Academy as a member.

On gaining entrance what I found there were collections much in need of curating. Objects were scattered everywhere in no particular order, most of the scientists too busy with other matters to tend them. Peter had bought the initial holdings during a visit to Europe straddling the years 1716 and 1717. One of the largest was assembled over 40 years by the famed Dutch anatomist Professor Frederik Ruysch, whose dissections Peter witnessed as a young man years earlier. It had come with a *catalogue raisonné* describing the collection's content. The other major collection was that of the Dutch apothecary Albertus Seba, whose famous cabinet of curiosities was filled with mammals, birds, reptiles, and insects collected throughout the East Indies.

When not attending to medical duties for the Archbishop and his retinue I helped Dr. Amman prepare, identify, and catalog specimens in the Academy's herbarium, many of the new additions being ones we had collected during our local excursions. It was Dr. Amman's mission to obtain plants from throughout Russia's vast reaches, an objective I enthusiastically shared. The easiest place to begin this monumental undertaking was at home, and by year's end 1735 we had gained a good working knowledge of flora indigenous to the hills, valleys, and marshes surrounding St. Petersburg. We were also making progress at upgrading the apothecary garden, which Peter the Great, by *ukase*, had opened for all Russians to view and enjoy as part of his plan of universal education.

While at Halle I was told by Professor Hoffmann about a man named Daniel Gottlieb Messerschmidt, a former medical student of his who had immigrated to Russia, arriving in St. Petersburg in 1716. Dr. Messerschmidt had signed a decree in 1719 under auspices of the Medical Chancellery. At the personal expense of Peter the Great he was dispatched to explore Siberia for 7 years, collecting specimens and information on everything he encountered. Among his assigned tasks was to thoroughly study the geography of the lands, rivers, and streams. He was to map them and catalog their plants, animals, and minerals. He was to describe the traditions and languages of Siberia's indigenous peoples, paying strict attention to their diseases and treatments, including all *materia medica* of possible use to the Russian medical establishment.

Remarkably, he did all this. Peter had been dead 2 years when Messerschmidt returned to St. Petersburg in 1727 with huge collections of specimens and artifacts and a mountain of notes and maps that when organized and transcribed eventually filled dozens of folios and other printed volumes. But of himself only a hollow shell came back; the effort had drained and robbed him of all energy and enthusiasm, and a melancholia in the form of pensive thoughts descended on his soul and never lifted.

Naturally, I sought out this unusual man. His knowledge of Siberia was a bottomless reservoir. Messerschmidt knew more about it than everyone in Europe and the Academy combined. As I discovered, he was blessed with an innate facility for languages and could still speak several native tongues, effortlessly switching from one to another. Among his writings were dictionaries that might be invaluable to future explorers, including those of the Second Kamchatka Expedition now underway. His input here in St. Petersburg could be timely and useful, provided he was interested in assisting. He wasn't. Later, after personally experiencing the bureaucratic blunderings of our putative leaders, Messerschmidt's ennui and disdain for my naïve enthusiasm seemed not unreasonable.

After turning over everything to the Academy Messerschmidt retreated from public life, refusing even the prospect of another assignment. In truth, by the time I came along he was mentally and physically incapable of accepting one even had it been offered.

The Messerschmidt I knew briefly was living the existence of an obscure, morose hypochondriac, although not alone. While staying in Solikamsk, Perm, in 1726 he claimed that a young woman appeared to him one night in a dream. Soon after he was startled to encounter her in the flesh. This was Birgitta-Helena von Böckler, whose father was a colonel in Russian service. They married, had a daughter, and were living in St. Petersburg impoverished and friendless. But their reclusive life was entirely Messerschmit's idea. His wife had a wild and lively personality and clearly resented the lifestyle forced on her, as I soon learned. Dissatisfied with Russia, Messerschmidt moved the family to his home city of Danzig. On 27 October 1729, while enroute, they were shipwrecked and lost everything. Danzig proved disappointing, and 2 years later they returned to St. Petersburg.

During the time of our acquaintance I relayed details of his current situation to the Archbishop, who extended charity to the family, assuaging some of its poverty, and I helped Messerschmidt catalog the few remaining plants in his personal collection. He died 25 March 1735; I knew him only a few weeks. But that was not the end of my association with Messerschmidt's family, not by any means.

7

SOON AFTER THE FUNERAL I was summoned by the widow to assist her with sorting out items her husband had left and isolating anything of possible use to the Academy. I had no compunction about doing this, and hastened to her house. She greeted me at the door, saying her daughter was away staying with friends. She offered tea, and we went into the sitting room and sat on a tattered sofa. The room was mostly barren and in process of becoming moreso.

Birgitta-Helena was a very appealing young woman, a year or so my junior. I couldn't help looking at her during my visits with her husband and sometimes got the impression she was looking back, but at the time I put any wicked thoughts aside as uncharitable. After all, she was a married woman, at least until recently. Their house had the appearance and musty odor of a neglected mausoleum where only whispering is allowed. Messerschmidt's voice had been barely audible, and his wife and daughter spoke rarely, usually remaining silent or drifting to other rooms soon after I arrived.

Her face and figure were pleasing, and the hint of cleavage peaking above the neckline of her dress offered the enticing possibility of firm globes beneath. She smiled and laughed easily, at which times her large brown eyes widened, fixed on me, and seemed to sparkle, a mannerism both stimulating and disconcerting, imparting a feeling that my very soul was on display. To what purpose and for whose amusement I dared not guess. This side of her had until now been hidden from me, and I was unsure how to respond to such disarming flirtation. Was she merely being friendly? I couldn't tell, but she obviously wasn't still grieving for Messerschmidt, if she ever had.

My Russian was improving rapidly, but I was aware of possibly missing certain subtleties of social conversation. I tried switching to German, but without effect. Her husband had been German and the two of them had lived for a time in Danzig, and although her father was also German, her mother was Russian. In both households, she told me, only Russian had been spoken; consequently, her knowledge of the German language was only rudimentary.

She got up and went to the kitchen to refill our cups, smiling over her shoulder and offering a flash of trim ankles as her dress swished around the corner. She returned and set the cups and saucers on the low table before us, and when she bent over I got a glimpse of the tops of her breasts. I was now fully alert. The beast in my trousers began to stir, and I prayed fervently it would calm itself and subside before I had to stand and participate in the task of going through her dead husband's belongings. As events played out, anticipating any need to stand was superfluous.

During our second cup Birgitta-Helena's hand gently touched my thigh and remained there, and I was suddenly confused and distracted from pure thoughts. I looked down at it, trying objectively to assess its purpose as I would any natural specimen. Yes, five fingers and clearly a woman's hand, but one strangely misplaced. What was it doing practically in my lap? Just a moment before I'd watched it gracefully lift a teacup; a moment after that I'd been conscious of eyes watching mine over the rim, eyes certain of their place in nature, predatory eyes.

The hidden beast surged suddenly, straining to be let out. The hand moved as if to calm its agitation, having instead the opposite effect. What could be happening? I was experiencing the vertiginous sensation of teetering at the edge of a high cliff or standing on a pitching deck in a gale. I raised my head and looked at Birgitta-Helena again, but the serene gaze had disappeared, subsumed beneath a look of vague kinetic fury.

The beast had extended to its full length, and the hand was stroking it softly, as someone might stroke the head of an eager dog tugging at its chain. The fingers of the hand moved with practiced caution, gently unbuttoning my trousers. I felt her hair against my face, her breath softly in my ear. Goose pimples rose over every surface of my body. Then her lips were against mine, her tongue pushing them apart.

The beast was now fully on display, restrained only by her hand. She was kissing me deeply, her lips warm and wet. Abruptly she pulled away and bent her head to my lap. I felt her lips slide slowly over the head of the beast and down its shaft. Up and down they moved in slow rhythm until the beast exploded in fiery ecstasy, throbbing uncontrollably before convulsing, shuddering to a stop, and retreating limply back to its den.

I awoke in her bed in darkness feeling disoriented. Despite having replayed the memory countless times, to this day I don't know specifically how we got there. Did we walk? Crawl? Fly? Evidently I was dazed, caught in a fixed instant of eternity. I can say only that I was happier and more relaxed than I ever thought possible. This after I'd sinned by wallowing in sexual escapades denied by the church to all believers! I smiled, thinking how our Christian deity had declared wanton thoughts and their fulfillment a sin, undoubtedly because of the unbearable pleasure. My first sexual experiences had just been consummated. I wanted more, lots more, and hoped this was just the beginning.

Birgitta-Helena's head rested on my chest. She was breathing gently in sleep. I plunged my nose into the tangle of thick hair and inhaled the sweet animal scent of a sexual being who had recently seduced me with nuanced tact and premeditation. I rubbed my hand along her body under the blanket and felt it shiver.

The door to the bedroom opened, and against the dim background light was the silhouette of a little girl. She was clutching a stuffed toy to her chest. In a tiny voice she said, "*Ty moy novyy papochka?*" I took the words to mean, "Are you my new daddy?'

I began visiting Birgitta-Helena and her daughter every day. Between bouts of making love I pawed through the tired remnants of Messerschmidt's life searching for anything of possible benefit to the Academy. Truthfully, I was also interested in what could be of use to me if, as I hoped, I was offered a chance to participate in the Second Kamchatka Expedition. While at Wittenberg I had developed an interest in languages and was excited by the prospect of learning the speech and customs of strange cultures. Messerschmidt's fluency in several had been mesmerizing, and he emphasized during our conversations that had he not learned them he would have never discovered which plants comprised the native pharmacopeias and how the shamans prepared them.

During those days of my trysts with Birgitta-Helena the Archbishop was losing strength and vitality despite the frantic efforts of his medical team. The enormous responsibility of overseeing the Orthodox Church of Russia was draining away his very life. He died gracefully in his own bed, at peace and with full mental faculties on the afternoon of 8 September 1736. Three dignitaries of the Holy Synod and his doctors were at his side when he took his last breaths. The grief that poured from our collective hearts was both agonizing and sincere. Theophan had been loved by everyone he touched; no man could have lived a fuller, holier, more exemplary life.

I took some degree of consolidation knowing that my good friend and benefactor had recommended me to the Academy. Its leader, Baron Johann Albrecht von Korff, had subsequently notified me that I might be sent to Kamchatka. A personal word from the Archbishop could not be dismissed easily, and on 28 July 1736 the appointment became official. My greatest dream had come true. I was going to Siberia.

The Second Kamchatka Expedition was known officially as the Second Great Northern Expedition. This was the massive adventure for which thousands had prepared or were preparing to undertake and in which I would now participate. Its realization had become possible only because the First Kamchatka Expedition (officially the First Great Northern Expedition) was considered to have failed. Peter the Great, on his deathbed and in his own handwriting, had ordered the first undertaking to determine with finality whether Asia and America were connected by land or separated by a sea.

Peter was obsessed with finding a northwest passage, a connection west through the Icy Sea from eastern Siberia to northern Europe. Such a route might exist between the Novaya Zemlya archipelago and Siberia's northern coast. If ice-free part of the year then ships from the Pacific could reach the Russian ports of Arkhangelsk and Murmansk and, of course, the same passage eastward would be viable. By sailing west past Murmansk and south along the northwestern coast of Norway a trading vessel could eventually enter the Baltic, proceed up the Neva River, and dock at St. Petersburg; or it might continue south to the major ports of Europe. Not unreasonably, raw materials and eventually manufactured goods from Siberia someday might be sent down Siberia's many rivers emptying into the Icy Sea and from there to Europe. A northeast passage was a thrilling prospect and a major reason for expending every effort to confirm the prevailing belief that Asia and North America are indeed separated by water.

Peter appointed Fleet Captain Vitus Bering, a Dane serving in the Russian Navy, as leader. He named as Bering's lieutenants Morten (Martin) Spangberg, another Danish naval officer, and Alekseij Ilitch Tchirikov (Chirikov), a naval officer and Russian national. Arrangements were made rapidly, and Tchirikov left St. Petersburg on 24 January 1725 leading part of the expedition. Peter died 4 days later. Empress Yekaterina immediately picked up the torch where it had fallen with Peter's death, and on 5 February Bering and Spangberg departed with the remaining party members.

The diligent, ever-faithful Bering carried out his orders, constructing the necessary vessels at Kamchatka and sailing up the coast of Siberia to north latitude 67°18′. Finding no land to the north or east past this point he turned around, concluding Asia and North America are not joined. He arrived back in Moskva 1 March 1730, presented his report to the Admiralty, and was astonished when authorities there discounted his findings and refused to accept his conclusion that only open sea lay between Asia and America. In their opinion, Bering had not continued far enough north to prove his assertion.

There were whispers that Bering might be too timid, although as he later explained to me during our voyage to America his reasoning then seemed both logical and prudent. He had decided to turn south to Kamchatka because winter was approaching. Wintering along Siberia's northeast coast risked losing the ship and all aboard if they became ice-bound. Moving ashore either on that inhospitable coast or rounding Cape Tchuktchi and wintering on the coast of the Icy Sea was no more appealing. Either location comprised empty tundra without wood for shelter and fires. The indigenous Tchuktchis were hostile, their language and customs still largely unknown. Furthermore, wherever they wintered the officers and crew would face the dangers of hunger, exposure, the scurvy, and marauding wolves and ice bears.

Bering stoically deflected the criticisms and innuendos directed his way by the armchair explorers attacking him, but inside he seethed. To preserve the honor of his crew, himself, and the mission he offered to repeat the expedition and prove his findings beyond doubt. Two months later the Admiralty received his plans for a second attempt.

Yekaterina had died during Bering's absence, and Anna Ivanovna now occupied the throne. She liked Bering's proposal, believing another expedition would shed glory on Russia (not to mention on her) and ordered that this second effort be grander and more comprehensive than the first. And so the plan released by the Admiralty in 1732 was breathtaking in ambition and scope.

The Second Kamchatka Expedition would be divided into three divisions: Arctic, Japan, and America. The mission far exceeded Bering's first objective of determining whether Asia and America were joined or separated by water. It would encompass this too (the America arm of the Expedition), but in addition the plan called for surveys of eastern Siberia north to the farthest point in Asia, the coast of North America south to California, and the coast of the Icy Sea as far west as possible and east around Cape Tchuktchi and into the North Pacific, or approximately the place where Bering's first expedition had turned back. This last was contingent on the absence of a land bridge linking Asia and America. Also to be mapped and explored were the Kuril Islands southwest of Kamchatka, parts of Japan, and perhaps other regions near Japan as deemed pertinent.

In sum, these tasks bordered on the fantastic. Some wondered if they could be completed even in several generations, but the plan wasn't yet finished. The Academy soon made its interests known, with goals no less elaborate than the Admiralty's. The Academy proposed examining most of these same regions, except instead of mapping coastlines its representatives would assess plant and animal life, farming and fishing practices, soil conditions, crops and animal husbandry, minerals and mining, logging, manufacturing, and the cultures, traditions, medical practices, history, and languages of the indigenous peoples.

The expedition would proceed under the umbrella and auspices of the Admiralty, but the Academy would establish its own hierarchy and objectives. Although these were separate from the Admiralty's, Bering, as the Admiralty's representative and expedition leader, was in charge overall, yet responsible for assuring the Academy got whatever necessary to conduct its work separately and unimpeded. Bering and his designated underlings were thus ordered to assist Academy representatives as required, which included arranging their housing, feeding, transportation, and other logistics. And all this came with a caveat: the services Bering provided directly or solicited locally as the Academy's proxy must meet the standards of exalted European intellectuals roughing it in the countryside and residing in primitive *ostrogs* (palisaded villages).

Poor Bering would be pulled this way and that. Everyone expected his own needs to come first and for Bering to acknowledge that his particular projects and problems were of special urgency, obviously more important than anyone else's. As such, Bering suffered the inevitable insults, disrespect, selfishness, and general horseshit tossed his way with all the politeness and equanimity he could muster. To Bering's credit he did his best under impossible circumstances, and despite several shortcomings of personality and leadership I admire his memory for that.

The Academy contingent was led by three professors assisted by six Russian students with knowledge of Latin and German who served as secretaries and assistants. Also along were servants and chefs, two artists/draftsmen whose job it was to paint natural history specimens, an interpreter, a surgeon, an artisan skilled in making instruments, and five geodesist/surveyors. To provide labor and security 14 soldiers (including a drummer) were assigned.

A complete list of accoutrements and equipment carried by the academicians might fill several thick ledgers. Each of the professors who volunteered for this adventure was allotted 10 horses, other staff members six. The three professors were also permitted delicacies and refreshments of their choosing, including wheels of cheeses and kegs of fine wine imported from Germany. In addition to their everyday traveling and work clothes each brought wardrobes stuffed with shoes, stockings, and European dress appropriate for an evening at the theater in Berlin. They brought complete sets of tableware and cooking utensils, books for light reading, and board games; in other words, everything anticipated to sustain the sybaritic lifestyle of European gentlemen forced to live among barbarians and idolaters. That they had volunteered was irrelevant. To conduct their work they packed a library of several hundred scientific books, plus portable laboratories equipped with all necessary instruments, chemical reagents, and preservatives to last 6 years.

Professor Johann Georg Gmelin was 24, 5 months younger than I, when he departed for Siberia. Gmelin was the Expedition's naturalist responsible for the description, illustration, and preservation of all plants, insects, fishes, birds, and mammals collected. He was to catalogue the collections and periodically send them by courier to the Academy along with accompanying illustrations, notes, and journals.

Professor Gerhard Friedrich Müller, age 28 when the Expedition set off, specialized in history, linguistics, geography, and ethnography. He was instructed to apply these disciplines in all territories through which he passed. In addition, he was to search all archives he came across in Siberia and periodically send their contents by courier for deposition in the Academy's archives.

I don't think any of us ever knew the age of the third professor, Louis de l'Isle de la Croyère, the Expedition's astronomer and geographer, but he was several years older than the rest of us. De La Croyère's credentials were shaky, his appointment at the Academy having been arranged by his half-brother, the noted cartographer Joseph Nicolas de l'Isle. As a young man de la Croyère had become embroiled in a scandal of some sort and spent 17 years in Canada during which time he had assumed his mother's name, de la Croyère. To perform his impending duties in Siberia he was taking nine wagons filled with instruments, including four telescopes of lengths 5, 7, 13, and 15 feet; five astrolabes; 20 thermometers; and 27 barometers.

Although companionable, de la Croyère quickly proved useless. Gmelin and Müller realized this not long after departing for Siberia and once there rarely saw him except when they occasionally crossed paths. What he was doing was anyone's guess, although he seemed always in motion, intently headed somewhere. He was in and out of debt and evidently other troubles never discussed in my presence.

De la Croyère retained peculiar notions about the geography of the North Pacific Ocean, mainly an unfounded belief in the presence of certain land masses yet unseen by any reliable geodesist or navigator. Their uncharted coasts seemed to exist only in the imaginations of sedentary European mapmakers who had never left their drafting tables long enough to set foot aboard a ship. De la Croyère's insistence on their reality, and Bering's reluctant willingness to waste valuable time testing his ridiculous beliefs, were partly responsible for our ship later coming to grief during the disastrous voyage from America back to Kamchatka. These hardships and human failings are described in brutal detail later in my narrative.

I had been appointed an adjunct of the Academy and assigned my own tasks in the field. A professor outranks an adjunct who in turn outranks the students, artists, and other lesser members of the Academy's retinue. Because my assignment encompassed natural history (in addition to mineralogy), Gmelin considered himself my nominal supervisor, an erroneous presumption that became contentious at times after he and I went in different directions to cover more ground. We often worked apart for months, only occasionally communicating by letter or word of mouth. Under the circumstances I suppose occasional misunderstandings were inevitable. These were not alleviated by my lifelong dislike—call it open disdain—of authority. This personal shortcoming and the admitted eagerness to advance my career (perhaps too aggressively) were largely the causes of our strife. For his part Gmelin was a calm, friendly, and open colleague, although not someone willing to tolerate what he perceived to be insubordination, as we shall see.

My professional association with Gmelin—in fact, even my assignment to the Expedition—might never have occurred were it not for a fleeting mishap. The initial plan for the Academy's part in the Expedition had included only two professors, de la Croyère and Gmelin. Then Gmelin was suddenly felled by a liver attack, and Bering recommended Müller to replace him. Shortly thereafter Gmelin, who was serving as his own physician, made a stunning recovery that Müller attributed to his having consumed two bottles of good Rhine wine while lying in sickbed. And so in the end all three went.

The tasks assigned the Academy contingent were daunting. The unforgiving land and harsh climate made even the shortest trip and smallest task frustrating and exhausting. De la Croyère, like Gmelin and Müller a full professor of the Academy and their equal in rank, soon proved his incompetence. His colleagues were uninterested in monitoring his activities. Still, they were concerned his obligations were not being met. They wrote to St. Petersburg requesting two additional persons, one knowledgeable in astronomy and geography, the other qualified in natural history, chemistry, and mining. Empress Anna gave approval in a *ukase* of 15 April 1735. The first position was filled by Professor Johann Christopher Liebert of Berlin, who arrived in St. Petersburg a year later.

On 24 January 1737 I was hired to fill the naturalist position at an annual salary of 660 rubles, including lodging, firewood, and lamp oil. My sponsor was my good friend Dr. Amman, who formally examined my knowledge of natural history and issued a certificate declaring it extraordinary. This, he concluded, combined with my proven diligence and resourcefulness, would make me a valuable member of the Expedition. My title was to be Adjunct in Natural History. The mandate stated that I would be allowed to make collections and undertake studies in Kamchatka independently, to go where and when I pleased.

News arrived that Gmelin and Müller had asked to be relieved. The collections they had sent to date were impressive, but were they losing interest, slacking off, and ready to pass the torch? No one knew. When—or if—their request to return home would be approved was anyone's guess, but certainly not soon. Nothing in Russia happened quickly unless the empress took a personal interest.

It was Gmelin who had requested the position in natural history be filled, and whether he retained authority to give me orders or assignments wasn't clear; that is, clear to him. My contracted stated explicitly that I would be an independent contractor. Whatever the case it would be wise to avoid internal politics and once in Siberia to keep my mouth shut and avoid pissing off anyone who could disrupt my career. Staying friendly with everyone was the best policy. This excellent advice had come from my wise friend and mentor Archbishop Theophan, who had witnessed my loose lips and quick temper first-hand. Infighting at the Academy had reached the boiling point. Baron von Korff, the Academy's leader and the man who appointed me to the Second Kamchatka Expedition, was facing possible dismissal for having recently fought a duel with Baron Karl Ludwig von Mengden, a favorite at Empress Anna's court. On 9 September 1737 I took the oath pledging loyalty to Russia, the empress, and my duties.

Gmelin was already being assisted by the illustrators Johann Christian Berckhan and Philip Wilhelm Lürsenius, but had requested another. The painter Ivan Kornilev Decker was given the assignment. He and Professor Liebert were to accompany me to Siberia, except that Liebert, having been in St. Petersburg a year preparing for the trip, changed his mind. Claiming ill health his petition to be released from his contract and return to Germany was granted. Professor Johann Eberhard Fischer later relieved Müller, and another astronomer was never dispatched to replace de la Croyère. Gmelin and Müller were instead ordered to tolerate him, whatever his deficiencies, and focus on their own work.

9

BIRGITTA-HELENA HAD MEANWHILE BECOME my obsession. Excited as I was about the prospect of Kamchatka and eager to start my new career, I was in no hurry to leave St. Petersburg. Anyway, travel by wagon was slow during late spring and summer, much faster in winter and early spring when the roads and rivers are frozen and you could fly along by horse-drawn sled. Birgitta-Helena and I were married before a Lutheran congregation in November 1737. I explained that I could be away 10 years or more. After much persuasion by me and considerable trepidation on her part she agreed that she and her daughter would accompany me. Bering, Spangberg, and some of the other naval officers had already taken their families to Siberia, as had de la Croyère from the Academy's contingent, so the presence of a wife and daughter would be nothing unusual. My annual salary of 660 rubles was exceedingly generous, the usual being half that. Empress Anna had decided that doubling everyone's pay would encourage Expedition members to perform with exceptional diligence and energy considering how difficult their tasks would be in the coming years.

Birgitta-Helena began having second thoughts as the time of departure approached. Messerschmidt had told her tales of his hardships during the 7 years spent in that bleak country, and she had little interest in reprising them. As I deduced later, I had been an obvious upgrade over the morose, hypochondriacal Messerschmidt for someone in need of a husband. She was young and pretty and looking forward to a life of comfort and distractions in a cosmopolitan city. She had no interest in extending her present impoverished existence in a strange and dangerous country filled with wild animals and peopled by Cossacks and heathens. And the experience of being shipwrecked and nearly drowned still gave her nightmares. Why risk this and more, especially with a young daughter?

I didn't give in. I argued and pleaded with her to come. On bended knee I pledged undying love and vowed to protect her and see to her comfort and that of her daughter—now *our* daughter—regardless of circumstances. No setting could be unbearable with love to bind you. And besides, I added, the situation in Siberia had changed considerably since Messerschmidt was there. Furthermore, Messerschmidt had traveled mostly alone or with local guides. We, in contrast, would have the support and backing of the largest expedition the world had ever seen. My new position at the Academy was one of importance. We would overwinter with Bering and the other leaders. There would be parties and holiday celebrations, good food and drink, cheerful conversation, dancing, warm fires. The Expedition had shipped endless provisions, and more were on the way, a limitless chain, a mobile cornucopia. An army would guard us, a navy with trained officers and sailors manning newly built ships of the latest design would see to our safe transport. The experience of a lifetime had fallen on our doorstep. We would be fools not to grab it.

Persuasion has never been my métier. Friends and colleagues consider me humorless at all times, irksome and argumentative when my head is flooded with drink. But that night on Birgitta-Helena's tattered sofa I was a poet. I watched her eyes soften in the firelight. She looked at our daughter asleep beside her, then at me. "I'll go with you, God help us," she said.

We departed 15 January 1738. The evening before I wrote and posted a letter to my brother Augustin in which I enclosed a check for 300 rubles that I asked he hold in my behalf if I should ever need it. I expressed my excitement about the upcoming adventure and promised to write periodically. About my marriage and new family I said nothing. Why? I don't know except that I felt uneasy, as if my hold on my new wife's commitment and loyalty was only tenuous. Like a caged bird shown the open door she seemed undecided whether to stay behind in safety or depart in freedom toward the unknown.

We set out for Moskva in a covered sled pulled by a three horses harnessed together, what Russians call a *troika*. Much of the winter road to Moskva had been ordered built by Peter the Great. It was straight, level, heavily trafficked, and the equal of any in Europe. It also was safe. The trees lining it had been cut down to eliminate places where highwaymen could hide, and government stations had been erected at regular intervals along the way where weary horses could be exchanged for rested ones at a fixed government price, and travelers could warm themselves before continuing.

Decker, the artist chosen to fulfill Gmelin's request, was traveling with us. We were all bundled in heavy clothes and covered in blankets, prepared to be on the move day and night. Everyone had packed clothing appropriate for the coming seasons. Birgitta-Helena had included toys for the girl in addition to makeup and other women's things for herself, even two party dresses with matching shoes. Decker's luggage included his paints, brushes, pencils, canvases, spirits, and other tools of the artist's trade. Mine was burdened with books, paper for writing and pressing plants, notebooks, quills, bottles of ink, knives and firearms of various sorts, munitions, magnifying glasses and dissecting equipment, preservatives, and other items large and small too numerous to mention. Messerschmidt, who had traversed western Siberia some 20 years earlier, had helped me compile a list of needed supplies and accessories unavailable during his sojourn and no doubt still impossible to procure. When we sat down side by side with pens in hand Siberia was just a tantalizing mirage dancing in my head.

10

Moskva had lost much of its vibrancy since Empress Anna moved the imperial court back to St. Petersburg in June 1732. In addition, a huge conflagration had recently destroyed much of the city. It was in this gloomy and slightly poisonous atmosphere that I got a first unpleasant taste of Russia's bureaucracy at the national level. There was a narrow bottleneck called the Sibirski Prikaz stuffed with useless paperwork pushed in random directions by sluggish, indifferent beings who looked and acted vaguely human. Everything relating to Siberia must squeeze through this tight orifice and emerge on the other side somewhat recognizable and feebly functional. There is no bypassing the experience because only through this agency can expenses be arranged and salaries advanced. The process, which ought to be straightforward, is made excruciating by surly clerks who consider their life's mission to misinterpret clear directions, lose and misplace paperwork, and postpone decisions.

The Academy had forwarded letters to this agency authorizing both Decker and me to receive a year's salary in advance. On arrival I was informed that my salary would commence starting 8 August 1737, the date I was confirmed. I argued that it should start 7 February, the day I signed my contract. The matter ended in a stalemate with me shouting curses at my adversary while he stared stonily back, lips revealing the facsimile of a smile. At the end of January the dispute was kicked back to the Academy to decide, and it ruled in my favor. This proved a small victory considering what was yet to come.

Birgitta-Helena was unnerved by Moskva's charred desolation and the despondency of its citizens. My rage at the petty inconveniences tossed in our path by the Sibirski Prikaz and the delays they were causing frightened her. Her original hesitation at spending years in Siberia and general fear of the unknown now conflated to render her psyche immobile. As we exited the offices of the Sibirski Prikaz for what I hoped would be the last time she said, "I can't do this. I can't go with you."

I was stunned, as if struck by a heavy club. I felt my shoulders sag and the wind leave my lungs. My exhalations hung suspended in the frozen air; images of the burned city stung my eyes through the falling snow. It was a scene from the apocalypse after the angel of death has swooped overhead and cast his toxic breath into the face of humanity. We were standing in the street not yet having crossed to the other side. Carriages dragged by clopping horses lurched past, wheels rattling on the cobblestones, the drivers flicking their whips and whistling sharply. Rubble from the fire's devastation had been pushed to the side where it lay in jumbled heaps, disarticulated timbers and planks like old bones and remnants of incinerated flesh recently unearthed. My legs seemed rooted in place. What was I to do? The girl tugged my hand and looked up, her other hand shielding her eyes. "*Papochka*, I'm cold," she said.

We returned to our quarters wordlessly and shed our coats. Birgitta-Helena removed her scarf and tossed her head to loosen her hair. "I'm sorry. It's just that I'm afraid for us." She meant herself and the girl.

I reminded her that we had agreed to stay together as a family, to share the good times and the bad. I had promised to protect us all and provide for our needs. Love and trust would see us through. Danger lurked everywhere, even the streets and alleys of St. Petersburg and Moskva. The very act of living came attended by the prospect of danger and death, which in the end visits everyone. We can only trust in God and put one foot ahead of the other.

"I can't do it. I've made the decision, and it's final." She said this in a normal tone, firm but not hard or cruel. "I'm uncomfortable and afraid, and I can't live with those feelings."

"They'll pass. Give life a chance. Give us a chance," I said.

"No, Georg Wilhelm, I've decided. You convinced me once, but this time I'm not budging."

On hearing this, on hearing me addressed so directly, I lost my temper completely. I became red-faced, accusing her of lying and deceit, afterward breathing deeply and begging her in softer tones to reconsider. When she shook her head my temper rose again, and I demanded loudly that she obey me, telling her that as my legal spouse she had no choice except bending to my needs and wishes. I reminded her that since Abraham's time a pious woman has yielded to her husband and trusted his decisions. I waggled a forefinger in her face and yelled that such is God's will, and as a trained theologian I should know. I picked up objects from our open trunks and hurled them at the walls. I screamed profanities in German and Russian and beat my fists against my skull. I threw back my head, spread my arms, and gazed heavenward, imploring God to impart His wisdom to this woman and let her feel love. And then I wept.

In retrospect it was one of my better sermons, although without the intended effect. Birgitta-Helena stood by stoically, withstanding my fury with the incurious detachment of a spectator observing a baited bear.

There was nothing else to be said. Birgitta-Helena had emptied her house in St. Petersburg and sold everything. She had nowhere in particular to go, so she decided to remain in Moskva. The next day we found suitable lodging. I paid to furnish the rooms and gave her 300 rubles, nearly half my present salary and the equivalent of almost my full salary had we stayed in St. Petersburg. This was exceptionally generous considering Moskva's lower cost of living. She and the girl could easily survive a year or longer in modest comfort. Later I heard she moved back to St. Petersburg for its more lively social scene.

I had been blinded by love and my own innocence. Perhaps to widows like Birgitta-Helena men are stepping stones across life's tumultuous river. It would make sense. A hop, a skip, a jump, and suddenly the other side comes clearly into view: good times, heated rooms, a little wealth with which to buy luxuries and a modicum of social status. No more inconvenience, discomfort, and loneliness. Distractions and money can cure all that. Life with Messerschmidt was a barren field. Her husband had been a tired, sick old man without interest in dancing, dining out, parties, and masquerades. I was another German, but at least healthy, employed, and closer to her own age. Messerschmidt's social standing had never risen very high. Any respect he'd gained was limited to inside the Academy, not the St. Petersburg social scene, and he died leaving her destitute with a young daughter. Compared with most of the available Russian men I was educated, relatively refined, and not an alcoholic. At least I offered hope of a steady income and social advancement, if only she could dress me properly and get me to focus on smoothing my German-accented Russian.

I remained in Moskva with Brigitta-Helena and our daughter through early spring, reluctant to leave. When not with them I botanized locally and compiled a list of plants, then one morning, the date of which I neither recall nor wish to, Decker and I departed for Siberia and ultimately Kamchatka to learn our destinies.

11

THE KAMCHATKA PENINSULA DANGLES like a cow's tit from mainland Siberia, a land mass comparable to England or Italy and stretching south from approximately 58° to 51° north latitude. Bordering its western edge is the Penzhine Sea (*Penzhinskoye More*, later renamed the Okhotsk Sea); to its east is the North Pacific Ocean (more specifically a section of it known later as the Bering Sea). If measured in a straight line, Kamchatka is perhaps 5,000 miles east of St. Petersburg, but expeditions don't travel in straight lines. At times the roads (where there are roads) meander without apparent direction, rivers bend sinuously against their banks, paths switchback through mountain passes. Realistically, the mileage is closer to 6,000.

Viewed in panorama the Second Kamchatka Expedition literally spanned an entire continent, encompassing all of northern Asia. No roads nor system of roads stitched together connect the two locations. The space between begins at the Russian Plain, then come the Ural Mountains, and farther east other snow-covered mountain ranges. Rivers great and small crisscross the land. Summer travel is slowed by countless marshes and bogs intent on swallowing wagons and carts to their axels and sucking down the horses and oxen to their bellies when they must often be unharnessed, killed, and abandoned. Mosquitoes and biting flies give no respite where all this standing water provides infinite places to breed. The forests of conifers and hardwoods are virgin and vast and in many locations almost impenetrable. In the far north they thin, and the landscape vanishes without relief into immense stretches of windswept taiga and tundra, presenting a white vacuum seemingly without end. Winter travel by sled on frozen rivers is the most efficient method of getting around in Siberia, although many people and draft animals are lost each year from falling through soft places in the ice.

Adding to the traveler's misery is the weather: the whole of Siberia kneels under one of the harshest climates on Earth. Mid-summer heat can be staggering, the air so infested with bloodthirsty insects as to obscure the sky. Winter temperatures at some locations have been recorded at − 70° Fahrenheit. In such conditions snot expelled from the nostrils freezes in midair, and exposed skin is frostbitten within minutes. Vicious winter winds sometimes make standing upright impossible, reducing mobility to crawling or inching wormlike on elbows and stomach.

Transit time between St. Petersburg and Kamchatka just in one direction is 2 years, including a sea voyage of 10-15 days across the Penzhine Sea between Okhotsk Ostrog on the Siberian mainland at the mouth of the Okhota River and Bolsheretskoi Ostrog on Kamchatka's west coast. Siberia offers no services and developed resources capable of supplying the enormous needs of the Second Kamchatka Expedition. Empress Anna had done what she could through a *ukase* issued to the *voyevoda* (head official) of every regional chancellery ordering complete cooperation with Bering and making clear his requests and those of the Academy were to be granted fully and promptly, but as we shall see her mandate was largely ignored, much to the Expedition's detriment.

In the absence of infrastructure Bering was forced to establish it. At various locations in mainland Siberia and later Kamchatka he dispatched surveyors and engineers to develop iron mines, construct furnaces to smelt the ore, and lay foundries to forge cannons and other weapons plus ammunition, chains, anchors, tools, every sort of ships' fittings, and, perhaps most important, nails of all sizes. At Kamchatka he ordered land cleared to make way for roads and *ostrogs*. He had lumberyards built so timber could be processed for erection of houses and barracks, palisades, churches, magazines; for barrel staves, wagons, axe handles, warehouses, and ships.

Even before his arrival at Yakutsk, a port on the Lena River and major staging area for the Expedition, Bering ordered the officers preceding him to acquire large supplies of hemp from Irkutsk and then construct a ropewalk to twist it and a distillery for making pitch with which to treat the rope so that it doesn't rot and weaken. Later, at Kamchatka, he approved harbor sites, modified coastlines for shipyards and docks, and built chandleries, smithies, lighthouses, and breakwalls. To supply skilled manpower he established schools for teaching navigation and the needed trades.

12

AFTER SAYING GOODBYE TO Birgitta-Helena and her daughter in Moskva, Decker and I traveled overland to the Tatar city of Kazan then on to Nishnij Novgorod via the Oka River. I botanized along the way with Decker making the necessary paintings and illustrations of the plants collected. We entered Siberia at Yekaterinburg on the Iset River where it joins the Tobol, which in turn conjoins the Irtysh at Tobolsk. My lists and descriptions of the plants of this region were lost when sent by courier to St. Petersburg. Many of my later collections and manuscripts also met this fate, including a journal of the nearly 3 years Decker and I trudged eastward toward our ultimate objective, Okhotsk Ostrog on the Penzhine Sea, the point of embarkation for Kamchatka.

Along the way we continued collecting specimens of plants and animals, and I recorded observations of the people and places visited. Traveling on the rivers in the warm months was especially rewarding because we could stop wherever we wished to observe, collect, and describe the flora and fauna. This was especially true when going upstream and the boat had to be dragged from along the shore. Then progress slowed almost to a halt. Much could be accomplished during the extended daylight of northern summer, often in quiet and pleasant surroundings interrupted only by bird calls and leaves rustling in the trees.

I botanized in the vicinity of Tobolsk, compiling a list and descriptions of the local plants. These later disappeared along with Decker's artwork somewhere in transit to the Academy. On the cheerful side it was here that officials of the chancellery introduced me to Aleksej Fedorovitch Danilov from Yakutsk whom I engaged at once as my agent, mediator, and assistant. His principal function was to arrange transport and other logistic matters during my travels, starting by accompanying Decker and me on the next leg to Irkutsk. On several occasions Danilov had led travelers between Moskva and Okhotsk Ostrog, our eventual destination before Kamchatka. He knew the routes and their pitfalls, which trails to take and which to avoid. Danilov stayed in my service for several years, proving trustworthy and capable.

We arrived in Tomsk on 8 November 1738 in time to participate in the decadent Festival of Archangel Mikhail when, as Gmelin had written of his earlier visit, it was as if a *ukase* had been issued ordering every citizen to get as drunk as possible. During the Christmas season I acquired a fever so violent that Decker and Danilov worried I would die. As the year ended Decker wrote to Gmelin and Müller waiting for us at Yeniseisk reporting that the fever had broken and I was on the mend, although still too weak to travel, especially with the outside temperature sometimes dipping to − 46° Fahrenheit. They replied that my health came first and by no means should I travel until recovered completely. Near mid-January 1739, although still weak, I declared myself fit enough, and we left Tomsk for Yeniseisk. The trip by sled took 10 days in temperatures that I doubt ever rose above − 30° Fahrenheit. The only stops were to feed ourselves and change horses at winter government stations along the route.

We pulled in at Yeniseisk on 20 January and took lodging with Gmelin and Müller. By then I was my old zesty self, still humorless and sarcastic but with renewed confidence and vigor. On seeing my enthusiasm and good health Gmelin, who wished to be relieved of his responsibilities as quickly as possible and go back to St. Petersburg, was overjoyed. He said he considered me nearly his equal as a naturalist, which I suppose in his mind was a compliment, and he burbled that by pairing Krasheninnikov's and my skills the Academy's natural history objectives in Siberia could be achieved without him. Stepan Petrovich Krasheninnikov was the Academy's star student whom Gmelin had brought along to assist him. In his excitement he rationalized that his continued presence away from St. Petersburg would cost Empress Anna far more than the sum of Krasheninnikov and me because he, Gmelin, required more support personnel and comforts, including soldiers to guard him and dozens of horses, carts, and drivers to transport his mountain of baggage and luxuries.

Our needs, in contrast, were wonderfully simple. We accepted any living conditions, no matter how squalid. What we ate and how we traveled were irrelevant to us. In concluding this tendentious exercise in logic, his opting out and returning to St. Petersburg could be seen as both frugal and altruistic. For Krasheninnikov and me it would open opportunities to pursue natural history mostly unimpeded while advancing our careers under his brilliant and benevolent supervision from afar. Essentially, he would send us lists from St. Petersburg of what specimens to collect, and we would set forth diligently to find and ship them to him.

If this reasoning wasn't dubious and arrogant enough, what emerged next from Gmelin's mouth was even more thoughtless and pompous. He said that if the need should arise and emergency warrants, Krasheninnikov and I, being lower in the Academy's hierarchy, could openly and unabashedly kiss Bering's ass to achieve his favor and thereby reach our objectives. In contrast, he and Müller, having been granted their gracious positions and high status as full professors directly by the Senate, could not possibly risk their dignity and reputations by groveling. I said nothing, but confess that my jaw tightened and my tongue bled metaphorically for several days.

It was just the three of us, my traveling companions having retired to the temporary quarters assigned us. Gmelin settled back in his chair and stared at me benevolently. I glanced back then quickly looked away, thinking I should do something with my hands, which seemed to be flopping aimlessly on my thighs like dying fishes seeking water. Gmelin's gaze wasn't so much unnerving as unnecessary. Finally, he barked an order in Russian. "Wine!" he said to no one in particular. A servant appeared at once dressed in a dirty serving jacket and carrying a tray with a bottle and three glasses, which he filled and handed to us.

Gmelin, still in recline, raised his. "To Steller and Kamchatka!" Müller and I raised ours and took a sip.

Müller, who had remained silent, now said, "And to the success of the Expedition! May we exceed expectations." Again we raised glasses in unison and sipped.

Gmelin now struggled to sit upright without spilling his wine. He had a kind and cheery disposition and by nature was sedentary, preferring to sit when standing was the other option, to lie down when the alternative was to sit. He had lost weight since our last encounter but still tended toward chubbiness, emphasized by his short stature and the baggy work trousers he now wore. His face was round and unblemished, its features paedomorphic, a trait highlighted by eyes that appeared guileless and soft like the eyes of certain small dogs bred to be companions of fashionable women.

"Gerhard and I shall do everything possible this evening to dissuade you from this insane Kamchatka adventure." He chuckled at this little joke.

"It's true," Müller said. "What you've experienced during these early years in Siberia is a holiday compared with the pain and disappointment awaiting you. It's rumored that Kamchatka devours Europeans." Müller had been leaning toward me, forearms on knees. He now sat back for emphasis, satisfied he had just offered something profound. He was a large, handsome man, like Gmelin pleasant and cautious. His willingness to take risks and tolerate discomfort extended only so far. It was clear that both were perfectly content to throw me into Kamchatka's gaping jaws if it hastened their return to St. Petersburg.

"We know what you're thinking." Gmelin raised his empty glass and waved it at his disheveled servant standing in a far corner. He waited while our glasses were filled before continuing. "You're thinking, 'How can I, a mere adjunct, possibly duplicate Johann Gmelin's intellectual efforts and sophistication in the absence of Gmelin.' Am I right?" He looked my way smugly.

They clearly had no idea what I was thinking. I saw myself as their unspoken collaborator, although not in the context they did; rather, I would do anything to assist their departure for St. Petersburg with the hope they never returned. Nothing would suit me more than to pursue the Academy's Kamchatka objectives without their fumbling supervision and fussy advice.

I said, "Exactly, Your Excellency," addressing Gmelin formally and looking humbly at the floor.

"Ah-*ha*! Just as I predicted, eh Gerhard?"

I glanced at Müller and saw him nod. "That you did, Johann," he said.

"But Gerhard and I have thought this over carefully and discussed the benefits and disadvantages of sending you off alone to face the wilderness. You have certain qualities we lack and that we think should benefit the Expedition. You have proven yourself not averse to risk and bodily harm. You don't worry about deprivations of any sort, plunging into the field despite intense cold, rain, snow, and other inconveniences. We've seen you work hard an entire day without food or water. When others stop to eat and drink you sit with them and instead use the time to write your notes and package specimens. You have an interest and facility for languages, and wherever you stay a month or so you learn to speak well enough to the indigenous people to obtain what you need from them.

"You travel with minimal baggage, and one each of a cup, plate, spoon, and folding knife. You eschew wigs and powder and go around bareheaded like a Cossack. You eat whatever is available, throwing it together in your single pot and cooking it yourself. Sleeping on the ground and shitting in briars aren't hardships. You carry a single blanket and for clothing take only what's on your back and feet. Boots of any size are adequate. If too small you cut holes in them, if too big you stuff them with grass. Lastly, we recognize your deep loyalty to our three secular gods—the Academy, the Expedition, and the natural sciences. Forget obeisance to the empress, who doesn't give a fuck about our work except for the light it might shine on her in Europe. Basically, we conduct this labor because it pleases and satisfied us. A more noble reason isn't necessary. These are the benefits, as we see them. Gerhard?"

Müller cleared his throat. "Excellent summary, Johann. The potential disadvantages now fall to me, and I shall lay them out directly and honestly. Are you agreeable?"

I nodded. "Certainly, Your Excellency."

"You have a quick temper that if you can't learn to control will inevitably land you—not to mention Johann and me and possibly the

Expedition itself—in trouble. We've received reports from various chancelleries you've visited. At first you deal mildly with the recalcitrant *voyevoda* in residence, but if your demands aren't met in what you consider a reasonable length of time you start to berate and insult him. By making him your enemy you then stand no chance of satisfaction and can expect to leave empty-handed when petitioning this man in the future. You have insufficient patience with those you feel less competent than you, bringing them to heel rudely and without explanation, when subtle blandishments might gain you more. Your sarcasm and churlish behavior wear on subordinates, colleagues, and superiors alike. Better to stay silent unless offering something pleasant. Sympathy for the plight of the indigenous peoples, European exiles, and serfs is admirable, but writing letters to the authorities angrily demanding better treatment of them is not within your purview. The biting pen must lie still for risk of pissing off unknown powers who might hinder our work. Last but not least is your open contempt of authority often to the point of disregarding instructions, which can only lead to negative consequences, certainly for you and perhaps innocent bystanders. Finally, please accept that Siberia is a calumnious place. It's our duty as enlightened men of science to remain objective and rise above it."

Müller again leaned forward, elbows on knees and face drawn close to mine. He looked down at his feet, lower lip quivering slightly. This awkward attempt at rebuke had made him uneasy, and he obviously felt guilty, like a father having just chastised a child but unsure if the effort was justified. The ruse seemed ridiculous, especially when presented by a man a mere 4 years my senior.

It was a sign of Gmelin's dominance that he'd left the unpleasant work to his colleague. He now broke in and applied the balm he believed necessary to soothe the sting. "But overall the beneficial outweighs the negative, and we don't by any means think less of you for having been burdened with these deficiencies. We willingly concede that some of them might indeed be congenital, but it's for you to decide which aren't and correct them. Please accept our criticisms in the constructive manner intended, and while here enjoy our friendship and hospitality." With those last words he waved his glass to be filled.

13

DESPITE THIS FEIGNED SUPERIORITY, Gmelin and Müller had not always distinguished themselves as models of diplomacy and tact since leaving St. Petersburg, as proved later by their own journals. On arriving at Irkutsk and still novices in Siberia they had visited the *voyevoda*, an unpleasant and stubborn man named Colonel Andrei Grigorievitch Pleshtcheyev. They laid before him their plans to explore the Lake Baikal region before proceeding to lands along the Mongolian frontier. For this they would need at least 74 pack horses. Colonel Pleshtcheyev allotted them half this number and stubbornly refused more. Thinking they could bargain, the professors then threatened to stay at Irkutsk with their contingent a full year and further drain the Colonel's provisions and budget, but he held firm.

The brief Siberian spring had arrived, and there was no time to lose. In the early morning of 24 April 1735 the professors dispatched their soldiers to the public market with orders to requisition every horse that could walk without stumbling and in this way made up the deficiency. The Colonel didn't try to stop them, and the party left Irkutsk later that day fully equipped with the necessary horse-power.

Not only horses were requisitioned as exigencies arose. After exploring Lake Baikal and the Mongolian frontier, including visiting several mines, Gmelin and Müller returned to Irkutsk and remained through early winter. Starting in late winter they traveled overland to Ust-Ilga Ostrog at the confluence of the rivers Ilga and Lena, arriving in time for Easter. Church services on Easter Sunday began at 6 o'clock in the morning so as not to interfere with the serious drinking, which began

59

2 hours later and continued uninterrupted for nearly a week.

The river ice broke soon after, and on 18 May 1736 the entourage started down the Lena in 12 boats to which Colonel Pleshtcheyev had assigned 96 *slushivs* (unmounted regulars) to row and steer. When only 73 showed up for duty the professors ordered their soldiers to seize 23 local peasants to take their places. The party arrived at Kirensk on 22 June. Along the way they freed the peasants and exchanged them for exiled Russian nationals, but both exiles and the original *slushivs* abandoned their oars and defected at alarming rates. To remedy this and send a stern message, gallows were erected in the larger *ostrogs* along the Lena where deserters, according to Gmelin's writings, *are to be strung up forthwith*. This heavy-handed attempt at deterrence was a comedic failure. Desertions continued, and no one was ever hanged.

The group reached Yakutsk 11 September 1736 and made plans to winter there. Yakutsk is the closest inland settlement of any size to Okhotsk Ostrog and the sea route to Kamchatka. Stores and equipment would be transported overland from there, warehoused at Okhotsk Ostrog, and sent across the Penzhine Sea to Kamchatka where ships for the three expeditions—Arctic, Japan, and America—were to be built, provisioned, and dispatched on their explorations.

On arrival at Yakutsk the Academy contingent found the only suitable lodgings already occupied by Admiralty personnel, the remaining houses being squalid and nearly uninhabitable. Regional and local authorities throughout Siberia had been ordered to extend the professors special privileges, including the best lodging and food, adequate firewood, and sufficient lamp oil to facilitate their writing and illustrating tasks through the tenebrous Arctic winters.

Many Siberian houses have no windows and chimneys. What paltry daylight is available seeps in through a hole in the roof that also serves as a vent for the smoke, usually originating from an open fire on the floor. The stove, if there is one, often emits so much gas that those inside suffer excruciating headaches. At some *ostrogs* holes are cut into the walls of the houses and in late autumn are fitted with transparent blocks of ice, the spaces around packed with snow onto which hot water is poured to form a permanent icy seal. There's little danger of the ice melting because room temperature is always below the freezing point of water until spring thaw.

Housing was always a point of contention between naval and civilian personnel. More than once the Academy's entourage arrived in a town or *ostrog* to find naval officers from the Admiralty's branch already ensconced in the better dwellings. Often the wealthier townsmen and their families remained comfortably at home, having bribed officials of the local chancellery not to evict them. At such times Gmelin and Müller badgered the top naval officer (often Bering himself), reminding him of the empress' instructions of providing them nothing less than the best accommodations, even it meant moving to lesser quarters themselves. When this failed they approached the *voyevoda*, showed him their documents, and made their demands known. Depending on his level of sophistication the *voyevoda* either brushed them off or smiled diplomatically and implied that the issue was an Expedition dispute and not within his purview to solve.

Gmelin and Müller were not just idly whining. Animal comfort was important, certainly, but more was at stake. Working is difficult when your eyes never quit watering from wood smoke, and the illumination inadequate to read a page from a book or write a line yourself. The artists had it even worst. They often labored not just in dim light but with soot drifting relentlessly into their paints and onto their canvases, muting and darkening the colors. Many illustrations had to be destroyed when exposure to full daylight revealed their deficiencies. Even when the fire was out soot and other tiny bits of debris rained from the ceiling blanketing everything. Attempts to wipe it off left black smudges. Within a year any books, manuscripts, and illustrations left uncovered were damaged irreparably, the books still adequate for field work but unsuitable for a library repository, the illustrations unfit for publication.

Overwintering was a time for sorting, preserving, and cataloging specimens to be shipped west to St. Petersburg. It was then we paused in our frantic travels and wrote reports, updated journals, and planned the coming summer's field work. It was also a time of socializing. On the night of 8 November during a party at the conscripted home of

Bering and his family the house in which Gmelin was living burned to the ground. He lost most of his belongings; even worse, his collections and documents from the previous year's field season were destroyed. Many books in the Expedition's traveling library were badly damaged or lost. Of these the most valuable was Tournefort's *Institutiones rei herbariae*. The locations Gmelin had recently scoured for specimens would have to be revisited and new collections made. He was naturally despondent, but his generally cheerful attitude soon put the coming difficulties out of mind.

On 11 May 1737, just after the Lena's ice had broken up and the spring flood subsided, the party prepared to embark for Kamchatka by way of Okhotsk Ostrog. Or so everyone thought. Earlier, in Tobolsk, the professors had passed along to the Admiralty a detailed list of provisions required during their coming stay in Kamchatka, which the *voyevoda* had been ordered to fulfill. Everything was to be delivered to Okhotsk Ostrog prior to the Academy contingent's arrival there and subsequent departure for Kamchatka. Because Tobolsk is Siberia's capital and most cosmopolitan city, no difficulties were anticipated. At that time the city comprised about 3,000 houses and 13,000 inhabitants. The navy was to arrange for these supplies and Academy personnel to be transported from Okhotsk Ostrog across the Penzhine Sea to Bolsheretskoi Ostrog on Kamchatka's west coast, which served as the peninsula's capital and the Expedition's principal staging area.

The navy, said the *voyevoda*, had taken all his stores. When might they be replaced? He shrugged. And the Academy personnel's own sea transport? Despite what the empress demands we look out for ourselves first, the navy told the professors. You want transportation to Bolsheretskoi Ostrog, arrange it with the *voyevoda* at Okhotsk Ostrog. You and your entourage aren't our responsibility. But the *voyevoda* there said he presently had no ships and didn't know when any would become available.

That the *voyevoda* weaseled out of his responsibility should not have been a surprise. The civilized part of Russia is a functioning dictatorship where authority is honored and orders ignored or disobeyed are punished harshly and swiftly. The hinterlands are different.

A *voyevoda* anywhere in Siberia had clear instructions to cooperate with Bering. However, Bering and his officers were prohibited by the same mandate from making decisions affecting these districts without approval of the local chancellery represented by the *voyevoda*. Instead of being organized as a vertical chain of command, the hierarchy was in fact a circle. It was a system designed to fail. Predictably, the result can only be a stalemate creating an environment in which progress moves forward hand in hand only if the hand belonging to the local official has been greased. In the end the *voyevoda* does as he pleases with little fear of reprisal. In practical terms the empress' *ukase* is at best a two-way street, at worst a dead end.

From the viewpoint of local officials, what benefit accrues to them when hundreds of entitled strangers descend suddenly into their lives like locusts, requisitioning the houses and expelling their owners into the fields to sleep, conscripting male citizens for labor, consuming the food and other resources, and rendering the countryside a wasteland? The officials have to live there after the ravenous horde moves on; those residents inconvenienced and often left more impoverished than before are their neighbors, relatives, and friends. The suppressed hostility of these officials toward distant authority, combined with an ingrained disinclination to cooperate, *ukase* or not, is understandable. And what power can coerce them? As the saying goes in Siberia, *God is in Heaven, and the empress is far away in St. Petersburg.*

The professors were flummoxed. The three of them held a meeting and decided to postpone going to Kamchatka and stay on the mainland for now. De la Croyère would travel north down the Lena to its mouth on the Icy Sea and fix its latitude. Müller, who had been ill, wanted some time in a warmer climate. Gmelin, needing to replace his specimens lost in the fire, went south to the upper Lena with him.

De la Croyère seemed indifferent to their present hardships, but Gmelin and Müller were tired of the sordid living standard and oppressive bureaucracies that infested every corner of Siberia. And they especially resented their objectives being placed secondary to the navy's. They longed for the easy life in St. Petersburg where scholarship could be undertaken in clean, safe surroundings. Even the Academy's political intrigue and backstabbing were preferable to this.

Wary of the challenges and discomfort they might encounter at Bolsheretskoi Ostrog and elsewhere at Kamchatka they decided to send Krasheninnikov ahead, hoping he could accomplish enough that their work might be completed sooner and they could go home. Stepan Krasheninnikov, mentioned earlier, was the most ambitious and reliable of the Academy students selected to participate in the Expedition. Although only 20, he was also the most resourceful, already having shown an aptitude for completing difficult tasks quickly and creatively. The professors therefore arranged to send him to Bolsheretskoi Ostrog to reconnoiter, collect specimens, gather information, start a small botanical garden, and have suitable houses built for their eventual arrival at Kamchatka.

Krasheninnikov's route from Yakutsk was the same one I would later take, except (God be praised) I avoided Krasheninnikov's misfortunes during the sea voyage and his awkward disembarkation. For this reason I shall reprise his adventure as told to me by Krasheninnikov himself.

14

INSTRUCTIONS IN HAND, KRASHENINNIKOV dutifully set out from Yakutsk on 8 July 1737 accompanied by a copyist to transcribe his notes, manuscripts, and reports and two *slushivs*. They crossed the Lena, procured horses at Yarmanka, and left for the mountains the next day. There they ascended to lakes still ice-covered in mid-summer, arriving eventually at the supply depot of Yudomskoi Krest established in 1726 during the First Kamchatka Expedition. It consisted of a few primitive houses for the officers and soldiers guarding it, a magazine, and warehouses.

After a brief stay Krasheninnikov's party continued on, arriving at Okhotsk Ostrog 19 August, where no ship was waiting. Within a week, however, the *Fortuna*, the first ship Bering built during the First Kamchatka Expedition and now transporting cargo back and forth across the Penzhine Sea, returned from Bolsheretskoi Ostrog.

Heavily laden and newly refitted, *Fortuna* departed for Kamchatka 4 October. Land had long since disappeared when she began leaking badly. Pumps were put to use and manned continuously, but water in the hold nonetheless rose with such frightening persistence it seemed a disgruntled God might be toying with them. Soon it was pouring in through the portholes. The wind direction discouraged backtracking to Okhotsk Ostrog despite temporarily pleasant weather. Jettisoning seven tons of cargo alleviated the situation, although not enough to abandon the pumps. The men worked in shifts around the clock through cold rain and sleet, arriving 14 October at the mouth of the Bolshaya River in a howling north wind.

Here the ship's crew mistook the ebb tide for the flood. The ship, battered by wind and waves crashing over the deck, was foundering and starting to break apart. The decision was made to run *Fortuna* aground, which they did, and praise God she became beached when the tide ran fully out, permitting everyone to scramble onto land. The next incoming tide finished tearing her apart, carrying her away in pieces when it retreated. A few planks remained. On examination they proved to be rotten. So much for the quality of the refitting. Those aboard were lucky to survive and thanked God for His mercy.

Fortuna is the Roman goddess of luck, but the luck she brings is unpredictable. It can be good or bad. Sometimes her likeness is depicted wearing a blindfold and holding a balance in the service and honor of fairness. This is Fortuna's incarnation as Lady Justice. Although sometimes blindfolded and a clone of Lady Justice, Fortuna doesn't carry a balance. Her decisions are fickle, not fair, based on destiny instead of justice. Who lives and who dies isn't her concern.

Krasheninnikov lost everything and arrived at Kamchatka wearing only the clothes on his back, which by then had mostly frozen to his skin. I admire his spirit and grit because he went promptly to work, having managed to save his list of instructions. There was no chance of procuring clothing and supplies from the academicians. Winter had set in, and mail could not be sent until spring. As things turned out, Krasheninnikov's letter describing his plight did not reach Gmelin and Müller until January 1739.

On 3 September Müller and Gmelin arrived at Kirenskoi Ostrog and decided to winter there, but Müller's illness was worsening. In early November he went by sled to Irkutsk where living conditions were more comfortable. There he gradually improved, writing later that a local physician bled him 17 times in 2 months. When no longer bedridden he enquired at the chancellery about obtaining provisions and transport to Okhotsk Ostrog via Yakutsk and eventually to Kamchatka in spring; the answer was again negative.

The Academy party had now been traveling almost 5 years. None except Krasheninnikov had yet departed for Kamchatka, and his arrival on that shore was as yet unsubstantiated. Gmelin had sent a letter to St. Petersburg requesting another assistant, but that was a year ago. Had the contents been seen? Sometimes the mail arrived, sometimes not, and expecting it to get there in only a year was highly optimistic. Gmelin and Müller knew for certain only that they were exhausted, discouraged, and feeling mortal. Their most fervent wish was to forget Kamchatka and go home. Sending in their places two hard-working, competent assistants inured to the hardships of field work could complete the Academy's objectives, permitting Gmelin and Müller to receive their shipments in comfortable, civilized St. Petersburg and begin the lengthy task of identifying, cataloging, and preparing monographs.

Allow me to expend a few words describing the logistics of the Second Kamchatka Expedition, doubtless the largest and most comprehensive undertaking yet attempted in the whole of human history. The trek from St. Petersburg to the Penzhine Sea would tax even Job's patience, but the final overland leg from Yakutsk to Okhotsk Ostrog, a straight-line distance of some 500 miles but in actuality much farther, is perhaps the most difficult terrain in all Siberia, and through this tortuous, trackless wilderness thousands of tons of stores and equipment had to be transported to the coast for transshipment to Kamchatka in all seasons each year of the Expedition.

Because most Siberian rivers flow north to the Icy Sea the way south requires dragging cargo-laden boats upstream against the currents. The rivers narrow as the traveler approaches their headwaters, becoming shoals and sharp bends that greatly hinder boat traffic. In addition, the rivers are navigable only when ice-free and then only partway. Where they become too shallow and narrow the material must be moved overland by wagons in summer and sleds in winter, but in the mountains even these must be abandoned and everything transferred to the backs of horses and men. All told, a good day's progress along the whole trek might be 10 miles.

Horses can be used only when the route is clear of snow and ice. In winter, provisions and equipment are transported manually. Each man is harnessed like a draft animal to a long, narrow freight sled called a *narte* (or *narta*) loaded with only five poods (about 180 pounds) because of the uneven terrain and steep inclines. At any given time as many as 500 men are in transit, traveling in convoys. Reindeer are also used to pull sleds in winter, which helps a great deal, although reindeer are weaker than horses, and one of these animals can't pull more than a man. Food is scarce, rations mostly limited to rye flour and groats. The men suffer greatly from hunger, exhaustion, and cold, and many die every year.

15

THAT NIGHT AT YENISEISK ended with Gmelin, Müller, and me slobbering drunk and loudly congratulating God for having scoured Germany to assemble three such companionable and accomplished colleagues. I suppose these laudatory praises directed at ourselves had some validity, although God didn't need to search far to find Gmelin and me: we had been born and raised in small cities not a hundred miles apart. Perhaps it bemused His Holy Presence to have dropped us like reindeer turds onto the Siberian landscape, a place He seems to have forgotten He created and now wished to forget.

Krasheninnikov's situation was a major worry. His personal belongings and Expedition equipment, along with flour that was to have lasted him 2 years, had been part of the cargo tossed overboard to keep the *Fortuna* afloat. He was in desperate need of food and clothing. Gmelin and Müller raided their own wardrobes and gave me clothes to pass to him at Kamchatka. Many of Gmelin's had perished in the fire, and he was loathe to part with what remained of his wardrobe. He and Müller were also writing urgent letters to the chancelleries at Irkutsk and Yakutsk asking that aid be dispatched directly and without delay to Krasheninnikov at Bolsheretskoi Ostrog, although without much hope of fulfillment.

The two professors now devoted their time and energy toward expediting my departure. They decided I needed another assistant, one fluent in Russian and sufficiently calm and sophisticated to intercede on my behalf at chancelleries. He need not be competent in Latin, but at least able to transcribe notes written in that language into my periodic reports to the Academy, and he was to serve as a secretary in the field, recording my spoken observations to spare the inconvenience and time lost by stopping to write them down myself.

It was helpful of Gmelin and Müller to bolster my rudimentary aptitude for diplomacy. I genuinely admired their resourcefulness when dealing with bureaucrats. Every backward *ostrog* in Siberia seemed inhabited by at least one such irksome specimen. Gmelin was particularly suave and adept at approaching these bumpkins using false flattery, although it seldom produced positive results. My quick temper when confronting such men of ignorance and open greed is an admitted failing, but I would much prefer addressing an angry wolverine in its den. At least the denouement would be quick and sincere on both our parts.

For this dubious assignment Gmelin selected Aleksej Gorlanov, a mostly competent and expendable student in his contingent. I was to find Gorlanov useful, except for his excessive drinking. He had also adopted many of Müller's mannerisms, including several annoying and pompous poses, such as leaning against a doorjamb while smoking a pipe and trying to appear thoughtful. I finally got him alone and told him he looked like a fool. He wasn't a professor and would never attain that lofty perch. I'm a mere adjunct, I said, but you? You're only a bear-skinner, so stop acting like an asshole and get to work. He took to the working part and reduced his drinking, but Müller's mannerisms were evidently too ingrained to abandon.

I had complained previously to Gmelin about Decker's dereliction of duty. He was slow in producing illustrations and unable to properly distinguish leisure from labor, spending excessive time with a glass of tea in the hand that should have held a brush. To assure I would not continue to be burdened Gmelin took Decker off my hands and replaced him with the German painter Johann Christian Berckhan. My only complaint about Berckhan was his weak constitution.

Gmelin also lent me several books from the Expedition's library to assist with identifications at Kamchatka, figuring he had one foot out the door. If by God's negligence he ended up in Kamchatka he could always retrieve them. These I welcomed. I was less enthusiastic about the detailed list of instructions he and Müller were preparing and

that evidently mirrored the list they had earlier given to Krasheninnikov. I took these pages with false gratitude, thanking their well-born
highnesses for their labors and feeling not the least remorse about the
deception. In my opinion, what they handed me represented information, not instructions.

My true orders had been imparted by the Academy, as stated in the
contract I signed prior to leaving St. Petersburg. I had not agreed to
join the Expedition as the subordinate of Gmelin or Müller despite
their rank of full professor and my lower position as an adjunct. According to the contract, which neither Gmelin nor Müller had seen, I
was in truth an independent operator. Nonetheless, I held my tongue.
There was no point in forcing a pissing contest having come this close
to my goal of reaching Kamchatka.

Yeniseisk was boring and intellectually impoverished, not different
from other Siberian cities, especially in winter. I could not leave soon
enough. On the night of our drinking bout the prim and conservative
Gmelin had described Yeniseisk as a cesspool ridden with venereal disease and populated by drunks and malingerers, either dismissing or not
noticing our own drunken condition and state of momentary idleness.

Danilov, Gorlanov, Berckhan, "the immoral clockmaker," and I left
together the morning of 5 March 1739, turning sideways on the sled
and waving goodbye to Gmelin and Müller behind whom the bleak
outline of Yeniseisk faded into the swirling blizzard. Fate is always concealed by a curtain, tantalizingly close and seemingly predictable, but
in truth hidden from everyone. Gmelin and Müller would eventually
be granted their wish to be relieved and return to St. Petersburg. My
correspondence with Gmelin would oscillate between friendly and
contentious, but I would never see his face or Müller's again.

I haven't mentioned "the immoral clockmaker" until now, and his
presence in our merry band of travelers therefore requires explanation.
Krasheninnikov wasn't alone in needing assistance. Just before my arrival at Yeniseisk a letter came from de la Croyère addressed to Gmelin
and Müller requesting someone with skills to repair his pendulum
clocks, which had been damaged along with other of his astronomical
instruments while enroute to measure latitude where the mouth of the

Lena River enters the Icy Sea. From the start, Gmelin had declared this venture unnecessary and foolishly risky, but de la Croyère was a full professor of the Academy and empowered to make his own decisions. The effort had come to nothing. Regardless, Gmelin was disinclined to fix blame for the mission's failure entirely on de la Croyère's incompetence. His principal assistants on that trip, a surveyor and a student from the Academy, had proved as inept as de la Croyère himself and also bore responsibility. Then there was a run of generally bad luck. Another surveyor and a soldier died, a soldier became frostbitten and unable to work, and one of the *slushivs* committed suicide.

No astronomical observations had been made at the designated site because de la Croyère, needing both hands to adjust his instruments (now in doubtful working condition) had no one along capable of counting seconds. In fact, during my entire time in Siberia I can't point to a single original observation de la Croyère contributed to the Expedition despite scurrying this way and that and disappearing for weeks at a time, returning with voluminous notes and reports of no value. In the end his presence amounted to a superfluous expense and on the voyage to America a clear danger, as I later show.

Academy professors were nonetheless obliged to help one another. During my stay with them at Yeniseisk, Gmelin and Müller received notice of a man recently exiled to Siberia after being convicted of an undescribed sex offense. He was said to be an accomplished clockmaker. Criminals could be conscripted by higher authorities demonstrating need of their skills. Gmelin and Müller immediately contacted the chancellery at Yeniseisk where the report originated and requested this person be delivered into their custody at once. The man's name was Mikhail Nevodtchikov. Here I shall refer to him as "the immoral clockmaker." I was to take him as far as Irkutsk where other Expedition personnel would hand him over to de la Croyère, who would set him to work repairing his astronomical instruments damaged on the Lena, including the malfunctioning pendulum clocks.

16

I HAD NOTICED AT Tomsk how the flora was changing. Until then the vegetation of western Russia was familiar, not very different from Europe's, but I was now seeing species strange to me and perhaps unknown to any naturalist. The prospect of life-forms yet undescribed to science was exciting, and I looked forward to tramping the landscape when the new growth started to appear. The hope was to reach Okhotsk Ostrog by year's end. My companions and I packed frantically, hoping to travel the winter road to Irkutsk before spring, a distance of about 800 miles, and after discharging a few official errands for Gmelin and Müller continue without delay to Yakutsk. But fate intervened, and I was stuck in Irkutsk a year, although the time wasn't entirely unprofitable.

By coincidence we encountered Captain Spangberg. He was going in the opposite direction, having been recalled to St. Petersburg. Detractors had demeaned his recent voyage from Okhotsk Ostrog to explore the Kuril Islands and Japan, one even claiming his ships actually reached Korea instead. At any rate, he had been instructed to repeat the voyage and was on the way to the Admiralty in St. Petersburg to receive specific instructions, review his maps, and formally address his critics. We stopped and talked, each lamenting the plight of the other and discussing in that brief interval the possibility of my joining him next time. He was agreeable, although I would need the Academy's permission. Hence my petition to join Spangberg's next expedition in a letter to Baron von Korff described a little later.

We arrived at our destination 23 March and found quarters. Irkutsk, a diverse and prosperous city, occupies the eastern shore of the

Angara River opposite the mouth of the Irkut, its affluent. While in the vicinity I hoped to explore Lake Baikal, that fascinating and mysterious freshwater sea a mere 40 miles upriver. Irkutsk is large compared with most Siberian cities, numbering about 1,000 houses in addition to the usual churches, monasteries, government buildings, and so forth. It also boasts a jail, several taverns and whiskey bars, a brewery, a bath-house, and a sizeable bazaar. This last is superior to most because of the proximity of China. The populace soon got news that a physician from St. Petersburg was in town, and my days were consumed with treating the sick and injured, including my artist Berckhan now down with an unknown illness.

On 10 May I wrote to Gmelin telling him about a recent earthquake that toppled many chimneys and damaged a cathedral, but mostly I gushed absurdly about my new findings, mainly plants and birds, and included some bird skins and a few of Berckhan's colored illustrations along with notes of dissections. I errored greatly in being so effusive, forgetting that Gmelin had previously surveyed the region and evident-ly made several of my putative "discoveries." This led to Gmelin's later accusation that I wasn't qualified to describe and name new species if unable to distinguish them from known ones. Furthermore, I had done this work independently without having first discussed any findings with an expert like him. Clearly, I was an amateur.

When posting the letter I had no premonition of Gmelin ever doing me such a disservice, so naturally I was angry and disappointed when his reply arrived and I learned he had slandered me. At the same time I realized that not only is it wise to keep your lips buttoned, but to be equally cautious when putting pen to paper. They were lessons I too often forgot.

Meanwhile, I prepared to visit the Lake Baikal region, and on 12 July wrote to Baron von Korff, my direct superior and head of the Academy, proposing a quick survey over the summer and asking as an aside if he could expedite my travel to Kamchatka. I promised to keep the cost of the Lake Baikal venture under 50 rubles and noted that the locations I hoped to explore had not yet been visited by Gmelin and Müller. Despite the short summer, I said I expected to find many new plants and animals and while in the field also investigate rumors of valuable mineral deposits. Locally, I continued to pester the Irkutsk chancellery for any aid it could provide toward getting me to Kamchatka. Gmelin and Müller had earlier petitioned this same man, the vice-governor Nikolai Alekseivitch Bibikov, and finally given up. Although abnormally kind and generous for a *voyevoda*, Bibikov was helpless to assist our cause, and I too went away empty-handed.

Soon after mailing my letter to Baron von Korff I set off with Berckhan and Gorlanov on a 250-mile trip along the shores of Lake Baikal. The only boats available, called *doshtcheniki*, are constructed strictly for rivers and lakes and would not last an hour on even a mildly restless sea. They sail clumsily, and the boatmen prefer pulling them along the shoreline tethered to long ropes.

I managed to catch some specimens of an unusual wood louse, probably new to science, in addition to a seal found in great numbers, which is not new but well known. It appears similar to the seal common to Heligoland in the North Sea and that I've also observed playing around the ships at Kronstadt where they enter from the Baltic, occasionally ascending the Neva River to St. Petersburg and beyond. I'm told they are indigenous to parts of Kamchatka also. Perhaps they are one species. If so then it occurs worldwide in the Northern Hemisphere. How this population came to be isolated in Lake Baikal hundreds of miles inland from the Icy Sea is a puzzle to be solved by future naturalists.

Interesting plants were everywhere, some known to me, others unfamiliar and yet undescribed. The latter included an onion of the genus *Allium* and a figwort (genus *Scrofularia*). I also collected relatives of two new legumes of the genus *Astragalus*, known to possess useful medicinal properties; these might too. We stopped at Olkhon Island where we came across an undescribed grass that when cut leaked a thick brown fluid. Thinking it might be manna I collected some and added it to my tea, but unlike true manna it had no immediate laxative effect. The Baikal region proved a paradise. It seemed placed in my path by God to enjoy and explore. I thanked Him profusely and took advantage of His gift with gusto.

The Barguzinian Mountains rise abruptly from the western shore of the lake. We disembarked at a small beach and started climbing. The trek was long and arduous, culminating in an alpine region. Just short of the summit we paused, and I was made dizzy and euphoric by the thin air and spectacular views. The sun's rays glancing from distant peaks turned the snow fields brilliant red, flooding my eyes with a rush of liquid ruby. Everywhere the stones were covered in patchwork scabs of multicolored lichens. Nestled in the scree beneath a large, crumbling ledge grew a stunning new gentian like no other, and on the descent we came across a new rhododendron with rare yellow flowers. A kind of bee I had never seen crawled through its petals, and on the bees lived a tiny parasitic mite, also new to science. I pressed several of these between thin sheets of transparent mica we picked up on the mountain and stored them carefully away for later examination underneath magnification.

We had brought along a pet roe deer that followed us everywhere like a dog. When we stopped to examine the rhododendron it ate some of the leaves and within minutes became drunk, stumbling and staggering about and shaking its head, finally falling into a catatonic state. For 4 hours it lay on its side and twitched. Afterward it recovered completely, but from then on avoided any plant of the rhododendron group.

17

THE BRIEF EXPEDITION TO Lake Baikal proved a needed respite. On returning to Irkutsk refreshed by our new discoveries we checked in at the chancellery, finding it no more helpful than before. Equally distressing, a new *ukase* announced that Academy leaders in Siberia were now responsible for provisioning their own parties. No *voyevoda* had ever assisted us anyway, but now their refusals were legal. To continue to Okhotsk Ostrog I would need to dip into my own funds. Subsequent preparations, in addition to treating my many new patients, now consumed all my time.

Piled atop these miseries was a letter from Birgitta-Helena demanding 400 rubles. I had previously authorized the Academy to pay her 200 rubles annually, more than enough for her and the girl to live modestly in respectable quarters. Her spending habits had obviously become profligate and more than I could afford, especially in these new circumstances. I ignored her request but privately fumed at such selfishness and complete lack of consideration for my hardships.

Shortly after her letter came one from Gmelin complaining that Müller had been recalled to St. Petersburg leaving him still awaiting the Academy's decision on his own petition. That was Gmelin's problem; I had many of my own. My reports to the Academy were late, and I was nearly out of paper for pressing plants. Most of the paper in Siberia originates in China. None was available locally, meaning the only option was a trip south to bazaars along the Mongolian border, but not until Lake Baikal froze and its surface became suitable for sleds.

Meanwhile, the student geodesist Krasilnikov had been sent here to

Irkutsk by de la Croyère to collect his party's pay and would soon return to Yakutsk where the rest were wintering. Krasilnikov told me that de la Croyère was living under a dark cloud. In addition to his generally shaky health he had sunk deeply into debt, his instruments remained in disrepair making work impossible, and the embarrassing behavior of Maria Dmitrievna Tatarinova, his drunken Russian wife, was causing him endless distress and melancholia. To assuage at least one problem I placed "the immoral clockmaker" in Krasilnikov's custody before he departed for Yakutsk. Perhaps some of de la Croyère's instruments could be repaired by summer, permitting him a tiny shiver of joy.

I continued to labor after dark in the inadequate light of oil lamps finishing the reports and putting my notes in order. The next task was to prepare and organize the collections and send them with all written materials to the Academy. When everything was packed satisfactorily I delivered the boxes and barrels to the Irkutsk chancellery and asked that they be closed both with its official sea and my own. By doing this I could be assured the specimens would arrive without having been disturbed or damaged at some customs house. The package containing the written materials was left unsealed. To demonstrate that my actions were above board I wrote a letter to Gmelin explaining what I'd done.

Gmelin and Müller were wintering in Krasnoyarsk, and it was there Gmelin received my letter explaining the shipping protocol. As fate would have it the shipment and the soldier guarding it had just arrived in Krasnoyarsk. In such a small place the appearance of a courier is immediately known to everyone. It would be a colossal understatement to describe the jovial, mild-mannered Gmelin as thoroughly pissed upon learning my shipment was bypassing his hands unexamined. He exploded in a towering rage and sat down to pen me a poisonous letter of rebuke.

To reiterate, I have considered myself an independent contractor with the Academy from the start and carried with me documents proving it. Nowhere do they state an obligation to report to Gmelin, much less bow to his orders. That Gmelin viewed himself *ipso facto* as head naturalist of the Expedition is a delusion of his own invention. His angry letter accused me of behaving surreptitiously and dishonorably after all he and Müller had done helping me get to Kamchatka, although here I still was on the mainland. My actions in not sending the specimens and manuscripts *to him* instead of directly to St. Petersburg represented blatant insubordination. I deserved to be harshly disciplined.

The shipment, as I mentioned, bore two seals, mine and the Irkutsk chancellery's, which could be legally broken only at the Academy in St. Petersburg. Until then, by law they must remain intact. In the opinion of Gmelin and Müller I had committed an unforgiveable error, and their grievance against me could be justified in several ways. Not only had I violated an (imaginary) chain of command and usurped their authority, but the dignity and respect of two full professors had been violated. Academic honor was also at stake. They and the Academy had been embarrassed in front of the entire intellectual world.

Puffed with rectitude and self-importance they decided to break the seals and inspect the containers, reasoning they could easily convince the customs officials at Irkutsk that I, a lowly adjunct, had lacked authority to apply my own seal and request Irkutsk's without higher authorization, namely Gmelin's. Having so convinced themselves, they opened everything except the package containing my written materials, which was addressed to the Senate and the Academy specifically and not simply the Academy like the boxes and barrels. They rifled through the contents, discarding what they considered unnecessary or redundant, then sent the soldier and repacked consignment on their way with letters to the Senate and Academy explaining what they had done and why and lodging a formal complaint against me.

Gmelin's pique did not soon dissipate. I needed to be taught a lesson. He wrote a stinging letter to the Irkutsk chancellery ordering that nothing for transport to St. Petersburg be accepted from me, that everything was to be forwarded instead to him, Dr. Gmelin, who would open and inspect the contents before forwarding them to the Academy. The reason? Mr. Steller is an adjunct and thus his subordinate. Mr. Steller has proven incapable of working without supervision and is unqualified to identify natural history specimens, having in the past labeled many with incorrect names. At the same time Gmelin notified me by letter that I was to cancel all plans for Kamchatka and instead go down the Lena to its mouth and examine the shoreline along the Icy Sea. During this furious one-way correspondence he also wrote Krash-eninnikov telling him I would not be coming to Kamchatka after all.

I was stunned by Gmelin's vehemence and angry and sad that my self-esteem and reputation as a loyal and dedicated naturalist had been bludgeoned so ruthlessly in the eyes of those who do not know me or are unfamiliar with my qualifications. I'm well educated. I have lectured at the University of Halle and been certified in botany by one of the most respected naturalists in Europe. Now Gmelin was trying to kill my dream of exploring Kamchatka and sending me instead on a journey he earlier considered useless and too risky for de la Croyère. Was he hoping I might never come back? Gmelin still didn't get that I was not sent to Siberia as his subordinate, and that his threats in this regard were empty.

So, what to do? My decision was simple: fuck Gmelin. I was going to Kamchatka. He could take his diplomas and other academic plaudits and stick them up his silk-covered ass.

Over two evenings I vented my anguish to my companions at a tavern while they consoled me with whiskey and tobacco. Having recovered my composure Gorlanov and I presented a diplomatic front and repaired Gmelin's damage at the chancellery, where Bibikov, the *voyevoda*, expressed good-natured understanding and sympathy. Still, we lost 2 weeks in straightening these minor kinks in our convoluted itinerary before leaving Irkutsk for Yakutsk in open disregard of Gmelin's orders. The entire distance by sled on the frozen Lena is 1,624 miles, but we traveled only 614 of them to Kirenskoi Ostrog where a tributary, the Kirenga River, enters the main flow. There we waited for the ice to break.

While idle, I composed a careful letter to Baron von Korff in which I defended myself against Gmelin's charges, pointing out that I am fully qualified to identify and label natural history specimens and also that I was not Gmelin's subordinate, but according to my contract expected to travel and perform my duties as an unsupervised professional naturalist. Kirenskoi Ostrog is a station on the post road. Couriers frequently pass through, and my letter went out 20 April.

My argument was detailed and extensive, requiring 19 large pages, the words presented in beautiful German calligraphy by my artist and draftsman Berckhan. I addressed von Korff in the most flowing and flattering terms as *High-well-born, High-governing Lord President, Gracious Sire*. . . . I explained my anguish at Gmelin's thoughtless and unfounded denunciation of me, why I had thus sealed the shipment (to protect it from the careless and thieving hands of small-town customs agents), my reasonable unacceptance of Gmelin's authority over me and my work, and why I was disregarding his illegal orders to visit the Icy Sea instead of going to Kamchatka. I ended the letter petitioning to accompany Spangberg on his return voyage to Japan. I made this request despite not having specific knowledge of Spangberg's plans, although as I mention earlier in the narrative I already possessed first-hand knowledge from Spangberg himself that such a voyage would occur and he was agreeable to my joining him, provided I received official permission from the Academy.

All available correspondence detailing the dispute with Gmelin was eventually read before a meeting of the Academy in St. Petersburg, then set aside to grow mold. Further action was never taken by either the Academy or Senate. The baron was a *boyar*, not a naturalist, and I did not know that 5 days after posting my letter to him he left St. Petersburg to become ambassador to the court at Copenhagen. Anyway, his personal disinterest in such controversies and the convenience of this one occurring well out of earshot would have been cause enough to provoke a yawn. At the Academy, staff members were distracted by their own vicious infighting and political intrigues, oblivious to the hardships and strife of colleagues and associates in faraway Siberia. To the Senate, feuding among a handful of foreign-born academics engaged in tasks nobody understood was trivial, whether under their noses or on the eastern frontier, similar in urgency to rumors of fisticuffs among some Cossacks in a Yakutsk tavern or another God-forsaken place. Life went on as normal in sophisticated St. Petersburg, and the whole matter sputtered and died with all the drama of a spent candle.

18

I WAS AT LAST headed toward Okhotsk Ostrog and the now almost mythical land of Kamchatka. How long I would stay there was problematic. The time might be short if my petition to accompany Spangberg to Japan was approved. If not, I could be there several years. Either opportunity was welcome. On 20 May 1740 my companions and I started down the Lena, now clear of ice, in a *doshtchenik* I had bought and paid to be refurbished, botanizing along the way.

Our provisions, equipment, and luggage had been sent ahead and were waiting when we arrived in Yakutsk. Now it was time to transport everything over the mountains to Okhotsk Ostrog. I chose the overland route instead of two of the Lena's tributaries, obviating the need to have barges built. I would still have to arrange for pack horses. The land route was shorter but considerably more arduous.

We would winter at Yakutsk, perhaps the coldest city on Earth. It had been Bering's headquarters for 3 years prior to moving his operation to Okhotsk Ostrog in preparation for the America expedition. Yakutsk consists mainly of primitive wooden houses of poor quality, perhaps 600 in total. It has a vodka magazine and a residence for the *voyevoda*, a shiftless man named Aleksei Yeremyevitch Zaborovski, and a chancellery where he appears at irregular intervals to perform a few perfunctory duties before banishing all visitors and opening the bottle. Outside the palisades are some churches and a monastery. Yakutsk has always been notable for its market, which boasts Chinese goods and serves as a clearinghouse for sable skins, good ones currently selling for up to 70 rubles. I would renew my supply of paper while here, the summer's botanizing having used up much of my inventory acquired at the Mongolian frontier.

Arranging for pack horses and drivers to load and lead them across the mountains took 3 weeks. On 15 June 1740 we departed taking the route followed by Krasheninnikov 3 years before; that is, to Okhotsk Ostrog via Yudomsk and the supply depot at Yudomskoi Krest. I walked nearly the entire distance to this way-station, *a cheerful foot-soldier* as described by my pen, collecting numerous rare plants along the trails.

As fate ordained, Spangberg, also on the way to Okhotsk Ostrog, overtook our little caravan at Yudomsk. He was hoping to arrive before Bering and his contingent sailed for Kamchatka. I left my companions, mounted a horse, and on 8 August 1740 joined Spangberg. The Captain is a splendid raconteur, and as we passed through the Urak River valley he soon had my head spinning with tales of fantastic peoples dressed in the most bizarre and intricate costumes, and of others by their behavior and hairy bodies a mere step above the beasts. He described foggy seas and lands teeming with near-mythic creatures probably never before seen by a European, of odd plants he does not doubt grow nowhere else.

I had not yet heard from Baron von Korff at the Academy regarding my petition to sail with Spangberg on his next voyage to Japan (nor would I for reasons stated above), but my head now swam with exotic images of that place, and I was determined to go anyway. We arrived at Okhotsk Ostrog on 12 August in time to intercept Bering. Spangberg knew Bering was finishing his vessels for the America Expedition and, as mentioned, would soon sail for Avatcha Bay, his chosen embarkation point on Kamchatka's east coast. Still, Spangberg expected to find the vessels assigned him in near-condition to sail, needing only minor refitting and repair. But Bering had emptied the warehouses, conscripted Spangberg's vessels the *Nadezhda* and newly-constructed *Okhotsk*, and dispatched them to Avatcha Bay to supply his two new ships the *St. Peter* and *St. Paul* now being readied to sail for America, the main reason for the Second Kamchatka Expedition and thus its principal undertaking.

Even were the *Nadezhda* and *Okhotsk* to return promptly to Okhotsk Ostrog it would not have mattered; the warehouses were empty, and as always replacement goods would have to be brought across the mountains from Yakutsk. Spangberg was stranded ashore indefinitely, and the reality of it enraged him. Bering patiently explained the situation. He was being hammered from all angles. Superiors and detractors in St. Petersburg were chastising him for proceeding too slowly. The America Expedition on which everything depended had not even left for Kamchatka. Then there was the budget, already exceeded with a cap nowhere in sight. And finally—incredibly—Bering had not received word of Spangberg's second Japan Expedition and was as surprised as everyone else at the news. All he knew was that Spangberg had completed his first voyage successfully the previous year and gone to St. Petersburg to report his findings. Bering told him the matter was out of his hands for better or worse, fates be damned. The onus, sorry to say, fell on Spangberg. Bering shrugged and said there was nothing he could do. God willing, he was on the way to America.

Bering would be returning the *Nadezhda* and *Okhotsk* after unloading them at Avatcha Bay, but everything considered, Spangberg would have to build another ship for a necessary fleet of three. Now Okhotsk Ostrog's warehouses were empty. He would also be forced to obtain supplies to provision his ships at Yakutsk and see them transported over the mountains. The earliest the next Japan Expedition could depart would be autumn 1741, although spring 1742 was more likely.

Interesting how the mind rationalizes when exigencies arise. Spangberg was hardly alone in being stuck at Okhotsk Ostrog. So was I, and my party and provisions would arrive soon. Autumn was almost upon us. With Spangberg now out of the picture these were the facts. First, my petition to the Academy asking to accompany Spangberg and dated 20 April was somewhere enroute, impossible to stop or delay. Regardless of the response, I had presented my case for going logically and well. I could think of no one bearing me a grudge to argue against it except Gmelin or Müller, and I had not informed them. Assuming no explicit objections, I estimated odds of approval at 50-50. Whether the request was accepted or rejected Spangberg wasn't leaving anytime soon, freeing me to sail for Kamchatka. I could proceed without approval after discounting Gmelin's pissing and moaning to the Academy about my insubordination and disrespect of his exaggerated self-importance.

Second, logistics for the trip to Kamchatka had been well planned and executed. My provisions and assistants were on the way and right behind me. No misadventures had befallen us. Everyone was happy, satisfied, and looking forward to the adventure. Nothing foreseen could prevent our safe gathering here at Okhotsk Ostrog before taking the final leg by sea to that long-sought destination. Third, I had laid out a good part of my personal resources and sweat to get us here, funds and effort that would never be recouped. If I abandoned Kamchatka now, only the collections and discoveries currently enroute to St. Petersburg held meaning.

Add to this Spangberg's disintegrating behavior. Having been spurned by Bering and now without a mission he railed at everyone. I suppose nothing could be worse for a sailor than to be stranded ashore without a ship, but his concealed anger had risen quickly to the surface, broken through, and was spilling over everyone. I blame Bering for not reining him in. It would not be the last time I lost respect for Bering because of his failure to instill discipline and display leadership.

Despite attaining the rank of captain, Spangberg carried a reputation as a bully and man of occasional violence. He had little education, inferior manners, and spoke Russian like a peasant, an inexcusable defect considering his long residence in the country. According to rumor he was once accompanied everywhere by a large, vicious dog that he set loose on detractors and those who openly insulted him. Whatever the truth of these disparagements Spangberg was unpopular in many places, and people crossed streets to avoid him. I tired of his shit after a few days in Okhotsk Ostrog and told him so. That abruptly ended our friendship. Having now burned this bridge I definitely would not be going to Japan.

Using the elements of deductive logic learned and honed in debates at the University of Wittenberg, I evaluated all possible options until just one remained: to approach Bering and demand transportation of my party and cargo to Bolsheretskoi Ostrog, where Krasheninnikov desperately awaited help.

19

BERING HAD ASSUMED COMMAND of the Second Kamchatka Expedition at age 43, already feeling the crippling effects from years at sea and the weight of both naval and civilian bureaucracies. He was now 60 and in declining health. Those familiar with his personality described his demeanor as polite and well-mannered, stolid, and soft-spoken although often keeping his counsel. In recent months he had become increasingly morose and craving solitude, sure signs of melancholia brought by an excess of black bile. When he and I met at Okhotsk Ostrog I was 31 and full of enthusiasm. I asked him if the America Expedition's roster included a naturalist. He shook his head and answered that its mission was strictly to survey and map new lands and determine if Asia and America were joined. I pointed out how much could be learned if such a survey included the plants, animals, and minerals, many of which might be of enormous economic value to Russia. He listened politely, but withheld comment.

I could tell Bering liked me, and he soon agreed to take my party and consignment to Bolsheretskoi Ostrog, our initial Kamchatka headquarters, and there give Krasheninnikov much-needed relief. Our unfortunate student was possibly still languishing in the clothes he wore the day he was shipwrecked, certainly by now reduced to rags. My companions and I could occupy the houses ordered built for Gmelin and Müller. The arguments intended to convince Bering to ferry us to Kamchatka had been superfluous; for once it wasn't necessary to defend a request and then confront the vicissitudes following rejection.

I stayed at Okhotsk Ostrog 4 weeks attending to duties pertinent to arrival at Bolsheretskoi Ostrog. There I met the Kurlander Friedrich Plenisner, a draftsman and artist destined to later become my courageous and trustworthy companion during the months we spent shipwrecked and marooned. There was also the matter of a consignment of specimens sent by Krasheninnikov from Kamchatka and addressed "to the professors." The bumbling de la Croyère, waiting at Okhotsk Ostrog with us to depart for Kamchatka and the America Expedition, had already broken it open and damaged much of the contents. I cleaned and dried the salvageable items as best I could, repacked the shipment, and prepared to send it with Danilov and my own horses to Yudomsk with instructions it be expedited to Irkutsk and on to Gmelin, wherever he might be. I'd learned the consequences of bypassing His Well-born Excellency. Anyway, considering I am not a professor the consignment was rightly his. Transport to Irkutsk could take 2 years, and I doubted the contents would arrive in acceptable condition. At the last minute I dispatched someone else and subsequently took Danilov to Kamchatka with me.

Despite these many tasks I managed to squeeze in a few hours of local botanizing, on several occasions encountering thickets and even entire fields of a tough, vigorous plant taller than a man's head. The Siberians call it "sweetgrass," although actually it is a form of cow parsnip (genus *Heracleum*) belonging to the carrot family and an old acquaintance of the Cossacks, who use it to distill an alcoholic beverage.

As a race the Cossacks are not commendable for intelligence, but their diligence is extraordinary. After his comrades attempted unsuccessfully to distill liquor from everything available, including old clothing and rotten fish, a Cossack from Yeniseisk named Chernyi tried cow parsnip and became an instant hero to his people. His beverage, variously called "brandy" and *raka*, and which not wishing to poison myself just yet I have so far avoided, is evidently not just alcoholic but also hallucinogenic. Its ingestion in large volumes turns the imbiber's face blue, shortly afterward inducing apparitions and nightmares that persist into the following day, attenuating eventually to normal thought (for Cossacks, at least) but leaving the victim disoriented, distracted, and melancholy. This liquor coagulates the blood, turning it black, and is so acidic it bubbles when poured on iron and makes it gleam. I'm told the brew can be strengthened by augmenting the cow parsnip residue with honeysuckle berries during fermentation. I intended to write a botanical description of this plant and observe effects of the liquor produced from it on Cossack volunteers, but fate did not allow me the time.

Several towns in mainland Siberia I passed through before coming to Kamchatka were large enough to have distilleries where poor-quality brandy was made from cut stalks of cow parsnip. A Cossack living in one of these places told me that distillery waste in the area is a favorite food of livestock, so I decided to investigate. He was correct, and it was funny to see a man on his way to a tavern adjacent to a distillery with his cattle trailing behind, the leader to enter the public house, the rest to stop at the waste pile, and later watch them stagger home together.

To be made useful for distillation and other purposes the stalks of cow parsnip are cleaned after cutting, and the rough external covering is scraped off with a knife, mollusk shell, or similar sharp-edged tool. The stripped stalks are bundled and hung to dry in the sun. Soon they exude a sweet syrup and are taken to the distillery. Alternatively, after a few days the syrup hardens into sugar that can be scrapped away as a white powder and stored. This product is used to sweeten dishes and as an additive to condiments. Pieces of unscraped stalks are cut and handed to teething babies to chew.

Three days before embarking for Kamchatka, eventually set for 23 August, I wrote a farewell letter to Gmelin. Our last correspondence had been his letter castigating me and ordering me down the Lena to the Icy Sea. However, on arrival at Okhotsk Ostrog I found two boxes of plants from him along with a letter offering to forget past disagreements and instead renew our friendship. The consignment and letter had been posted from Krasnoyarsk, evidently after Gmelin learned I had ignored his order. I was elated to have this black cloud lifted. Making an enemy of Gmelin would be detrimental if I hoped to advance within the Academy. Still, while penning the customary salutation in my reply I felt the bile rise in my throat. How could I not? *My Dear High Well-born, Highly-honored Doctor! Exalted Patron and Friend!*

20

WE CROSSED THE PENZHINE Sea without incident and established headquarters at Bolsheretskoi Ostrog, intending to venture forth into the countryside come spring. I immediately informed Krasheninnikov that as an adjunct of the Academy I held full authority over him, and as students he and Gorlanov were equals. He kept silent, although I could tell he wasn't accepting this new situation with equanimity. As the Academy's only representative in Kamchatka until now it was natural for him to harbor a proprietary feeling for this place, but a clear chain of command was necessary, and I could not have him taking orders from the peripatetic Gmelin whose eyes were now fixed longingly on the western horizon. The first order I issued to Krasheninnikov was to compile for me a complete report of all his activities from the moment of arriving at Kamchatka until now. Specifically, I needed a list of places he had visited along with an inventory of collections made and their dispositions.

The winter's preparation was interrupted when a letter from Bering arrived in February 1741. It had been posted from the port of St. Peter and St. Paul in Avatcha Bay, his new settlement there known as Petropavlovsk (the Russian combination of Peter and Paul). The captain commander requested my presence at once to discuss the America Expedition. I left 10 March by dog team accompanied by my servant and hunter, a Cossack named Toma Lepekhin from Nizhnekamtchatsk, whom I had conscripted from Krasheninnikov's service. We hurried east across the peninsula and arrived 20 March, taking up lodging in the barracks at Petropavlovsk with de la Croyère. As fate later decreed,

Lepekhin would be the only member from my group at Bolsheretskoi Ostrog to accompany me on Bering's voyage.

Now the relationship with Bering had turned on its head, and he was wooing me. He presented his reasons for needing my services on the impending expedition to America. Among the advantages, if I accepted, I would be his cabin mate throughout the voyage, which meant superior ship's quarters. Dr. Kaspar Feige, the physician who was supposed to join the Expedition and share his cabin, had withdrawn because of illness and petitioned the Admiralty for permission to return to St. Petersburg. His impending absence left only surgeons with various levels of skills, no one trained as a physician in the healing arts. Surgeons learn their skills through apprenticeship, not university curricula. Formal training isn't required. There was no position for a naturalist, but openings for a physician and mineralogist were now available, and I was qualified in both. My official title would be Mineralogist because that job hadn't yet been filled, and time was too short to petition the Admiralty for a replacement physician. Although I would not officially function as a naturalist, Bering offered time to pursue my interests in natural history during the voyage. When I reminded him I would be leaving my assistants behind at our Bolsheretskoi Ostrog headquarters he agreed to assign men to help me as needed, a promise ultimately broken.

At the very least I needed an artist. No professional naturalist takes the field without someone skilled to illustrate his discoveries. I was incapable of performing this task myself, and the request to bring Berckhan along had been denied. Bering assured me that Plenisner was fully competent and could pick up the slack. I accepted this compromise. Plenisner and I got along well, and Berckhan's sickly constitution often rendered him unable to work. Plenisner might actually be an improvement. I also needed a hunter, mostly to shoot birds and aid in preparing bird skins and other specimens. Bering allowed me a personal servant, a role Lepekhin could fulfill when he wasn't hunting. Finally, Bering and I were both Lutherans, and my training in theology and experience as a minister seemed an added comfort to him.

There were also political considerations and consequences to weigh. Bering emphasized how my willingness to participate would be noticed and appreciated in high places at completion of the voyage. Accolades would certainly follow if we were successful. Buttressed by his letters of recommendation, future promotions and possibly a permanent position at the Academy would follow. For this last he agreed to lobby in my behalf when we got back to St. Petersburg.

21

AFTER RETURNING TO BOLSHERETSKOI OSTROG I focused on preparing for the voyage to America, which included giving the personnel I was leaving behind their lists of specific assignments and routine duties. Heavy snowfall prevented excursions to the surrounding countryside, and I was getting antsy from being stuck indoors and breathing toxic fumes from smoldering wood and smoky seal-oil lamps. To consume the vacant hours I started writing letters, disregarding Gmelin's and Müller's advice about not becoming a pain in the ass to unknown authorities and instead keeping my head down and lips buttoned. The letter writing must cease, they emphasized, before it got us all in trouble.

Easier said than done. For months I'd been irked by disregard for decent human values and administrative incompetence permeating the frozen corners of Siberia like a ubiquitous fungus. Kamchadals everywhere were being routinely cheated, raped, beaten, and otherwise mistreated by Cossacks. As a quasi-Pietist I believe that knowledgeable Christians are obliged to put faith into practice, not merely pray and stand aside passively awaiting God's divine intervention. The heathens among us ought to be treated with sympathy and kindness instead of punished for their ignorance and idolatry. They should be encourage to join hands with white Christians here to help them discern the Holy Light, not driven away to cower in darkness.

I feel that as an enlightened man and a Christian I have no choice except to report the lamentable social conditions I continued witnessing throughout this bleak land. I therefore wrote to the Holy Synod informing it about the scandalous state of the clergy, many priests having "gone native" themselves by taking bribes, charging fees for baptisms, and generally not attending to the spiritual affairs of their unenlightened flocks. The Russian clergy sent here are too few, too scattered, too little inspired, and apparently never supervised. I acknowledged how the high officials of the Russian Orthodox Church need not agree with my Lutheran beliefs, but as devout Christians themselves this hardly excused their inaction.

The Senate had only vague notions of events in Siberia. I, on the other hand, know a great deal, which I shared with that powerful governing body openly and without mincing words. At every *ostrog* indifferent government officials stiffly resisted helping the Expedition despite Her Majesty's orders. Having passed through many a chancellery and interacted with the *voyevoda* in residence I offered valuable advice for improving the quality and efficiency of regional governments. I pointed out the widespread sloth, ignorance, drunkenness, and corruption of these officials, even naming some of them, and their rampant abuse of power. I noted that many were taxing the populace and pocketing part or all of what they collected. Foreign merchants were inconsistently and loosely regulated. Bribery is the engine that drives the Siberian economy, such as it is. The civil and military laws obviously require immediate examination and tightening if government revenue is to be maximized. I wrote about all this and more.

I offered guidance on the proper criteria that must be promulgated to choose, train, and monitor Siberian officials and castigated the current system of appointing them based on bribery, friendship, and nepotism instead of demonstrated merit and experience in public administration. I suggested standards and gradations of punishment for various offenses routinely committed by the local garrisons, listing the knouting of citizens for minor offenses or the mere accusation of offenses, hangings without trials, raping of women and girls, extortion, usury, bribery, unauthorized conscripting of serfs into virtual slavery, even unpunished murder.... The list was several pages long. I also proposed where new *ostrogs* might be built to take advantage of trade, offering asides on the methods used in their construction to assure that defensive palisades are erected with greater care so they don't fall into desuetude so quickly.

After several nights of labor I lay down my pen, satisfied at having made my indignation clear, in the process passing along useful knowledge and advice to the highest powers in church and government. I confidently assumed the words would be taken seriously if only because the disputation set forth was unassailable. Higher powers would undoubtedly thank me for my wisdom and forthrightness, and I might even be rewarded.

Chest swelled with righteous feelings I summoned Krasheninnikov and ordered him to translate my Latin sentences into suitable Russian and add the appropriate Russian salutations which, being Russian, he knew better than I. He was to then pass his work to Berckhan, who in addition to his artist's duties was serving as our copyist and calligrapher. After checking everything for accuracy, grammar, and esthetic presentation Krasheninnikov was to post the letters to their designated High Well-born Excellencies and Exalted Whosomethings.

The result was not what I expected. Perhaps not surprising, Gmelin had even from a distance managed to interject his ill-advised opinions. Two years later, when he and Müller were finally on the way back to St. Petersburg, Krasheninnikov, having also been recalled, caught up with Gmelin at Turinsk and told him about my letters. Amused but annoyed, Gmelin wrote to Müller, then staying at Verkhoturye, relaying Krasheninnikov's story. In a letter dated 13 October 1742 he repeated how I had sworn Krasheninnikov to secrecy about this correspondence with the authorities, thinking someone might steal my ideas and advice and thereby deprive me of the deserved credit. He also poked fun at my suggestions of where to build future *ostrogs*, noting that in some of these regions suitable timber isn't available. Then he added that Krasheninnikov had held back expressing his contradictory opinions to me at the time for fear of eliciting my wrath and relentless persecution.

22

DURING MY MEETING WITH Bering I mentioned having earlier petitioned the Academy to accompany Spangberg to Japan, and that if the request were to be granted and I left for America instead I could be subject to severe discipline and penalties. He dismissed this concern with a wave of his hand and said not to worry, he would obtain the necessary permission by writing to the Senate stating his reasons for taking me, making it sound almost if he was conscripting me into his service out of urgent need of my specialties. He promised to assume full responsibility.

Bering soon made good on these promises by taking all necessary steps. He wrote to the Senate, held a conference with his officers to gain approval of my inclusion, and by letter publically offered me the positions of physician and mineralogist. Although left unspoken, there was little doubt he was concerned about his failing health and was taking me along entirely for medical and theological reasons. I learned once we were under sail that none of the naval officers, Bering included, had the least interest in natural history. On occasion I would be denied access to previously undiscovered shores, and certain officers went out of their way to discourage my efforts, thinking them useless and trivial.

During our negotiations Bering brought up the matter of Spangberg's distress at having his stores confiscated, stranding him at Okhotsk Ostrog and delaying his second voyage to Japan indefinitely. Thinking Spangberg and I were close, Bering wished to clear the air by explaining why Spangberg's complaints of unfair treatment were unjustified. It so happens that the First Japan Expedition might have been postponed indefinitely had Bering not provisioned Spangberg from his own stores.

Bering had moved his headquarters from Yakutsk to Okhotsk Ostrog during summer 1737, as always lugging everything over the mountains. On arrival he found Spangberg, his ships, and the officers and crews prepared to sail for Japan, except they had no provisions. The warehouses were empty. Bering gave Spangberg his own supplies brought laboriously from Yakutsk and originally intended to provision his America Expedition, but on arrival had found the two vessels intended to take him there still on the stocks at the Okhotsk Ostrog shipyard and not nearly finished. His decision to ready the Japan expedition before his own allowed Spangberg to embark without incident the following summer. Spangberg, having already been pushed to the front of the line on this occasion, had little reason to feel abused when subsequent events had not gone in his favor.

After relating this story Bering leaned back in his chair and seemed to study me. If I agreed to accompany him, he said, it would be with the understanding that no matter the circumstances his decisions would always favor the Admiralty's objectives before those of the Expedition's individual participants. By staying in Bolsheretskoi Ostrog I was free to pursue the Academy's interests solely on its terms. However, if I accompanied him to America I would be just one of many laboring for the glory of Russia under the Admiralty's directives. He repeated his willingness to accommodate my natural history pursuits as best he could, although without ultimate guarantees. In all instances the Admiralty's goals took precedence. The Academy, from the start, had understood the role of its field personnel differently, and the Expedition had been organized to accommodate its many objectives. Bering obviously disagreed with how these would be implemented at the operational level. His stubbornness in this regard, and that of the other officers after his death, would hinder and disrupt my work until the America Expedition ended and I was back at Kamchatka.

The seaport of Okhotsk Ostrog requires a brief description, if only because certain of its deficiencies exerted an adverse impact on our preparations to sail for America. The facility was valuable for only two reasons. First, its location on mainland Siberia gave overland access to resources north all the way to the Icy Sea and west to Moskva, St. Petersburg, and everywhere in between. Second, its outlet on the Penzhine Sea provided sea access east to Kamchatka and south to Japan. In all other aspects it was gravely deficient.

The surrounding countryside is low, vulnerable to seasonal flooding, and timber for housing and ship-building was already becoming locally scarce. The Okhota River's strong currents, in combination with a tidal range of 9 feet, make for insecure anchorage. Sandbars at the river mouth shift unpredictably, so running aground is always a danger. During winter and well into spring the harbor's access can be sealed suddenly by wind-driven sea-ice from the Penzhine Sea and drift-ice carried downriver on the ebb. A better staging site was obviously needed.

After Spangberg returned to Okhotsk Ostrog from Japan in August 1739 and then left to report to the Admiralty in St. Petersburg, Bering had the *Gabriel*, one of Spangberg's ships, refitted and sent to Kamchatka that same autumn under command of First Mate Ivan Yelagin. He was accompanied by Second Mate Vasilij Khmetevski. Their orders were to survey the coast south from Bolsheretskoi Ostrog, round the southern tip of the peninsula at Cape Lopatka, and continue surveying north along Kamchatka's east coast to Avatcha Bay. Inside the bay they were to select a suitable site for a harbor and settlement. With this mission completed the two ships for the America Expedition would sail to the new harbor and provision the warehouses. Petropavlovsk would then become Bering's Kamchatka headquarters, conveniently situated directly west of where America was presumed to lie.

Bering's vessels the *St. Peter* and *St. Paul* were named in honor of the apostles. A description of one suffices for both because they were identical. Captain Commander Bering chose the *St. Peter* for his flagship and assigned Captain Tchirikov to command the *St. Paul*. As to class of vessel, they were packet boats such as used to carry cargo on the Baltic and drawing 9 feet. Each was designed for a load capacity of 220,000 pounds. Each ship would carry provisions sufficient to sustain 78 men for 2 years, the length of time we expected to be away.

The vessels were 80 feet from bow to stern, double-masted and brigg-rigged, and armed with 14 cannons of 2 and 3 pounds.

Delays followed. The original departure date for Kamchatka of 15 August was pushed forward to 23 August, then into September. Bering ordered the double-sloop *Nadezhda* to embark on 1 September under command of First Mate Sofron Khitrov. I was aboard with my assistants Berckhan and Gorlanov, as was de la Croyère and his student assistant Krasilnikov. For reasons of weather we stayed anchored in the roadstead, finally leaving the harbor 3 September. We were barely under sail when the inept Khitrov carelessly ran the *Nadezhda* aground on a sandbar at the mouth of the Okhota. The ship was not just stuck, it was damaged. We lost large amounts of provisions, including all the irreplaceable ships' biscuit intended to sustain us during the 2-year America Expedition. Not even into the Penzhine Sea and already disaster! The remaining cargo was transferred to the other ships headed to Kamchatka, and the *Nadezhda* was repaired and refloated. On 8 September our convoy finally turned east, arriving at the mouth of the Bolshaya River on 21 September 1740. On that day I got my first look at Kamchatka.

Bolsheretskoi Ostrog's harbor is better than Okhotsk Ostrog's, but not much. It too is subject to strong currents, and treacherous, shifting sandbars also lie perpendicular to its mouth. When the wind blows hard from the north and the ebb is running, entering the river safely is nearly impossible, as Krasheninnikov learned when the *Fortuna* had to be run aground and subsequently was torn apart.

So as not to risk his ships, Bering in the *St. Peter* and Tchirikov in the *St. Paul* continued around Cape Lopatka at Kamchatka's southern tip and north to Avatcha Bay and the splendid, sheltered harbor of St. Peter and St. Paul, arriving, respectively, 6 October and 27 September. De la Croyère and I with our assistants continued up the Bolshaya aboard the *Okhotsk* to Bolsheretskoi Ostrog on the west coast where we would winter with Krasheninnikov, who doubtless was looking forward to the supplies and companionship.

Khitrov accompanied the *St. Peter* and *St. Paul*, but suffered another "mishap" of some sort while attempting to double Cape Lopatka and nearly losing the *Nadezhda* for good, not to mention all aboard, forcing him back to Bolsheretskoi Ostrog instead of proceeding to Avatcha Bay. He and the crew put into port 8 October and were left no choice but to winter, it being too late in the year to sail back to Okhotsk Ostrog. Having previously lost the America Expedition's consignment of biscuit, he had now failed to deliver other essential provisions to Bering's warehouses at Petropavlovsk. Subsequently, it became necessary to transport them 140 miles overland across the peninsula.

At this time there was not a single horse in all Kamchatka. The only way the goods could be moved was by dogsleds and on men's backs. It takes a team of 8-10 dogs to pull a load carried by a single horse (about 400 pounds), and Bolsheretskoi Ostrog did not have nearly enough to even start emptying the *Nadezhda*'s hold. Dogs and their owners were therefore conscripted from inland locations. Few of these men had ever been farther than a few miles from home, and as it happened almost none in this part of Kamchatka even knew what a dogsled looked like and had to be taught against their will how to mush. So did the dogs, and considerable time was expended in the instruction of men and beasts. The result was a native rebellion during which soldiers knouted the Kamchadals and otherwise treated them cruelly. Several people on both sides were killed. Five thousand or so dogs were eventually assembled, and goods were transported throughout the winter.

Khitrov was wholly responsible for this catastrophe. His "mishap" at sea left considerable havoc in its wake that trailed us like a hellhound, including loss of life, unnecessary expense, inconvenience, and wasted time moving our provisions overland to Avatcha Bay. I hold Bering responsible for not dismissing him outright and continuing to stoically tolerate such dangerous incompetence. His indecisiveness demonstrates an appalling failure of leadership, causing me to fume inwardly for many days. No, I amend that last statement: I still fume. As punishment Bering relieved Khitrov of command of the *Nadezhda* and assigned him to the *St. Peter*, promoting him to lieutenant and placing him third in the chain of command, thus solving one problem by creating another! How could anyone think Khitrov would miraculously become intelligent and competent by attaining a higher rank and transferring to a different vessel?

Khitrov isn't only an asshole of a human being, he's a terrible sailor as well. I later expressed both assessments loudly to his face during a heated moment when we had been drinking in a tavern at Okhotsk Ostrog. He didn't appreciate the words, but truth be told I have no use for him, and *vice versa*. More of Khitrov's "mishaps" were to come, endangering everyone aboard Bering's ship.

23

I mentioned earlier that despite a *ukase* issued by Empress Anna to all Siberian chancelleries ordering cooperation with Bering, neither side had real authority over the other. Cooperation being a commodity in Siberia, nothing ever got done except through bribery. The Russian naval leadership is restrained by a similar odd hybrid democracy, except bribery isn't a component. According to protocol Bering must seek advice and counsel of the Expedition's Academy members on important matters, in addition to gaining the approval of Tchirikov, his top Russian assistant. This policy in slightly different form holds true aboard ship. In the Russian Navy a captain is not in complete command even of his own vessel. In some situations the captain is required to call a meeting of the ship's council, which includes both commissioned and noncommissioned officers, and they as a group decide. However, naval policy also dictates that the captain consult his entire crew on matters affecting everyone. Decisions are subsequently declared by vote, the captain's carrying no greater weight than an ordinary seaman's.

The course to America—or where it was believed America lay—had to be plotted and agreed to be taken by majority vote, as navy regulations required. This involved considerable discussion. East and north was the logical direction; unfortunately, it was too logical.

Spring was late, and ice blanketing the harbor of St. Peter and St. Paul had still not thawed by 1 May, although the ship's log of the *St. Peter* had started 22 April at noon when preparation of both ships for their sea voyages commenced. A meeting of the combined ship's councils was held 4 May. All officers and mates were invited to participate.

Because neither Gmelin nor Müller could be present, de la Croyère as the only full professor represented the Academy's interests. He reprised orders transmitted by his half-brother, the cartographer Joseph Nicolas de l'Isle, to insist the America Expedition search for João da Gama Land. Whatever its exact shape and size it was too big to be missed. Supposedly, it spanned north latitudes 47-45°. The map de la Croyère presented depicted João da Gama Land lying vaguely northeast of Japan beyond Yezo (Hokkaido), although apparently not one of the Kuril Islands, and putatively located somewhere southeast by east of Avatcha Bay. De l'Isle had drawn the map at the Admiralty's request in 1731.

The existence of João da Gama Land had been debated by mariners and cartographers for years. Several officers present, including Bering, were reluctant to waste time in the search. Their mission was northeast to America. The summer sailing season is short, but all were intimidated by de l'Isle's scientific reputation and near-regal status at the Academy. Following considerable debate and discussion those present agreed that attempting to find this place before turning northeast toward America would be worthwhile. The map later proved erroneous and was partly responsible for the disaster that befell us. João da Gama Land is a myth, although no one knew this at the time. A document was duly prepared recording the agreement of the combined counsels, and everyone signed it. These contracts are irreversible. Despite some trepidation, finding de l'Isle's Holy Grail would be our first mission.

Since arriving at Kamchatka I had interviewed many mariners and other knowledgeable persons and come to a private conclusion, namely that the American land closest to Asia would be found opposite the Tchuktchi Peninsula, the most northern and eastern point in Asia. My presence at this meeting had not been requested, but prior to it I offered this unsolicited opinion to Bering. During his first voyage in 1728, foul weather had shielded the view east from Cape Tchuktchi, and although he could not state for certain I was wrong, he doubted me and advised disregarding local rumors as not being credible. This was the first of many subsequent instances during the voyage when my opinions and good advice were ignored because I'm a landsman and thus inexperienced in nautical matters. Familiarity with science, proven observational capacities, and ability to reason deductively based on direct evidence apparently become worthless attributes the instant someone having such qualities but who isn't a sailor steps aboard a ship.

Bering was skeptical about deviating from the main mission, and with good reason. The America Expedition had already been shortened by half, several exigencies, including loss of the ships' biscuit, having now reduced it to a single year. The original Admiralty plan called for the *St. Peter* and *St. Paul* to winter on the American coast this year, continue cruising during the following spring and summer, and return to Kamchatka in autumn 1742. Unwilling to needlessly risk lives and ships by extending this year's work later into autumn, Bering now insisted we arrive back at Avatcha Bay by late September. For this disappointing mandate we could largely thank Khitrov, that eternal *svoloch* and fuckup, whose fateful decisions while commanding the *Nadezhda* stole glory from Russia in the semblance of a full year now lost in the exploration of unknown lands. And yet Khitrov would be coming along on the *St. Peter* as a lieutenant and Bering's third in command! That this bumbling moron might be commanding our ship if some tragedy struck Captain Commander Bering or Captain Sven Waxell, Bering's first officer, was frightening beyond belief.

The naval personnel had long known their ship assignments, but the real bickering, intrigue, and griping began when we civilians were given our places. I already knew I would accompany Bering and occupy a berth in his cabin to keep a close eye on his health. My illustrator Plenisner was also placed aboard the *St. Peter*. Lieutenant Waxell had been allowed to bring along his son Laventij, just a minor, who was about to experience (and survive) the voyage of a lifetime.

De la Croyère would sail with Captain Tchirikov aboard the *St. Paul*, as would his student assistant Krasilnikov, who was actually the more competent geodesist. But Krasilnikov resisted, stating emphatically that he wasn't going to America under any circumstances and told de la Croyère to fuck off. De la Croyère erupted in a rage, ordering his subordinate to gather his belongings and get his ass aboard the *St. Paul* forthwith, at which point Krasilnikov produced a letter from Dr. Feige stating he was too ill to participate. De la Croyère then confiscated

Krasilnikov's surveying instruments and books and turned them over to another geodetic student.

Later he cooled down and returned Krasilnikov's materials. Accepting that Krasilnikov would not be assisting him in America, de la Croyère ordered him to instead survey the coast of Kamchatka from Bolsheretskoi Ostrog south around Cape Lopatka and north to Avatcha Bay. This identical task had been accomplished previously in autumn 1739 by Yelagin and Khmetevski in the *Gabriel*, refitted after Spangberg's voyage to Japan and as ordered personally by Bering. Whether the absent-minded de la Croyère had forgotten I can't say. In any case, I doubt if Krasilnikov cared. Clearly, he was tired of taking shit from his boss and needed space.

Each packet boat took 78 men; the *St. Peter*, in addition, had Waxell's young son on its final roster, as mentioned. Also as mentioned, Captain Waxell, a Swede, was Bering's second in command followed in the hierarchy by my nemesis Lieutenant Khitrov. Included on our ship's roster were several servants, two for Bering, one each for the other two officers, Assistant Surgeon Mathias Betge, Plenisner, and me. Toma Lepekhin, my Cossack servant/hunter, had resisted going, but had no choice after being assigned to the Academy's Kamchatka's contingent by the *voyevoda* at Bolsheretskoi Ostrog. Lepekhin could always run away, although if caught he would be knouted and tossed into prison. If he did decide to desert his mind would be at ease in one respect: punishment by exile to Siberia was hardly a frightening prospect, considering he was already here and had never lived anywhere else.

Also listed on the ship's roster were a first mate, a second mate, and a purser. Medical personnel included me as unofficial physician, an assistant surgeon (Betge), and a surgeon apprentice (Arkhip Konavalov). The rest were sailors, boatswains, gunners, grenadiers, soldiers (including two trumpeters and a drummer), and skilled workmen (carpenters, a caulker, a blacksmith, a sailmaker, and a cooper).

The day of departure finally came, or so we assumed. We were already behind schedule because of persistent harbor ice and numerous other contingencies. Anxiety about completing the many tasks ahead in a single sailing season instead of two had put everyone in a foul mood.

On 29 May we anchored in the roadstead and on weighing anchor encountered unfavorable winds. The next few days were spent tacking in futile attempts to reach the open sea. On Thursday 4 June the fore-topsail and fore-topmast staysail were hoisted, and both ships cleared the entrance to Avatcha Bay propelled by a gentle northwest wind.

By 9 June we had reached north latitude 49°, supposed location of the fabled João da Gama Land. Soundings commenced at 10 o'clock in the morning, but no bottom was touched at 90 fathoms. We crept forward through the night, wary of striking a reef or impending shore in the darkness, then perhaps being boarded and slaughtered by bloodthirsty João da Gamans. The wind was slight, and no breaking surf could be heard. By 12 June near north latitude 46° there was still no land, no reefs, no discernible bottom, just open ocean. Sailors were sent aloft to the crosstrees where they stared at the horizon until woozy. Nothing. If João da Gama Land was here we were sailing over it. Maybe it existed at one time, then sank like Atlantis. I didn't mention to anyone that in some learned circles João da Gama's very existence is doubted. Perhaps he's no less mythical than his so-called "discoveries." I left that bit of trivia for another time. Who aboard would believe even the possibility? After all, I'm not a sailor.

Terms of the combined council meeting of 4 May to which all present had affixed their signatures had now been met. The *St. Paul* was standing off. Captains Waxell and Tchirikov took up their speaking trumpets and agreed to change course to east by north toward America. Meanwhile, I had been observing our surroundings, noting some species of seabirds and also harlequin ducks, both known to be mainly coastal, and floating seaweeds of various sorts detached from rocks, all signs indicating land nearby.

I approached the officers and offered my opinion, pointing to the evidence and suggesting we continue in an east-southeast direction at least another day. I was ridiculed and reminded I'm not a seaman and should therefore leave navigation and related nautical matters to professional sailors. As I was to discover, this episode was just the first expression of their insular thinking and patronizing attitude.

It bears mentioning that none of the officers deployed in the America

Expedition had ever attended a university. Their reading and writing skills were adequate for naval service where composing entries into ships' logs and issuing written orders are necessary. And all officers, of course, have training in navigation. Bering is a cut above the others in this regard, yet he sometimes relies on secretaries to transcribe his orders and keep minutes of council meetings. Considering his enormous responsibilities, whatever help he can get is deserved. As to the rest of the naval contingent, despite betrayal by their coarseness even the lowest sailors claim to have captured and retained exclusive scientific knowledge about navigation and seamanship, which is laughable when a signature represents the limit of what most can accomplish with a pen.

Their ignorance is often appalling. One sailor, when shown a map of the world, tried convincing me that we were near Canada; still another insisted that Canton is at north latitude 45° and the Maldives are located in the Mediterranean! I went fuming to my berth hoping that by updating my journal I could sweep the mind clear of such stupidity. Later that day when I told Plenisner about these experiences he merely laughed and said, "George Wilhelm, they're toying with you. They've discovered your lack of humor and inability to take a joke. It's best if you ignore them. Maybe they aren't as stupid as they pretend."

I considered Plenisner's words and vowed silently to abide by them and not take myself so seriously when interacting with the sailors. After all, what difference did it make if they were teasing me or really believed what they said? Why should I care? I was aboard for the higher purpose of describing God's plants and animals, the strange people he created, and the unknown coasts. What came from the mouths of degenerate sailors was irrelevant and unworthy of the distraction. As to the officers, how could I be insulted at being treated like a *slushiv*, knowing, as I wrote in my journal, *They, of course, have been in God's council chamber!*

24

On 20 June we lost sight of the *St. Paul* in thick fog and never saw her again. When the weather cleared we sailed about aimlessly in a vain search before turning back to north latitude 46° thinking we might cross paths, or at least give João da Gama Land a final chance to prove itself real. I again saw sea-signs indicative of land nearby, but on sighting neither packet boat nor coast the officers gave up on the *St. Paul* and rightly consigned João da Gama Land and its equally nebulous discoverer to history's trash bin. On 25 June we set a new course east-northeast.

Nonetheless, I kept pestering Bering about the sea-signs around us, emphasizing that my training and expertise as a naturalist should be taken seriously when making certain decisions and by ignoring such knowledge he wasn't making the best use of his personnel. There was much to be gained and little to lose, I argued, in folding outside opinions and observations into the navy's nautical expertise. During one of these sessions we were in the captain's cabin. Bering was lying in his berth, a place he was spending an increasing amount of time and leaving running the ship almost entirely to Waxell. He had begun to look sickly, having acquired a pallor and dark bags under his eyes. He was also losing weight. I stopped badgering him for the moment and asked if he felt right.

He sat up with a groan. "No," he said. "I don't. But you aren't making me feel better, Dr. Steller. In fact, you're starting to piss me off. I don't appreciate, nor do I accept, advice on nautical matters from landsmen. You're wearing on my patience and dignity."

I said, "Indeed, but call if you need medical assistance. I do know something about medicine. And incidentally, are you aware of Waxell and Khitrov keeping certain information from you, knowing you're ill?"

He waved a hand dismissing me and lay down. Without being asked I brought some cool compresses and placed them on his forehead, which felt feverish. I was considering whether to bleed him when he began to snore softly, so instead I slipped away. One thing the captain commander needed was sleep, and it was my responsibility to remember his age and frailties.

Half the drinking water had been consumed by mid-July, and there was no way of telling how many of the remaining barrels were completely full, partly full, or empty. Leakage is always a worry aboard ship, and especially so in our case. On both ships the staves had been bound with flimsy wooden bands because iron throughout Siberia is in short supply, especially so at Kamchatka. Assuming the casks were full the supply would last about 5 weeks, provided the daily allowance was reduced. Bering rallied from his berth and called a meeting of the ship's council, which decided to take a more northerly course in hope of finding land and filling the barrels.

I personally put a dent in my credibility during the evening of 15 July. While strolling the deck I thought I'd spotted land straight ahead above the horizon and loudly shouted my discovery. Others rushed forward and exclaimed to have seen it too, but the officers disparaged us, me in particular, and subjected me to open ridicule when soundings revealed no bottom at 90 fathoms. My embarrassment was fortunately short-lived and soon forgotten.

Still, the false alarm I trumpeted got the attention of everyone even if the first sighting of America isn't mine to claim. Uncertainty had grown during the night, although the officers were silent, wary of perhaps having to eat their words. Did Steller actually see land or was shouting that he had merely another odd and baseless outburst? Regardless, the next morning there was renewed interest in staring at the horizon. The weather was overcast and drizzling, but about noon the sun appeared long enough to allow a celestial reading, showing our position to be north latitude 58° 14′. The crew went about its tasks a little more energetically; the officers conversed among themselves with renewed alacrity. I was too restless to go below and write in my journal, and the sky seemed to be brightening propitiously. In the high humidity and calm sea every normal noise was magnified.

My senses were on high alert. I was conscious of the slap of seawater against the *St. Peter's* flanks, of the creaking rigging and rattling stays, of sails snapping and luffing in the light breeze as the officer of the watch barked his course corrections to the helmsman and deckhands jumped to adjust the sails. Then suddenly from a crosstree overhead we heard, "*Land ahead!*" At those words every head rose simultaneously. As if in a quickened dream the clouds vanished and before us a panoply of mountains appeared, their snow-covered caps glowing pink in the slanted light of afternoon. America at last!

The captain commander was summoned from his cabin, and he soon appeared and shuffled toward the bow. This was his moment of glory, the apotheosis of his already legendary career capping 15 brutal years of constant hardship and work, of worry and self-doubt made worse by slights and abuse hurled at him from his many detractors. He leaned his forearms on the rail and glanced toward the mountains, then shrugged and turned away. We were shocked, uncertain what to think. He explained the gesture when we were alone in his cabin. The infectious rapture of his shipmates had not affected him because he was already worrying about the vicissitudes of leading us safely back to Kamchatka. Our season of exploration was nearly over, and who could predict what events might delay a safe return to Petropavlovsk?

My thoughts, in contrast, were positive, my mood euphoric. Hidden in those mountains were undiscovered plants and animals and mineral riches so astounding that St. Petersburg would surpass Berlin and Paris as the world's center of enlightenment and learning. And I was hardly discounting my chance for personal glory. America was the opportunity of a lifetime to make my reputation and add the name Steller to the list of immortal naturalists whose discoveries and descriptions would remain timeless. My impending observations, God willing and given the opportunity, would shake the world of science to its foundation.

I understood Bering's concerns and his reasons for hurrying home, but wasn't exploration one of our missions? Weren't we supposed to follow and map the coastline of America? I needed to get ashore quickly to start observing and collecting. There were new forms of nature waiting to be described, undiscovered people speaking languages we Europeans had never heard in cultures we had never witnessed. Selfishly, I prayed that a minor disaster might force us to winter here.

By morning the next day, 17 July, we were almost within hailing distance of the coast, advancing toward it slowly in a light breeze. Fog and intermittent rain hindered the view, and dusk erased the visual field entirely. Conditions the next day were the same. Soundings did not reveal a bottom, and by evening we were within a few miles of land (later named Kayak Island). We crept closer, finding bottom at 55 fathoms. We tacked through the night and all the next day, eventually reaching the lee side of the island. During this process I noticed land debris floating toward us at one location atop a current of water less salty than the sea. I reported my observation to the officers, adding that it could be evidence of a river and maybe a suitable anchoring site. They dismissed my suggestion with the usual sarcasm, one of them asking if I had been here before, considering I knew the place so well. Later they avoided me when the prediction proved correct, and the river was named after Bering.

25

AT 6 O'CLOCK THE next morning I stood nervously on deck shifting from one foot to the other, notebook, pen and ink, cooking utensils, and collecting equipment packed and ready to disembark. We had anchored a mile offshore in 22 fathoms. Bering sent Khitrov with a crew in the longboat to check a nearby strait and see if it led to a sheltered bay where the *St. Peter* could be moved if a storm should blow up. I requested permission to go along, which Khitrov, as skipper of the longboat, surprisingly granted, but Bering vetoed the request. I felt my blood pressure rising and my head about to explode. I pleaded with Bering, who replied he could not take the chance of my being murdered by savages who might be lurking among the trees. If the island was inhabited the people had surely seen us and were watching.

Seeing the longboat pull away at 8 o'clock was too much. Before I could stop my tongue I yelled, "Goddammit, it's my *duty* to explore that island! My orders from the Academy state this clearly, and you're violating them! If you keep me aboard I'll report you to both the Admiralty and the Senate. Who in hell do you think you are?" I prayed God would forgive the profanity, while rationalizing that He surely understood the predicament. I was uncertain about Bering, but to his credit he laughed instead of instructing the grenadiers to toss me into the brig. I deserved it after that outburst.

Bering gave my shoulder an avuncular pat and said that Lepekhin and I could go ashore with the yawl when it left to fill water barrels at 10 o'clock. At the appointed time my Cossack and I stepped into the boat to a royal fanfare from the ship's trumpeters, Toroptsov and

Vasiliev. Everyone including Bering laughed and cheered and otherwise enjoyed the joke immensely. Everyone except me, although I forced a smile and pretended to accept their derision graciously.

I jumped ashore the instant the yawl scraped onto the beach, the first naturalist to set foot in this faraway land. I was exhilarated to the point of feeling lightheaded. Time ashore would be short, and I could reflect later. While the crew started unloading and filling barrels my Cossack and I set out along the shore toward the mainland visible in the distance. We soon came across a recently abandoned fireplace and a covered pit containing cooking utensils, tools, and cached food. I took samples of everything and sent Lepekhin back with them with instructions to ask the captain commander if he might deploy a couple of men to help us investigate the site in detail. I also requested some minor trade items to leave in exchange for what I had taken. I wasn't concerned about being left temporarily without an armed guard, confident I could convince any belligerent natives that my companions and I meant them no harm.

I continued hiking, looking around, and collecting plants. About 4 o'clock I rested, made tea, and began listing the known plants collected so far and formally describing those as yet unknown before they wilted. Among the latter was a species of raspberry (later known as the salmonberry, *Rubus spectabilis*). It was such a spectacular find that I dug up several with the intention of planting them in boxes of earth and shipping them to St. Petersburg to be cultivated. The berries were large, numerous, and tasted delicious despite not being fully ripe. I could easily envision this species as a future crop plant of commercial value to the Russian Empire.

The yawl returned from delivering water to the *St. Peter* with instructions to get my ass aboard or I'd be left here to rot. Bering had supplied Lepekhin with the exchange items, but no men to assist. I put the goods in the covered pit and dispatched Lepekhin to shoot birds. I had seen several that were new to me. I recognized the magpies, ravens, and some others, but the rest had never been observed by a naturalist. When Lepekhin and I met near sunset he handed me a single specimen. I recognized it immediately from a painting in a folio volume in the Academy library titled *Birds of the Carolinas* by the Englishman Mark Catesby and labeled "Blew Jay." Lepekhin's specimen was less colorful, although similar and doubtless undescribed. Because there are no such birds in Asia, as soon as he handed it to me *I knew we were in America*. Unfortunately, the skin and Plenisner's drawing of the whole specimen never reached the Academy, both having been lost in transit. Luckily, my description did get there.

Lepekhin and I hurried to the beach where a boatswain reminded us a final time to get into the longboat immediately or prepare to winter where we stood. He shrugged and smiled. Those were the captain commander's words, he said. He was only the messenger. So my Cossack and I climbed aboard with our collections (elated in my case, relieved in his) just as the northern mid-summer sun reached its lowest point on the horizon.

On the *St. Peter* I immediately encountered Bering, who in place of a stern lecture offered me hot chocolate! Then breaking the cheerful mood, he ordered my new raspberry plants thrown overboard, saying there wasn't room for boxes of growing vegetation or any other objects of no value to the voyage. I could keep the materials I intended to press between sheets of paper, so long as they did not clutter his cabin. And he gently reminded me that Admiralty obligations came first. He didn't have to say more. I could interpret the rest. He had managed to make celestial readings of our positions on this new coast, thus extending knowledge of Earth's frontiers, knowledge of definite value to future cartographers. The Academy's contribution? A few native trinkets, an inedible bird, and some wilted plants. Of more immediate concern was the water supply: only 35 empty casks had been filled.

Khitrov returned as I was being lectured, reporting the strait too shallow for the *St. Peter*. He and his men had gone ashore on an island, discovering a hut made of boards planed nearly smooth. Inside were cooking utensils and tools, but nothing made of metal. There was also a stone with copper residue, perhaps a whetstone. The stone and planed wood suggested the availability and use of metal tools, although no such tools were found.

26

ON THE MORNING OF 21 July Bering gave orders to weigh anchor and plot a new course for Avatcha Bay. The weather being fair, Waxell suggested staying long enough to fill the remaining 20 or so empty water casks, but Bering said he anticipated the weather turning unfavorable and didn't want to risk being driven ashore. He was right: the next morning we stood well away from land in rain squalls and dense fog.

We had been at sea 7 weeks. In Bering's opinion the return voyage would take this long and maybe longer. He had been brooding and moody of late, which I attributed to melancholia brought on by poor health. But there was more. As captain commander the safety of the ship and all aboard were his principal responsibilities. In addition, the decision of the council on 4 May was a binding contract, and he had no choice except to meet its terms, and these included returning to Avatcha Bay by the end of September in time to hunker down for winter. Our wants, individual or collective, were irrelevant. He was bound by the signed agreement, and that was that. Not even God had a say.

The mostly favorable winds that had taken us north might shift counter to our advantage as new courses were set south and west. If autumn winds indeed blew from the southwest as Bering predicted, they would be directly in our faces, requiring more tacking and greatly slowing progress. Furthermore, lurking ahead were uncharted shores and submerged reefs, murky skies offering tenuous visibility, and fickle weather as the still-warm breezes swept north across the frigid sea stirring up local atmospheric disturbances. We could not be certain of anything. Bering was being cautious in allowing extra time for the homeward trip.

He explained all this to me before we turned in that night. I was disappointed but clearly saw and understood his reasons for not extending our stay in America. Bering carried more weight on his shoulders and bore it more gracefully than any other man I knew.

Over the next few days we sailed through intermittent rain and fog seeking a place to fill the water barrels. On 2 August we anchored off a small island. The sun was shining and the sea was flat. We would not be seeking water here, but I nonetheless asked to go ashore for a couple of hours. Bering denied the request, and again we argued, I claiming my superiors at the Academy would surely discipline me for not having taken every opportunity to survey these places as we encountered them. Bering held a meeting of the ship's council at which everyone agreed to swear I had done everything possible to fulfill my duties. There was nothing more I could say or do, so instead I fished with hook and line from the ship and caught two undescribed species of sculpins, some specimens of which I preserved in alcohol. They were later lost during the shipwreck, but thankfully their descriptions survived.

During the next several days we sailed through thick weather, and on 7 August Bering's prediction was realized when the wind turned about-face and suddenly we were headed directly into it. Now there was no time to waste cruising leisurely homeward. Add to this worry a more immediate terror had appeared suddenly among us.

At a 10 August meeting of the ship's council Assistant Surgeon Betge said that 21 men now had the scurvy, five being unfit for duty. Bering had been spending increasingly more time in his cabin and leaving daily operations aboard the *St. Peter* in Waxell's command. As his cabin mate I noticed he was displaying early signs of the disease and reported the observation to Betge. Bering proposed leaving immediately for Avatcha Bay and abandoning any further consideration of exploring America. His reasons were those given to me previously with addition of the scurvy. We were still a long way from home and facing autumn storms, headwinds, and dangers from uncharted shores, reefs, and sandbanks. There was no disagreement.

We would be stopping at least once more to fill the empty water casks. Meanwhile, the scurvy outbreak would likely worsen, not improve. Nautical wisdom held that no preventive or cure had yet been established, although I knew better. In fact, I knew exactly how to prevent and cure it. The secret lay in incorporating antiscorbutic plants in the diet. I had observed during my tenure in Siberia that native peoples seldom contracted the disease. By adopting their diets, neither had I. They recognized which plants to eat raw in salads or as condiments, or lightly cooked. If I could get ashore I would undoubtedly find enough vegetable material to keep all of us healthy. As usual, my opinions and advice were ignored, and I could only hope to make myself heard before too many sickened and died.

We now proceeded slowly westward, beating into the wind, determining our position as openings in the overcast sky permitted. By 27 August the estimated distance to Avatcha Bay was 1240 nautical miles. At the present speed we wouldn't arrive for another 75 days, well past the deadline of 30 days until near the end of September. Winter would have set in, placing the mission—and ourselves—in considerable danger, assuming we were still afloat.

On several occasions over the past 2 weeks I had been certain of glimpsing land. The officers, of course, dismissed these reports, often without even going on deck to see for themselves. They laughed and made such jokes as, "Thank God, we're saved! João de Gama Land at last!" When I complained to Bering about their ignorance and dereliction of duty he too dismissed me with his customary wave of the hand.

By 28 August we were down to 25 barrels of water and needed to find land. We saw land-signs in the form of sea lions and gulls and hove too. A sounding at 4 o'clock in the morning of 29 August revealed bottom at 75 fathoms, and 4 hours later we saw many islands. The weather was calm and pleasant. We anchored near one of the closer ones and in the night saw fire there, proving it was inhabited. The following morning Khitrov, who was officer of the watch, prepared a crew to take the longboat ashore for water and asked me if I wanted to go along. I was stunned. Khitrov and I had done nothing except growl at each other, and I was convinced we were destined to remain bitter enemies for life, but maybe I was wrong. I accepted eagerly.

Khitrov justified his invitation by acknowledging that if natives were encountered I was the only one competent to write a description of their appearance and habits. I had already devised a theory that these Americans, as yet unseen by an educated European, were descendants of people who had migrated from Siberia, and that when someone did eventually observe them their appearance and traditions would mirror the Tchuktchis, Koryaks, and Itelmen, which even earlier had probably migrated north out of Mongolia. Unable to prevent my mouth from spilling the contents of my brain I had babbled about this in front of Bering and the other officers. I was therefore excited at an opportunity to make observations before these naval officers or future unwitting ethnologists beat me to it and gained the credit and acclaim.

Future glory aside, my first duty was to locate a source of good drinking water, an especially important task with the scurvy now a silent enemy among us. While preparing to disembark I learned that Khitrov's motive for sending me ashore had not been altruistic, but rather to get me out of the way. My momentary good feelings toward him were misplaced, and I should have suspected as much. After agreeing to visit the aforesaid island, which looked scoured and bleak from this distance, he proposed to Waxell that he and a crew take the yawl to the island where the fire had been seen and search for the people who made it. What a despicable bastard!

Waxell was hesitant, saying it was too far. If a storm blew up we might not be able to reach them, and if the storm generated a headwind toward the island placing the yawl on the lee shore, their return to the ship might prove impossible. Khitrov insisted and demanded of Waxell that he consult Bering, who was sick in his berth. Bering, probably not wanting to be bothered, gave his consent, and Khitrov and a crew departed about 11 o'clock with instructions to be kind to any people he encountered and offer them gifts. By these he meant the inexpensive trade goods kept in the purser's inventory for such purposes.

I took along Plenisner and my Cossack, both carrying guns to shoot birds, and we left for the unnamed island with the watering crew and a load of empty barrels. I walked inland a short distance and immediately found a spring producing excellent water. I hurried to the beach to discover the crew already filling the casks from an evil looking pond, the level of which rose and fell in synchrony with the sea-surge. The pattern of gravel around the edges indicated total inundation during especially high tides. Probably only frequent rains kept the salinity below that of seawater. I tasted the water and announced it was brackish and unacceptable, especially with sick men aboard. As ship's physician I demanded that the barrels just filled be emptied and that they all be filled instead from the spring I found. I even sent comparative samples of both sources back to the ship.

The officer of the watch, presumably Waxell, ignored this advice, telling his messengers that the water wasn't that salty and ordering them to continue filling the casks as they were doing. Frantic, I searched for a source closer to the beach and found one, sending back samples of it too. This time I received word to stop interfering with the men's work. They had been instructed to fill the barrels quickly from the brackish pond, load up, and return as soon as possible. Waxell was nervous about having two boats ashore at different locations. He later admitted his mistake as men were dying and the water was undrinkable.

Waxell's decision at the time was nonetheless unconscionable despite his later remorse. He cited lack of time as his excuse, when in truth we collected water throughout this day and the next. The St. Peter's inventory included 100 water casks, and all of them could have been filled, even if those containing brackish water had been emptied. The fact is, Waxell fucked up in a big way, and by the time he confessed his error it was too late.

27

THE SCURVY IS THE disease most dreaded by sailors, and everyone who has seen its ravages would take any measure to avoid contracting it. Bad water, although not a direct cause of the scurvy, worsens those suffering from it by dehydrating them. The Arctic arm of the Second Kamchatka Expedition was a recent and horrifying example of what it could do, and Waxell knew the fate of those men. Peter Lasinius had led his group of explorers down the Lena River to the Icy Sea in 1735-1736 during which 38 of the 46 expedition members, including Lasinius himself, died of the scurvy. Waxell also should have known that naval vessels fitted out under direction of the Admiralty are staffed by surgeons, rarely physicians, and the function of the former is to treat wounds, not diseases. Consequently, nothing in the *St. Peter*'s medical chest was useful for treating asthma, the scurvy, the fluxes, or any common illness that victimizes sailors. Instead, we were well supplied with enough plasters, ointments, and bandages to treat several hundred battle wounds.

While we were anchored I asked for several men to help collect antiscorbutic plants I had seen growing on the island. With assistance I could gather enough to treat everyone currently down with the scurvy and keep those still healthy from falling victim. Not surprisingly, my request was denied. Plenisner, Lepekhin, and I therefore collected enough spoonwort growing near the beach to treat ourselves and the captain commander. Everyone else could go to hell. My two assistants and I never became ill, and Bering, although gravely sick and having lost the use of his limbs, responded quickly. Within 8 days of my spoonwort salads he was on his feet and back on deck. I later retracted the earlier uncharitable thoughts about letting men sicken and succumb because of their own ignorance and instead treated everyone while our inventory lasted, at minimum firming up the teeth of all aboard.

We continued exploring, coming across many interesting plants and animals, although not seeing any people. I even considered building a crude shelter and staying overnight, but we eventually returned to the beach and made an unpleasant discovery.

For reasons unknown to the medical arts, scurvy patients kept in foul air often die soon after being brought to a place where the air is healthy. You would expect the opposite. The sick men had been taken ashore to enjoy the fresh air and good weather, whereupon Nikita Shumagin, a sailor, promptly died and was buried on the island the next day. This small archipelago was christened the Shumagin Islands in his memory.

After learning of Shumagin's death I relinquished all thoughts of staying on the island and at 10 o'clock at night returned to the ship and again made my case to discard the brackish water recently loaded aboard and replace it with a potable substitute from one of the two springs I'd found. I also renewed the request to be assigned several men starting at dawn to collect antiscorbutic plants. With help we might obtain enough to doctor the entire ship's company for the duration of the voyage and keep ourselves healthy. I was told curtly to stop complaining about the quality of the water, and that if I wanted plants I could collect them myself.

I stormed below and noted in my journal how angry and unhappy I felt about being treated like an uneducated surgeon apprentice subjected to the Admiralty's abysmal stupidity, vowing once again not to look after anyone except Plenisner, Lepekhin, the captain commander, and myself. Those words, of course, were written in a fit of temper, and I would never deny anyone my aid. As a physician and a Christian it's my duty to assist my fellow man however I can, even if not receiving gratitude in return.

The next day was Monday, 31 August. Khitrov and his crew still had not returned. My companions and I again went ashore to explore and collect. As before the water detail began filling empty barrels with brackish water from the coastal pond, and the sick, having once again been loaded into the longboat, were discharged onto the beach. Plenisner and Lepekhin shot me amused glances while I fumed and bit my tongue. On disembarking they went toward the opposite shore; I struck out alone, enjoying the fine weather, which wasn't to last. By midday the sky clouded over, and the wind was rising. A storm was coming, as Waxell had feared. At 6 o'clock the longboat came to retrieve everyone. A *slushiv* was sent to fetch my party and me. We were about 4 miles away on the lee side on the island, and on being notified ran to the landing site to find the surf crashing and the sailors trying to unload the empty water barrels stumbling and falling in a ferocious backwash. The sick were carried one at a time to the longboat, which writhed and heaved at its painter like a harpooned whale, the cold and their pain causing them great distress. Eventually, everyone was safely aboard.

My admonishments had made the officers wary of drinking brackish water, but not until after ordering a sizeable inventory of it stowed aboard. To assuage their worries they had sent several empty barrels in the longboat to be filled at one of the healthy springs, planning to reserve them exclusively for their own use. I could imagine the rationalization entangled with false casuistry. What if that opinionated loudmouth Steller is right? If the officers become ill with the scurvy, who would be left to lead? Suddenly the matter became clamant. Their own asses were in danger. They had to act, knowing another chance might not come. But fate worked against them. The unruly sea conditions and difficulty shifting the sick from the beach left no time for filling water barrels. The effort was thus abandoned by the boatswain, who in making a command decision invoked a triage, placing his boat and his sick shipmates ahead of the officers' selfishness. The casks were left ashore, soon to be joined by the yawl. Think of them as unintended gifts from Her Highness the empress to the Americans, compliments of the Russian Navy's conceit and ignorance.

By midnight the storm, having metamorphosed into a gale, was blowing full force. There was concern the anchor lines would break and cast the *St. Peter* adrift, but strengthened by God's hand they held. The gale lasted through the night and into the morning of 1 September. By then the hold was flooding, 12 men were on the sick list, and the status of Khitrov and his men could not be known. When the wind later slackened the ship's anchorage was moved to the lee of the island.

Khitrov once again distinguished himself, and I thanked God I wasn't with him. Having arrived on the island where the fire had been seen he located its ashes but discovered nothing of interest. I should be specific and state nothing of interest *to him*. Anyone with even inferior observational skills would certainly have found an interesting plant or stone to examine.

In the approaching storm Khitrov and his men tried vainly to return to the *St. Peter* but were instead forced ashore on a different island, the one I and the others had just abandoned. Everyone in his party reached land safely. The yawl, however, was badly damaged. The men built a fire on the beach to warm and dry themselves and to signal their location. Their position was visible from the ship, but the gale made rescue impossible. By noon of 2 September the wind and sea had calmed enough to launch the longboat. A carpenter sent ashore declared the yawl beyond repair. The next morning everyone returned to the *St. Peter*. Shortly afterward we weighed anchor, leaving the yawl behind and in doing so confirming again that everything Khitrov touches turns to shit.

28

CONTRARY WINDS ON 4 September kept us from circumventing a large Island in our path and continuing west. The order was given to drop anchor in its lee and wait until morning to proceed. It was here we encountered our first Americans.

About half past 4 o'clock in the afternoon we heard shouting from the island. Soon after, two men in small kayaks covered in seal skins paddled out, but stopped well away from us and continued to hurl a coarse, unbroken stream of language in our direction. Our two interpreters, a Tchuktchi and a Koryak, understood none of it. They shouted back in their own languages to no avail, the words in both directions devoid of comprehension. Then one of the Americans tossed a stick toward us with a hawk's wing tied to it. Although the gesture was without clear meaning, we took it to indicate friendship. We beckoned them to come aboard, but they refused and pointed to the island, evidently inviting us to join them there.

One of the kayaks came closer, and the man extracted some shiny clay from inside his upper clothing and painted streaks across his nose and cheeks. Then he stuffed grass up his nostrils, which were pierced with thin strips of bone. He picked up a stick about 5 feet long from atop his craft and using strips of baleen attached two hawk wings to one end. He held it in the air, laughed, and tossed the stick in our direction into the sea.

We in turn tied two Chinese tobacco pipes and some glass beads to a small piece of wood and threw it toward him. He handed the bundle to his companion, who meanwhile had paddled up beside him, and the second man placed them atop his kayak. Becoming more confident the first man moved within reach. He paused to tie an entire hawk to another stick and handed it to our Koryak, receiving in exchange a piece of Chinese silk and a mirror. Then he pulled back the stick, intending to put the cloth between its claws, but our interpreter retained possession. This startled him. He paddled out of reach and refused to come closer, beckoning us to join him ashore. All this time the Americans still ashore never stopped shouting and gesturing.

The officers decided to lower the longboat under command of Captain Waxell and go ashore. The Koryak interpreter and I went along accompanied by nine sailors and soldiers armed with sabers and firearms. We were 12 in all. An accurate count of how many Americans were on the beach was impossible considering the distance and fading daylight. Others could have been hiding out of view among the rocks. We were equally unable to judge the status and sophistication of any weapons. And so we rowed toward shore armed but carrying brandy, biscuits, tobacco, and tobacco pipes as gifts, plus a few minor trade goods.

What from our anchorage had appeared to be a relatively serene beach turned out to be large rocks and steady surf. There was no chance of beaching the longboat. The Americans rushed to greet us, beckoning us ashore. The men and women were almost indistinguishable in their identical clothing and manner in which they cut their hair. We indicated by gestures that joining them was impossible, at which point one man picked up his kayak and paddled out to us. We gave him a cup of brandy, and following our example he tossed it off, then rapidly spit out what he hadn't swallowed. From his subsequent reactions he left the impression we had tricked him and he was not amused. We then gave him a lit pipe and showed him how to smoke it. This too annoyed him, and he left to rejoin his comrades.

His response to these treats, as I later wrote in my journal, was no different from that of a European being offered rotten fish soup and willow bark, considered delicacies by the Kamchadals. Not that I hadn't warned Waxell beforehand, saying that residents of remote islands had likely never experienced brandy and tobacco. The pleasure derived from them is an acquired taste, and the habits of primitive Americans were not comparable to those of hardened Russian sailors and soldiers. The advice was ignored as usual, with predictable consequences.

An anchor had been thrown among the rocks to steady the long-boat. Waxell ordered two sailors and our Koryak to undress and wade ashore carrying the trade goods, the gifts having angered our hosts.

The men were well received and remained perhaps 15 minutes when Waxell became concerned by the rising wind and surf and called them back. The Americans, however, ignored the trade goods and instead wanted them to stay. They seemed especially intrigued by the Koryak, perhaps because he resembled them. They restrained our men by the arms to prevent them from returning to the longboat. Others took hold of the anchor line, evidently to prevent us from pulling the anchor. Waxell ordered three muskets fired over their heads, causing them to instantly let go of the rope and our companions and fall to the ground. In the confusion our men dashed to the boat. The anchor had become stuck, so Waxell ordered the line to be cut. Having recovered their composure the Americans began shouting in belligerent tones and ges-turing at us to go away. We did this, gladly. No sooner had we reached the St. Peter safely than a storm hit from the south, and rain poured steadily through the night. The Americans lit a fire on the beach. As I wrote in my journal, *and made us think this night about what happened.*

I was also rapidly recording my observations made in those 15 min-utes before they vanished from memory. There had been nine people on the beach, mostly young adults or adults in middle age and resem-bling Kamchadals in facial features, skin color, and stature. Both men and women were attired in long shirts like dressing gowns made of whale gut and thus waterproof. Their boots were sealskin died red-dish-brown, probably with alder bark, resembling the boots Kamcha-dals wear. A few of the men carried crudely made iron knives. I tried unsuccessfully to barter for one in exchange for up to three knives we carry as trade goods. After observing these people I am more certain than ever that my theory of their origin is true: their strong resem-blance to the Kamchadals, Koryaks, and Tchuktchis in appearance, culture, and dress point to an Asiatic origin. As I recorded in my jour-nal, *I have no doubt that I would have been able to give perfect proof of this thesis, if I had been allowed to act according to my own judgment, but this the nostalgia of the naval men would not permit.*

The American kayak is nearly identical to the ones used by the Samoyeds and so light a man can carry it under one arm. It is propelled by a wooden paddle with a blade the width of a hand at each end. The boats are 2 fathoms long, height and width 2 feet, and made from the skins of seals sewn tightly together and stretched over a frame, probably of wood or baleen. The bow is sharp, the stern rounded. A sleeve of whale gut is sewn around the opening on top. The paddler inserts his legs into the hole and extends them forward inside the craft. He sits upright and raises the whale gut sleeve around his lower chest, pulling it tight to his body with a drawstring to establish a watertight seal. To propel the craft he dips first one end of the paddle into the water and pulls back, then the other. This alternating back and forth motion keeps the boat on course. He can also turn in a circle using just one end of the oar or paddle backward using both ends by reversing the forward motion.

At 6 o'clock on the morning of 6 September we pulled anchor and in a favorable wind sailed around the island into the open sea. The *St. Peter* kept a southerly course until veering west the next day, a direction that would eventually take us below north latitude 53°. For 2 weeks we sailed seeing only sea and sky and mostly tacking into a westerly wind before veering northwest on 22 September. The scurvy claimed its second victim of the voyage on 23 September when the grenadier Andrei Tretyakov died. Land was sighted on 27 September, what we assumed were two islands backed by a distant snow-capped volcano evidently on the American mainland.

Now the evil fates began extracting revenge. Tretyakov's death had been only a harbinger. Shortly after consigning his body to the sea we encountered gales out of the west. An especially fierce storm straddling 30 September and 1 October damaged the rigging, leaving the *St. Peter* helplessly adrift. Even men who had abandoned their faith now prayed for God's assistance. The storm's fury caused those of us still ambulatory to ricochet randomly off the walls and fixtures, raising bruises that later made us look like we had been severely knouted and then beaten with clubs. There was no comfort anywhere. You could neither stand nor lie down and hope to remain stable The sick had to be tied fast in their berths, their howls of pain blending with the wind to create a satanic symphony. Lightning and thunder hijacked the heavens, their rage adding to the shrieking wind and exploding seas. At the height of the maelstrom blue points of St. Elmo's fire hopped like delighted demons along the spars and tiptoed up and down the thrumming stays. Half the crew was incapacitated with the scurvy, and even in fair weather there were barely enough able-bodied men to sail the ship. Cooking was impossible. For those still capable of eating the fare was an occasional moldy biscuit.

Every shudder of the ship's superstructure as a wave broke over the deck brought the terror of imminent drowning. The sea was huge and terrifying, plunging the *St. Peter* abruptly into dark canyons then lifting her seconds later onto crests far taller than the masts. Each cycle of falling and rising and falling again dropped my stomach into my bowels before raising it an instant later nearly to my throat. Strong men wept and cried out asking why God had chosen to punish us so harshly. Mixed with these pitiful pleas for mercy were equally fervent curses against Heaven, surely negating any expectation of a merciful reply from Above. No doubt God keeps track of our profanities without revealing the limits of His patience. As I later penned in my journal, *There was much praying to be sure, but the curses piled up during ten years in Siberia prevented any response.* What I had meant to write is any *compassionate* response.

Several lesser gales followed on the tail of this one, and by 11 October we had been blown 7° longitude east of our farthest westward progress. Waxell asked Bering if he might consider wintering on the American coast, but he insisted on continuing toward Avatcha Bay. The short-handed crew made what repairs it could, raised the remnants of canvas, and we limped on.

Bering was again suffering from effects of the scurvy, but he certainly wasn't alone. The assistant surgeon's sick report of 18 October listed 29 men in addition to the captain commander. Twenty-four hours later the grenadier Alekseij Kiselev died, followed by the *slushiv*

Nikita Kharitonov on the 20th, and the soldier Luka Zaviakov on the 22nd. Their bodies were consigned to the sea and the ship's course was shifted northward. On Sunday the 25th a towering snow-covered island was sighted and named St. Markian in the ship's log to honor the saint of the day.

The assistant surgeon's morning report of 26 October listed 30 on the sick list, and two more were added the next day. On the 28th Stepan Buldirev, the ship's cooper, succumbed. We were sailing in a sea of islands ordinarily hidden because of the low sky and precipitation, and we lived in terror of running aground. The ship's company was now in serious trouble. Almost all the decent drinking water was gone, and the remaining casks were brackish. Soon there would be no one to steer the ship, sail her, and stand watches. The weather was turning cold, and we were under continuous hail, sleet, or swirling snow.

Khitrov, the most moronic of our officers, suggested stopping at one of these nearly invisible places to search for water, evidently forgetting we now had too few able-bodied men to pull the anchor after dropping it. Waxell at least had the good sense to ignore him.

The officers now made what turned out to be a fateful decision. On 30 October two islands were seen that Waxell claimed resembled the northernmost Kuril Islands. To my regret I concurred even though I had no say in his subsequent decision to reset the course northward. Had we possessed the knowledge gained in hindsight we might have reached Avatcha Bay in less than 2 weeks simply by holding a westerly course.

In truth, we were now entirely in God's hands, and it would be unfair to place the blame for our dilemma on the shoulders of the officers. Bering was completely incapacitated, and Waxell and Khitrov, although still capable of performing their duties, had too few able-bodied sailors at their command. Men had to be helped to their stations, some even carried and set on the stool when taking their turns before the helm. Men at all stations stayed until they could no longer stand or sit, then comrades just as ill replaced them.

We were carrying minimal canvas aloft because there were too few men to lower the sails in event of a storm and raise them afterward. Waxell, to his credit, encouraged the crew by speaking gently, coaxing instead of shouting, and reminding everyone that God on High was watching. What made the situation even more perilous was the uncertainty of our position. By 4 November some believed we were at north latitude 56°, which would have placed us east of the mouth of the Kamchatka River. The order was given to shorten sail so as not to run aground, and all who were able appeared on deck to watch for land, some limping, others crawling, still others carried by their shipmates. Avatcha be damned. We'd have welcomed finding anchorage anywhere on Kamchatka. Sure enough, at mid-morning land appeared in the foggy distance, and Khitrov bellowed self-congratulations for his prowess as a navigator. We were overjoyed and praised God for guiding and protecting us.

The hallelujahs were premature when it became apparent that the view bore no resemblance to the mouth of the Kamchatka River. Laughter and joy turned to tears and despair. The same desperate souls who earlier had praised God now cursed Him. When the sun appeared at noon after many days of dark skies, our latitude was found to be 54° 30'. Waxell speculated we could be somewhere between the Kamchatka River and Avatcha Bay, but his improvident attempt to buoy hope fell flat. In fact, this was an alien land that none of us had ever seen.

We had drifted into a bay. The wind was rising. A storm was blowing up, and as night approached Waxell reset the course northeast, fearing we might be driven against the lee shore of this forbidding place where mountains rose steeply from the sea and heavy surf crashed at their feet. Toward evening we started tacking in an effort to escape into open water. In the night the scurvy claimed the grenadier Aleksej Popov. He was followed into death shortly before dawn by the soldier Ivan Nebaranov.

29

ANOTHER LAND WAS SEEN at dawn on 5 November. A storm the previous night had broken the shrouds supporting the mainmast, and those capable of repairing them were either down with the scurvy or dead from it. Bering, at the urging of Waxell and Khitrov, held a meeting of the ship's council. All who could muster went to the captain commander's cabin, where Bering moderated while lying prone in his berth. The officers gave a situation report. Just six casks of water remained, all of it brackish. The ship was undermanned to the point of being out of control, and even with a full crew it was presently in no condition to sail. They recommended anchoring offshore of the land ahead and finding water.

Bering held a contrary view, saying we should instead sail for Avatcha Bay. We could endure the hardship a little longer, he said. The officers expanded their opposing case: the rigging was rotting, and lines were parting even as they spoke. The sails were damaged, some past repair. Men were dying so quickly that soon the *St. Peter* would become a drifting ghost ship. Winter had arrived, and by continuing west we would be sailing directly into freezing headwinds thick with sleet and snow. Still, argued Bering, if we drop anchor in this unknown place, who has the remaining strength to raise it? Our only choice will be to cut the line, leaving us two anchors.

The men, although incapacitated, said they would follow the captain commander's wishes, provided the officers could guarantee that the land ahead really was Kamchatka. Khitrov blustered that if it wasn't he stood ready to be voluntarily beheaded. The officers eventually won the day, the only dissenter among the crew being the sailor Dmitrij Leontievitch Ovtsuin, a demoted lieutenant, who took Bering's side and was driven from the cabin by threats and insults from the others. They called him a useless prick and a son of a bitch. When my turn to speak came I declined to offer an opinion.

The course was set west-southwest. Universal despondency now gripped the men. It seemed obvious that neither man nor deity was watching over us. They returned to their berths no longer caring what fate threw at them. If this sounds unduly pessimistic, I can soften it by saying that even the most optimistic didn't expect miracles. I stayed on the nearly deserted deck, knowing the officers were sick with the scurvy but wondering why no officer of the watch was on duty. Eventually I reported this to Bering, and he ordered the situation remedied. At 4 o'clock in the afternoon we anchored off what appeared to be a sandy beach in 37 fathoms. The wind had dropped, and the sea was calm.

Within an hour the ship started bucking violently. The anchor line parted, and we were carried onto exposed rocks now swept by thundering surf. It seems we had dropped anchor just seaward of a submerged reef lying parallel to the shore, now exposed in the falling tide. In the ensuing confusion a second anchor was tossed overboard and lost immediately when that line broke too. A third was about to be sacrificed when Boatswain's Mate Aleksei Ivanov and the sailor Dmitrij Ovtsuin ordered it to remain on deck.

The men were terrified, and because keeping corpses on board is considered bad luck the bodies of the last two dead men were heaved over the side without benefit of Christian ceremony, like the remains of unreasoning animals. I admit I had to laugh at some of the shenanigans taking place. Men too weak to stand on the heaving deck were wailing and weeping. As I later recorded in my journal, one asked me *whether the water was very salty, as if death in fresh water would be more delightful!* I also enjoyed watching that buffoon Khitrov making himself scarce, but after the danger passed exhorting everyone to take courage despite he himself having acquired the bearing of a skulking manikin. His skin, apparently transformed by fear, had assumed the tone and appearance of papier mâché. Under the supposed leathery hide of every sailor lurks a frightened landsman.

We were preparing for death by drowning when an enormous wave lifted the *St. Peter* clear of the reef and into a quiet lagoon in its lee where the surface was still as a summer pond. The third and last anchor was dropped in 4 fathoms. Everyone relaxed. We had survived, at least for now. The moon rose into a mostly clear sky; we were nearly home. This was surely Kamchatka, or so everyone thought. Everyone but me.

We awoke on 7 November in heavy swells, remembering we had been lifted into a lagoon, not a harbor, and were therefore protected from the sea's surges only during the ebb. I spent the morning packing the camping and collecting gear and ordered Plenisner and my Cossack to pack their cooking utensils and whatever else they needed for an overnight stay. When the longboat was launched around noon we hopped aboard along with Waxell and his son, a few of the ill who were nearest death, a makeshift crew of the barely able-bodied to handle the boat, and a several empty water casks.

The situation had become desperate. Another few days at sea would have placed the *St. Peter* entirely at nature's mercy. The morning sick report listed 49 incapacitated by the scurvy. This number alone accounted for more than half the original ship's roster. Since embarking from Kamchatka 12 had died of the disease, and from this day forward another 20 were destined to perish. Of the original 79 aboard, 46 would survive to return to Petropavlovsk.

Near the landing site a stream of clear water poured from the mountains and flowed into the sea, solving one immediate problem: the water casks could now be filled with good potable water. After tasting it I motioned the crew to start filling the barrels. I hiked behind the dunes onto the tundra and looked around. Despite the late month I could foresee warm weather bringing a thick, rich blanket of vegetation comprising mostly grasses, shrubs both erect and patulous, and low-lying willows. The land as far as I could see into the distance was devoid of trees. What little driftwood we noticed along the tideline was adequate for fuel and perhaps crude shelters, but little else. Soon it would disappear underneath winter snow. Having discovered a convenient source of water the next two problems were housing for everyone and securing a local supply of nutritious foods. Only then could the sick be made well. Even more urgent, it now fell on my shoulders as ship's physician to cure the sick of the scurvy and prevent those still healthy from succumbing to its ravages.

I sent Plenisner off with the gun to shoot whatever game he came across, while Lepekhin and I wandered in the opposite direction to search for antiscorbutic plants. I can't repeat too often that anyone ill with the scurvy requires fresh foods to survive, recover, and hold off a later attack.

Around 10 o'clock that night we met at the longboat. Plenisner had shot six ptarmigans. We sent the longboat back to the *St. Peter* with three of them to be prepared for the captain commander on my orders, along with some plants related to nasturtiums and a bunch of fleshy brooklime growing in a wet area near the stream's outfall. I instructed the boatswain that a side salad was to be made of the vegetables and fed to Bering, emphasizing that unlike the ptarmigans the vegetables were not to be cooked but given to the captain commander in their raw state.

Lieutenant Waxell was feeling sick and dizzy from the scurvy and returned to the ship along with the now-full water casks. My two companions and I stayed ashore along with young Waxell and the sick. Plenisner and I prepared salads and a broth from the remaining plants and ptarmigans, feeding the sick and Waxell's son before ourselves. Afterward, Plenisner devised three rickety walls from driftwood and covered them with an old sail, and there we spent the night.

From the start the officers and crew thought we had reached Kamchatka and needed only to recover from our illnesses, determine our position, and start trekking toward the closest *ostrog*. I knew from looking toward shore from the longboat that we were on an uninhabited island. Uninhabited by humans, that is. It was the animals that gave away the secret.

As the boat came near the beach we were surrounded by curious sea otters that some of the men mistook for bears, others for wolverines. We no sooner scraped ashore than dozens of blue foxes ran to greet us, sniffing and nipping at our ankles and calves. They persisted despite our killing several with an axe. I even stabbed one to death with my knife. In my experience as a naturalist, only animals that have existed for centuries in an Eden without humans are ever this tame. Clearly, we were alone, although where exactly was the question.

I explained this to Waxell and Plenisner, both of whom doubted me. I told them that as a naturalist and a landsman what I said is true and it was Waxell's duty as a mariner to discover our island's position. Wherever we are, I insisted vociferously, it isn't Kamchatka. We needed to give up this hopeful notion and start preparing for the full winter nearly upon us. As further proof I pointed to the gigantic animals lazing in the kelp beds offshore, rising occasionally to snort like horses. After observing them from a tall dune I had concluded they were manatees, also called sea cows. I had never seen a manatee alive or dead, but these magnificent creatures resembled illustrations in books I'd read. They inhabit the coastal rivers of western Africa and parts of North and South America. There is even a kind found far up the Amazon River that reputedly tastes so delicious that despite its warm blood and air-breathing habit the Jesuit missionaries have declared it a fish so its flesh may be eaten on Fridays. All these examples suggest a tropical distribution. The species I was watching had evidently never been seen by a naturalist. Describing it would be one of my objectives while marooned here. If indeed we were standing on mainland Kamchatka, why had I never seen these animals or at least heard tales about them?

A quick survey of the officers and men established a collective ignorance of such a beast. Neither the Cossacks aboard nor our Tchuktchi and Koryak translators had a name for it, which I took as additional evidence of our isolation on a large island, perhaps part of an unknown archipelago. Creatures the size of whales would be memorable, and if they inhabited Kamchatka or existed anywhere along the Siberian coast then dead ones must occasionally wash ashore where the indigenous people would undoubtedly use the blubber and meat. Considering their slow movements, harpooning them from *baidaras* would be easy, meaning there would be myths and traditions in which manatees were specific referents.

30

PLENISNER AND I DECIDED to transfer our belongings from the *St. Peter* onto land and discussed how a suitable shelter could be constructed. I ordered Lepekhin to accompany us. The ship might be driven ashore in the next big storm, and there was no logical reason to continue living aboard. If anything, it would be detrimental to being close to my work. The longboat was too unreliable for planning explorations. It came and went at the convenience of the officers and vagaries of the weather. When the tide was at flood and the wind blew strongly onshore the longboat couldn't be lowered because of the swells; if already on the beach, it couldn't be launched into the surf.

Others weary of the *St. Peter*'s cramped quarters and her increasingly derelict state also wished to live ashore. The able-bodied began excavating pits for themselves and their infirm shipmates, following Plenisner's and my example. Soon the dunes were becoming a congeries of bleached driftwood and tattered canvas. As mentioned, a sudden change of air often causes someone very ill with the scurvy to fall dead when recovery might be the expected response. We saw this happen several times to men brought topside or ferried to the beach. For this reason Bering, on my orders, was covered in heavy blankets and carefully taken ashore on a stretcher. Once in the shelter prepared for him in the sand he asked if I might stay and share ptarmigan broth with him, which I did. He asked my opinion of our location, and I told him I was certain we were on an island, although not far from Kamchatka because in walking the beach I had come across a decaying window shutter of obvious Siberian origin. Afterward, I returned to my own campsite where Assistant Surgeon Betge asked Plenisner and me if he and his servant could live with us and our servants, and we agreed.

Bering had been able to feed himself, but the experience was awkward and painful. Just sipping broth from a spoon must have hurt his gums considerably, requiring both perseverance and courage, yet he never complained.

The scurvy is a brutal disease. The victim becomes lethargic and melancholy, preferring to lie still instead of moving, eventually losing use of his arms and legs and relinquishing any remaining muscle strength. The lower legs and feet swell, and the joints become acutely painful. The skin of the face yellows, the body acquires reddish or purple patches resembling bruises. Relentless bleeding of the mouth and gums is accompanied by the teeth loosening and falling out. The gums swell, turn brownish-black, and nearly overgrow what teeth remain, making eating so painful as to be avoided. Unable to eat and his mind numbed by apathy, the victim becomes anorexic and dehydrated.

The prognosis is worsened by unhealthy air in the living quarters made stale by unwashed bodies and clothing unchanged for weeks while the sick lie moaning in their own piss, puke, and shit. And ultimately, of course, by the telltale rotten odor of impending death. The bites of lice and fleas and the scrabbling and nibbling of rats on parts of the body that still retain feeling add to the misery. I observed in the midst of such misery that pain is its own reality; it has no metaphoric equivalent but exists instead on a plane separate from the soul's suffering.

On 8 November Bering ordered Gunner's Mate Boris Roselius to take two men and set off to the northwest until they found people. If successful, they were to enquire about our location and report back. Meanwhile, bringing the sick to shore and construction of dwellings continued. Unruly sea conditions often made ferrying the sick men impossible. On this day the boatswain Nils Jansen died. He was followed by the trumpeter Mikhail Toroptsov on the 10th. On 14 November we lost four to death: Sailor First Class Ivan Emilianov, Gunner Second Class Ilya Dergatchev, Yakut Regiment Cadet Vasilij Popkov, and Sailor Second Class Seliverst Tarakanov, the last just as his feet touched the beach. Soldier Savin Stepanov succumbed on the 16th, Sailor Nikita Ovtsuin on the 19th, Sailor First Class Mark Antipin on the 20th, and First Mate and Navigator Andreyan Eselberg the 21st.

Eselberg's death saddened me deeply. He was 70, the oldest of us, a sailor for 50 years. His wisdom and knowledge were irreplaceable. Unfortunately, his advice on nautical matters was often ridiculed and dismissed by the officers. I wrote of his end in my journal: *This came to pass solely and alone because the Captain Commander, as well as the others, in their foolish conceit and pride took no more notice of his remonstrances than of the opinion of anybody else who did not agree with them and as a consequence did everything alone that they wanted to, with the result of what afterwards happened.* I refer, of course, to the shipwreck and our unfortunate circumstances resulting from that event.

A large pit was dug for the sick and covered with double sails. The scene all around was horrifying. Foxes now attacked the living as they lay practically immobile, and guards of the barely able-bodied had to be posted to drive them away. The sick wept and cried out in pain or because of hunger or thirst, although those complaining of hunger typically rejected food because their gums were too painful and their teeth too loose or few to chew it. The best we could do was give them warm broth and raw salads crushed to a pulp, advising them to swallow the contents whole with water if they were unable to chew. Our skeleton crew had become a crew of living skeletons.

Of the officers, Bering was dying; Captain Waxell, Lieutenant Khitrov, and Second Mate Kharlam Yushin were ill and barely ambulatory. I did what I could, neglecting my naturalist's duties to become a full-time physician and minister offering medical assistance, proper nutrition, and kind words of encouragement in God's name.

31

BERING KNEW HE WOULD soon be dead, as would anyone of sound mind whose body is decaying and in short order will cease to function. Never loquacious, he had become quieter than usual, but then I'm German and he's a Dane. We conversed in Russian. There were many other differences. He was a broken old man; I was vigorous and young enough to be his son. Bering was cautious and thoughtful by nature; I'm aggressive and impetuous. He learned navigation at an Admiralty academy, but was essentially an autodidact; I was educated at two of Europe's most modern, forward-thinking universities. Bering was a life-long sailor in tune with the sea; I shall always be a landsman.

There was something niggling at him besides looming mortality. He wanted to talk; more specifically, he had something he wanted to tell me. So one morning when I brought him a small salad of watercress and broth I'd made from a ptarmigan Lepekhin had shot, he said he had something important to confess. We were both devout Lutherans, so I understood what he meant if not what he was going to say. I also understood tacitly that I was to silently take what he told me to my own grave when that day arrived.

He began talking about his first voyage, reiterating that if higher powers in St. Petersburg had believed his reports we wouldn't be in our current predicament. I had always thought it strange that Bering volunteered so quickly to undertake a second expedition simply to confirm what he had already proven, but attributed this alacrity to dispelling all doubts about his conclusions and thus seal his reputation as a reliable and loyal explorer and navigator. The possibility again came to mind as I fed him broth a spoonful at a time.

He abruptly closed his lips and waved my arm away. "As everyone knows, Peter the Great, from his deathbed, issued me instructions written in his own hand. They were in three parts. First, I was to go to Kamchatka or another place within reasonable distance from the eastern ocean and build two decked, seaworthy vessels. Second, I was to sail these vessels north up the coast of Siberia to where it ends and there discover whether Asia and America are joined or separated by water. If finding a land bridge I was to proceed east, plot its contours carefully, and bring the chart back to him. Those were his instructions. I was then a captain, Spangberg and Tchirikov my lieutenants.

" Siberia is anomic, a land of sloth, ignorance, and lies. Nothing is ever as it appears. Each day something goes wrong. You think you have control, but you don't. Even the simplest task becomes contingent when you know in advance the outcome can't be predicted. Piled atop these minor but cumulative events come disasters over which you have no control. For example, in March 1727 an epidemic of measles struck Yakutsk. I had left Tchirikov there with orders to join me at Okhotsk Ostrog in the spring. By April everyone in town was ill. Right on schedule, I thought to myself. After all, this is Siberia. I feared Tchirikov might die or at best survive but be too ill to travel.

"That wasn't enough. Also in April my clerk went insane and I had to send him with two armed guards back to St. Petersburg, a trip of 2 years. Did he make it? Who knows? This was a man I trusted completely. I depended on his counting and writing skills for keeping track of inventories and assisting me with correspondence and preparing budgets and reports. The clerical work, as you know, is never-ending. Sometimes I forget I'm a sailor and believe I'm a clerk myself. Anyway, life in Siberia eventually destroyed his mind. His melancholia transformed into rage and insubordination. He became capricious in all matters, disappearing for days and not attending to his duties, eating hallucinogenic mushrooms, drinking *raka*, and fucking Kamchadal women. Through this last activity he contracted the French pox. Many people afflicted with this disease eventually become senile or go insane. As a physician you know this. One night my once-reliable assistant lost his mind completely, driven to such despair that he set fire to his living quarters, very nearly burning down the barracks.

"Such unexpected events set back schedules, result in expenditures not in the budget, cripple the emotional resources of everyone, and diminish the available manpower. So how do our so-called 'betters' in St. Petersburg repay us for these trials that would make Job tremble? They inveigh and slander us, accuse us of laziness, dishonesty, and incompetence. Then they bury us in more paper.

"I followed His Majesty's instructions through every detail, and we suffered many delays and hardships. Want another example? In December 1726 I was obliged to send a rescue party from Okhotsk Ostrog to Spangberg and his retinue at Yudomskoi Krest. His boats carrying a good part of our provisions had become trapped in ice on the Gorbeh River. Spangberg's command unloaded everything and cached it, and for 2 months they walked across the mountains toward Yudomskoi Krest, often through head-high snow, eventually running out of food and being forced to eat the horses that had been pulling the boats upriver along the shore, then they ate the harnesses and traces. When these had been consumed they ate the skin from their fur clothes and the upper leathers of their boots. Fortunately, through unforeseen circumstances I had earlier cached 5,500 pounds of flour at Yudomskoi Krest. This saved Spangberg and his men from starvation, and they eventually made it over the passes and through the forests to Okhotsk Ostrog."

Bering's lungs released an involuntary suspiration. I gently removed my hand from the back of his neck so his head could lie prone. I didn't comment and instead busied myself collecting the utensils. When I returned and sat down in the sand beside him to check his pulse he seemed to gain vigor and continued the monologue. As expected, his pulse was firm but thin, cold, and dry. Its slithery, serpentine rhythm confirmed my original diagnosis of a melancholy temperament caused by excessive black bile. There was nothing I could do for Bering at this point except provide as much physical and spiritual comfort as possible.

"Ah, but certain armchair critics in St. Petersburg reclining on their soft sofas beside their warm fires were dissatisfied with my results.

Our many sufferings, the deaths, the frostbite, lost and broken limbs, crushed fingers and toes, wives left widowed and destitute, children orphaned.... What does any of it matter to them? Nothing. They had only two questions. First, who can we blame for the expedition's cost overruns and how should he be punished? Second, how quickly can I profit from the results? And not just the *boyars*, even the serfs and beggars snipe openly. Any Russian feeling cheated by life can bitch and declare my efforts worthless unless he receives a ruble or two in compensation for doing nothing.

"As an example I hold up that exiled septuagenarian prick and insidious bastard and gadfly Grigorij Pisarev, who from no less a remote place than Okhotsk Ostrog, our own backyard, wrote letters to the Senate and Admiralty starting a rumor that the land Spangberg had discovered was Korea, not Japan. The sad thing is, many believed him, including some in the Admiralty, which is especially shameful. If the navy can't trust the observations and reports of handpicked men from its own fleet, who's left to believe?

"Spangberg, of course, was ordered to reprise his voyage during this Second Kamchatka Expedition. What a fucking waste of funds. I recall Spangberg once demanding I jail Pisarev's wrinkled old ass to get him out of the way. A suitable alternative, he said, would be somehow exiling Pisarev from his present Siberian exile to an even more desolate place, maybe Mongolia. Either choice would have been illegal, but perhaps worth the consequences. The man was a thorn in my hide until the day we embarked on this God-forsaken voyage."

Bering stopped and apologized for the profanity. There was no need, I said, offering assurances that God will surely forgive him. He was breathing rapidly, and his skin felt febrile. I dipped a cloth in the sea, wrung it out, and placed it on his forehead. Earlier he had taken a few sips of a decoction I made from fresh willow bark, which if imbibed in sufficient volume effectively lowers fever and reduces pain. An infusion of meadowsweet leaves is even better for lowering fever, especially if mixed with white wine. At least one species is a common forb throughout Kamchatka, although I hadn't seen it here during my brief forays behind the dunes. Even so, there was no wine in which to prepare the medication. The plant I know is tall, grows in large stands, and is difficult to miss. I again considered bleeding Bering to alleviate the overload of black bile, but as before while aboard the *St. Peter* he fell asleep before I could act.

32

When I checked on Bering in the early afternoon he was alert and eager to continue his tale, asking me to place a pillow under his head so he could see me better.

"On 14 June 1728, having finished provisioning our new vessel christened *Gabriel*, we put to sea carrying sufficient supplies to support 44 men for a year. By 8 August we arrived at north latitude 64° 30' and hove to when eight native men in a sealskin *baidara* paddled out and asked who we were and why were we there. If you wonder how I remember these dates and latitude and others I shall mention in a moment, they're fixed in memory so long as I live, components of my legacy and also my fate.

"These men were Tchuktchis. Our interpreters were Koryaks and barely knew their language. We beckoned them closer. A man buoyed by inflated bladders made of seal intestine swam to us and climbed aboard. When we neither harmed nor kidnapped him, the others paddled closer. They pointed north of our present position and said that eventually the land ends, and from there the coast veers sharply west. On the way to that location we would encounter an island with some huts. Their information was accurate. We later passed this island and named it St. Lawrence after the patron saint of the day.

"On 15 August we arrived at north latitude 67° 18' and saw no land to the north or east. I felt we had discharged our duty to his Imperial Majesty and could return satisfied to Kamchatka. I worried then as I have on this second voyage that if we encountered contrary winds late in the sailing season we might not get back to base and be forced to winter in that northern region where the natives are reportedly hostile, we had not seen a suitable harbor, and the only wood for fuel consisted of low-lying thickets of thin willow and alder scarcely adequate for small fires."

I visited the captain commander again that evening and tried to induce him to take nourishment. He waved away the antiscorbutic salad saying there was no use in treating the disease that was killing him, but he would accept a few spoonsful of warm ptarmigan broth. He was in pain everywhere and refused to let me turn him over to examine his backside. For a time now his anus had been discharging black bile with a foul odor, evidence of internal gangrene. I removed his boots and replaced his tattered socks with newer, thicker ones. Any movement, no matter how slight, was accompanied by an unconscious groan. Even while lying still he moaned softly with every breath as if air, the substance of life, had become his enemy. I was about to discover that Bering's afflictions manifested in more ways than disruption of the four humors. He also suffered from bunions and narrow dreams, the first caused by too-tight boots, the other by a stunted soul.

"Steller, I must confess to you that the critics I earlier castigated were right in claiming I hadn't met the First Expedition's principal objective," he said.

I was astonished. I had expected a confession of some sort, but certainly not this. "What's that you said, sir?"

"I failed. During that first voyage I turned back for Kamchatka leaving my mission unfinished. Oh, don't misunderstand. I followed His Majesty's instructions perfectly. I was to determine if Asia and America are joined or separated by a sea. If the former, I was to chart the connection, prepare a map, and present it to His Majesty or his successor. I know the meaning and substance of orders, but I also learned at an early age how to read between the lines. His Majesty's instructions were remarkably brief, and the simpler the instructions the easier it becomes to distort their intention. Invented omissions can seem reasonable in the absence of specific statements to dispute. Remember when I said we had reached north latitude 67° 18′ off Cape Tchuktchi?"

"Of course, captain commander."

"Well, we did. That wasn't a lie. What I purposely buried in my report to the Admiralty was mention of the longitude readings. The ship's log implies that *Gabriel* tracked the Siberian coast north, thus showing the expected latitudinal increases. But the coast also curves east, introducing a not unexpected eastward shift in longitude. We indeed attained north latitude 67° 18', but at that point were considerably farther east than if we had followed the coast. I reported honestly that after sailing 24 hours beyond Cape Tchuktchi I couldn't see land to the north or east, although truthfully I couldn't see it to the west either because from our position we stood too far off the Cape for it to be visible.

"My conclusion that the two continents are not joined therefore withstands all scrutiny insofar as the letters of my orders are concerned. I failed not by what I didn't do but in what I might have done. I *did not* round the Cape, sail west, and therefore confirm where the sea on which I was sailing merges with the Icy Sea. I instead took the word of Tchuktchis we met on that first occasion and later another group who paddled out in *baidaras* to trade with us as confirmation, and this despite not understanding all they told us. Our two interpreters were Koryaks, as I've noted. Tchuktchis speak a different language, related perhaps, but as different as Danish and German. Meaning is obscured in the nuances. That's why on this voyage I placed one native speaker of each language aboard both vessels. I didn't intend to make that mistake again.

"Neither did I try to discover the American continent, which I might have within a day or so of sailing east. According to the Tchuktchis the Big Land (as they called it) to the east wasn't far off, and they had traded with those people. They said we could get there easily in a ship like ours propelled by wind instead of paddles. So there I was, a captain in the Russian Navy with a sound ship under me, a full and healthy crew, reliable officers, provisions for a year, and 6 weeks left in the sailing season. *And my decision was to turn back!* In hindsight it was disgraceful, even cowardly."

"Perhaps it was the right decision," I said. "You returned with your men safe and your ship undamaged having completed the mission."

"Steller, don't patronize me. Sarcasm, not generosity, fits you better.

Let's be honest. My decisions throughout both Kamchatka Expeditions have been those of a cautious bureaucrat, a callow administrator attempting to keep everyone calm and content, scurrying from one disaster to the next like a frightened squirrel dreading the onset of winter and forgetting where its seeds are stored. I want my men to love and respect me, and I in turn want to be their protector. But these aren't necessarily the qualities of leadership."

"You fulfilled your duties," I said. Bering was right that I was acting out of character, but isn't the responsibility of a Christian and a physician to comfort the sick and dying?

"You aren't distinguishing yourself, Dr. Steller. Stop being an asshole. I'm not soliciting forgiveness. What I've done can't be forgiven, and comfort isn't a palliative in my case. The wound goes too deep. What I need right now is merely to tell my story, nothing else. So put aside your false concern for the guilty remorse of a dying man. Forget trying to uplift my spirits, just swallow your anodyne words before they reach your goddamn mouth and listen.

"When His Majesty appointed me to head the First Kamchatka Expedition he expected scintillating leadership, not hesitation and indecisiveness. Peter's sobriquet is eponymous. He was indeed great because he manifested what it looks like to lead. He took chances, many times risking his own life and the lives of others. He didn't give a shit if he or anyone else lived or died. He existed to serve the Russian people and drag them out of the Middle Ages no matter the cost. He was bold. He expected loyalty from those he placed in high positions, also superb organization and doggedness. I can say without boasting that in me he got these three attributes. But above all he needed leaders willing to take chances, men more like him, and in choosing me he failed. My shortcomings became his legacy.

"Peter was barely literate, having given up formal education at age 10 or so, and look at what he still achieved. He didn't want a facile scribbler and logistics wizard to lead the First Kamchatka Expedition. For such functions he could hire clerks. He needed *and deserved* someone of ruthless character to push frontiers ahead, no matter the price in rubles and pain, the losses in ships and goods and lives. He was a man who treated everyone and everything as expendable in the pursuit of knowledge, who challenged critics with courage because the man he chose would assure his results were backed by facts of unassailable accuracy. He got none of these qualities in me."

Bering uttered the last sentence after a pause, his exhausted voice trailing away. He seemed smaller, lying there covered with sand in the creeping darkness. I recalled on first meeting him how straight and muscular he stood, like a man who had labored at heavy tasks all his life. I judged his height when fully clothed at about 5 feet and a half, and he seemed as perfectly proportioned as a Greek statue. His attire had instantly struck me as oddly juxtaposed against the squalor of Siberia. Both in port and aboard ship he wore at all times a full dress naval uniform decorated with epaulettes and the insignia of his rank, the jacket adorned with medals and ribbons earned in service, a clean blouse underneath the jacket, the brass always polished. As his cabin mate I knew he had two sets, one on himself, the other clean and pressed and hanging in the wardrobe, their upkeep assigned to his two servants who bent to this task as diligently as Jesuit priests before their relics and icons.

I stood and looked at the sky, then down at Bering, whose eyes were closed. I assumed he was asleep, but I was wrong. A sliver of moonlight momentarily pierced the high clouds, and in its glint I saw tears on that furrowed face, until this moment so outwardly stalwart and self-confident. I looked again to be certain they weren't beads of sweat or drops of condensed mist.

I now understood why he falsely claimed how during the first voyage foul weather shielded his view east from Cape Tchuktchi. In fact, by his own recent admission he had not been anywhere near the Cape, but instead much farther east. And when dismissing outright my theory that America had been peopled from Asia in ancient times, which I formulated from my own observations and after interviewing many knowledgeable seafaring people I'd met at Kamchatka and elsewhere in Siberia, he laughed and said only fools believe stories and opinions from the mouths of Cossacks and Kamchadals. They're all liars. Yet here was a man who staked his whole career on believing *without confirmation* what some Tchuktchis had told him. First, there is no land bridge to the east, although a Big Land isn't far; second, the coastline you're following—Tchuktchi land—turns abruptly west beyond Cape Tchuktchi, and there the Pacific Ocean meets the Icy Sea. Lies by omission are still lies.

33

Discipline was crumbling. The officers were too ill to defend themselves in the event of mutiny and worried that the men might kill them. I overheard some of this whispering but didn't interject. It was illogical. The men certainly had become surly and lax in their duties, but they were ill too. And what would a mutiny have gained them? We were all marooned here together, and I sensed that no one was so optimistic as to believe he would recover shortly and tramp off to a distant *ostrog* even in the unlikely chance we were actually somewhere on Kamchatka. The concern appeared nonsensical.

Nonetheless, cooperation instead of antagonism would benefit everyone, and even the officers recognized it was worth striving toward. To their credit (but also to protect themselves) they agreed that decisions affecting everyone would be made by consensus, as if we were still aboard the ship. As the men's respect for the officers plummeted so it rose concomitantly for certain of their comrades who by their attitudes and actions demonstrated strength of character. In this regard two petty officers stand out: Boatswain's Mate Aleksei Ivanov and Boatswain's Mate's Helper Luka Alekseyev. These men and one or two others were instrumental in keeping order.

Plenisner, Betge, and I each had a Cossack servant. Theirs were named Ivan Partinyagin and Aleksei Lazukov. All three were displeased with their circumstances. I'd already heard enough shit from my Cossack, Toma Lepekhin, who shortly after we came ashore lashed out at me for bringing him on this perilous and unnecessary trip. Morale everywhere could hardly fall lower. A household meeting was called during which we Germans explained to our Cossacks the advantages of living with us instead of dispersing to the other dwellings, assuming they would be welcomed. Like us, they were civilians and had no standing in the naval hierarchy. We agreed to share duties equally and vote on any important or contentious matters that arose. They agreed to this arrangement enthusiastically, and from then on we existed in harmony.

On 15 November the reconnaissance party dispatched by Bering returned to report it had found neither people nor forests, and that we appeared to be on an island. This news deepened everyone's despondency and elevated the volume of bitching. Most now anticipated the inevitable death of the castaway and lost any hope of ever seeing Kamchatka.

By 20 November both the sick and able-bodied were settled on the beach, Waxell having been the last holdout aboard the *St. Peter*. Bering's principal concern was now for his ship and the stores in her holds. On the 22nd he called a meeting of the ship's council. The lagoon was unprotected from storm winds arising from any direction; the anchorage was precarious, relying on a single anchor and a 288-pound grapnel, both attached to rotting lines. The council agreed to haul the vessel ashore at the highest flood and tie it down with hawsers by whatever means could be devised. None of the ballast and cargo, including water casks, were to be removed. Khitrov, despite suffering greatly from the scurvy, was assigned the task of seeing the mission through.

Khitrov waited for calm weather and a favorable tide, and on the 26th he summoned Boatswain's Mate Ivanov and ordered him to notify the captain commander that he, Khitrov, was prepared to board the *St. Peter* and start the process of laying her up. Bering relayed the message through Ivanov that if this couldn't be done Khitrov was to start bringing provisions ashore. Ivanov, however, had only five able-bodied men available, and that number was soon down to four when one collapsed when helping launch the longboat from the beach. Khitrov informed Waxell of the situation, who advised him to explain it directly to Bering. The following day Khitrov declared himself too infirm to leave his dwelling, and there the matter rested. Sure, he was sick with the scurvy, but so was nearly everybody. My diagnosis of his situation was laziness and fear of failure, but I kept silent.

Fate intervened during the night of the 28th when a powerful gale snapped the anchor and grapnel cables and put the *St. Peter* high onto the beach, completing the work our men could not. Much of the flour, groats, and salt was ruined, but the other provisions were saved. The ship now lay firmly beached with its rudder destroyed. A large hole punched in the port side allowed sand to wash in and out with every change of the tide. Each day that passed, each hour, our once proud ship became ever more derelict.

Emphasis now turned to finishing the dwellings. By the end of November there were five dug into the dunes parallel to the shore: a large barracks for the sick, then four overseen by Waxell, me, Ivanov, and Alekseyev, all fronted by rows of fox-proof water casks for storing meat and other foods.

Waxell was near death, but with my ministrations aided by Betge and Plenisner and efforts of the able-bodied who helped procure fresh foods, he was saved. His recovery came as a relief. Everyone feared that without him or Bering, whose condition was in steep decline, Khitrov would take command, destroying what little discipline and hope was left.

Khitrov's health was precarious too, and he came to our dwelling begging admittance. We were already crowded, having voted in Gunner's Mate Boris Roselius and Midshipman Ivan Sind. Another unanimous vote was required. The vote indeed turned out unanimous, but unanimously negative, and Khitrov had no choice except the barracks, where the men called him an incompetent asshole, threatened him with bodily harm, and told him to fuck off and go live elsewhere. But he had nowhere else to go.

Bering's end came 2 hours before dawn on 8 December 1741, still expressing the belief we were marooned somewhere on Kamchatka. In our private conversations he admitted saying this so the men wouldn't give up hope, although an insular location admittedly seemed more in line with the evidence. He had long awaited death and in the final hours asked for me. I hurried over to the place apart from the others where Betge, Plenisner, and I tended him, the sandy depression that we three and Bering himself referred to with macabre humor as "the grave." The walls were disintegrating, and he was nearly covered in sand, but he asked me to leave it, saying it made him feel warmer despite knowing the sensation was fallacious. The edema in his lower legs and feet had worsened just in the last day and turned them black.

He told me in a hoarse whisper that a copy of his report of the First Kamchatka Expedition could be found among his papers. He instructed me to retrieve and read the contents and afterward destroy the entire document, telling no one of its existence. The Admiralty archives in St. Petersburg did not contain a record of this copy, so it was never officially in his possession. Only after reading his words would I understand the larger meaning of what he had been telling me during our conversations, and why they proved him to be a dishonorable man and a disgraced naval officer. He had been praying for God's forgiveness, but had chosen me to confirm this specific act of dishonesty and serve as his confessor, and he apologized for placing such a burden on my shoulders.

Then others arrived. The captain commander was kind and courteous and urged us to be of good cheer, saying our misery would end and God would see us safely home if only we kept His faith and persevered.

The next day after the burial our household voted to accept his servants Ivan Maltsan and Maffei Kukushkin, who had stayed loyally by their master's side through his long illness and deserved our sympathy and Christian charity.

34

THE SCURVY WASN'T FINISHED with us, and death's scythe continued to reap more victims. Aleksej Klementev, a caulker, had preceded Bering to the grave on 4 December; Under Skipper Nikita Khotyaintsov passed away the day of Bering's funeral. Waxell immediately assumed command, and although discipline had become ragged his calm presence proved a positive influence. Waxell was 40, much closer to my age than Bering, who died at 60. He shared my faith in God and belief that with fresh food we could still save many of the men, just as we had saved him, and get through this ordeal alive and healthy. He and I were to get along well and be in agreement most of the time.

The colony's tasks had been reduced to three: hunting fresh meat, collecting firewood, and caring for the sick. Seals and sea otters inhabited the beaches and inshore waters, and ptarmigans were still plentiful in the hills beyond the dunes. Driftwood for fires was getting scarce. We had used up what was nearby to build shelters and as fuel for heat and cooking. Men were now dragging it from as far away as 2 miles.

Throughout Russia all foreigners are referred to as "Germans." Our dwelling housed five "Germans" (despite two of us being Danes) and five Cossacks. For work details we formed pairs of one "German" and one Cossack working in shifts and switching around duties to prevent boredom. One pair cooked, one or two pairs hunted, and one or two pairs gathered firewood. By professing an open agreement of equality the Russians were guaranteed we "Germans" wouldn't abuse them. This was satisfaction enough, and they happily slid into their former places as servants recognizing "German" authority. By this I mean they washed the kitchen utensils after meals, set out the food, fetched water, built fires, and when cooking accepted the job of sous-chef without complaining. Everything went well, and there was no dissention.

The combination of fresh food and continued medical attention by Betge and me was slowly gaining ground on the scurvy, and by the end of December it was clear that most of the sick would recover. Still, on the 17th we lost Ivan Tretyakov, a grenadier; Prokofei Yefintsov, a gunner second class, died on the 27th. As had been the practice with everyone except Bering, the men took their clothes and boots before consigning the corpses to eternity underneath the frozen sand.

During the brief ceremonies it occurred to me that death is demeaning in part because the dead are so much shorter than the living, who stand erect while they lie prone, close to the earth and already part of it, at eye level now with the worms and other lowly creatures. But death is infused with another final and inevitable abasement, which Ovid describes in his *Metamorphoses*. When Prometheus created humans he gave us the shape of gods, "standing tall as the other beasts do not" and enabling our gaze to be heaven-oriented instead of directed toward the baser dirt at our feet. That apes and bears can also rise onto their hind legs is an awkward, inauthentic bipedalism. Our upright form is proof of humankind's dignity in life, having been created in God's image and made ruler over all living things (*praeter cetera animantia rectum habet*).

We celebrated Christmas with stores rescued from the ship. There was no oven in which to bake cakes. Besides, our flour had hardened after 3 years and having been drenched in seawater when the ship came aground. In addition to sea salts, it was contaminated with gunpowder. We chiseled out pieces, soaked them in water, flattened them into crude cakes, and fried them in seal oil. They tasted awful, more the worse without wine or beer to wash away a disgusting flavor that truly defied description.

The following day dampened spirits still more when Timofei Antchyugov, a sailor, staggered into camp with two other men. As his last directive Bering had sent them out to determine if we were on Kamchatka or an island. They had wandered 18 days across mountains and tundra, meeting no humans but concluding we were most likely on an island. How they survived the cold, wind, and snow in tattered clothes and leaking boots without shelter or sufficient provisions is a testament to their toughness. Most of us presumed they died of exposure and starvation, but here they were without even frostbite.

Fedor Panov, a soldier, died 2 January 1742. His death was followed by Purser Ivan Lagunov's the night of the 7th. Lagunov was the scurvy's final victim; he was buried next to Bering. Of the 78 listed on the original ship's roster (not counting Waxell's minor son), 32 had met death.

The good health of the survivors brought bad habits. With the scurvy finally under control our colony became afflicted with the gambling disease. It spread as a contagion, consuming both officers and men. Initially the currency comprised rubles and kopecks, but these had no value without a place to spend them. The next commodity became sea otter pelts, and these innocent creatures were slaughtered for no reason other than fodder for the card games. The meat, which has a gamey taste, was usually thrown away. The craze for sea otter pelts led to thievery, which in turn led to bad feelings, grudges, and altercations. The officers could do little, partly because they now feared their subordinates, but also because they were complicit, eagerly taking part in the card games and stashing away as many pelts as they could.

Despite lacking all authority in the naval hierarchy, I addressed the men and berated them for not being kinder to nature and each other, reminding them we were all still in danger, and that having beaten back the scurvy was not sufficient reason to become uncivilized and toss aside proper behavior and Christian morals. How, I asked, did they intend to transport the pelts to mainland Siberia and cash in? Even if, as many still believed, we were actually on Kamchatka there was no market for them anywhere on the peninsula.

They paused in their gambling and watched me attentively during these harangues because I alone recognized which of the local plants were antiscorbutic and could keep the scurvy from returning. By now they were all converts to botanical Christianity, espousing profound trust and belief in what to them bordered on magic. My combined knowledge of plants and medicine had saved their lives and restored their health. The study of natural history wasn't such a fool's errand after all, and so they treated me respectfully despite the shabby terms I freely tossed around in denouncing them. After listening politely they returned to their cards and berating one another with curses.

A ship's council meeting was held 18 January to discuss the *St. Peter*'s fate. Other meetings followed. Because she was a naval vessel a strict protocol had to be met and every decision and its justification recorded. Many ideas were presented. Should she be refloated? If so, how was this to be accomplished with a short-handed crew and no timber available from which to hew rollers? What was the extent of the damage? Could it be repaired? How were repairs even possible with the hold now filled with wet sand, the strong tides sweeping in and out of the lagoon making footing and general working conditions perilous, the sea too cold to tolerate longer than a few minutes? Any sand shoveled out on the ebb would be replaced on the next flood, and a damage assessment below the waterline was impossible unless the sand could be removed and prevented from returning. The meetings seemed endless, but on the 29th it was finally agreed that the *St. Peter* would be dismantled and a smaller vessel constructed from her salvageable wreckage.

No one looked forward to standing in the cold surf pulling away planks and timbers despite agreement not to commence work until early spring. Then God in His mercy lent a helping hand. On 1 February a fierce gale and commensurate flood tide, as if perfectly timed by Heaven to coincide, lifted the *St. Peter* well beyond the mean high tideline, making her impending dismantling far more convenient and putting to rest any remaining thoughts of refloating her. When the water receded the vessel's new position showed her to be almost entirely filled with sand. There was no hope of her ever sailing again.

On 29 January some of the men killed a young sea lion. We had grown weary of eating the gamey flesh of sea otters, hair seals, and cormorants, and this was a welcome change. The ptarmigans we counted on so heavily at first were delicious and still numerous on the tundra, but had recently become wary from our relentless shooting at them.

On 25 February another scout team was dispatched to again determine if we were on the mainland or an island. Earthquakes are common throughout Kamchatka, and a quake that shook our camp on

7 February and knocked us off our feet reignited hope of the former. Five men set out led by Second Mate Kharlam Yushin with orders to proceed along the beach to north latitude 56° 10′, the position of the mouth of the Kamchatka River. The reasoning was, why take the trouble of building a ship if we could walk home? It was all foolishness. Wishful thinking is the most tenacious form of delusion. The trek neither reinforced nor refuted either hypothesis, in part because the men ignored their objective in favor of a sea-otter hunt. They returned 8 March no more informed than when they left.

On 15 March the eminently reliable Aleksei Ivanov trudged off with four men in another direction. Their way was blocked by insurmountable headlands, and they returned 4 days later to report the arrival of northern fur seals on the southern beaches. This was good news because fur seals offered possibilities of another supply of meat. Ivanov's team was then ordered to follow Yushin's route and proceed until determining whether we were on the mainland or an island. If the mainland, he was to send two men to Petropavlovsk for help; if an island, everyone was to return immediately so work on building the new ship could start with all hands present.

Ivanov's discovery of fur seals piqued my curiosity. No one yet knew where they bred, only that they were commonly encountered in Kamchatkan waters in late spring. They arrived from the direction of the Kuril Islands, gathered along the coast between capes Shipunski and Kronotski, then disappeared east in early June to an unknown destination. In autumn they returned lean and swimming south. Females harpooned at sea in late spring were carrying full-term fetuses, indicating they came ashore in early summer not far from the mainland to give birth, nurse their pups, and probably mate again. Discovering their breeding grounds would prove a boon to the fur industry and Kamchatka's economy.

When Ivanov and his team left camp 22 March, I and three of my household accompanied him as far as a large river we had named the Lyesnaya, where we left the others and continued walking southwest. We were still exploring this new location when Ivanov and his party returned to camp 6 April confirming that our location was indeed an island.

My companions and I were back by the 9th when a ship's council meeting decided unanimously to start building the new vessel at once. Everyone except Waxell and Khitrov was assigned to rotating work details servicing the entire camp. I was also excused to continue my natural history tasks. Members of my household would be relieved periodically from their rotating duties to assist me as needed. Labor for everyone else consisted of gathering firewood, hunting, and building the ship. The hunters were assigned household chores in their home dwellings when not actually hunting. These included cooking, fetching water, mending clothes and boots, and so forth.

On 18 April some of the hunters killed a mature male fur seal, or *sikatch*. Its flesh was rank and nauseating but nonetheless could feed the camp for at least a week. This was a heartening event, indicating plentiful food during the warm months when ship-building would be at its most intense. As we were soon to learn, the females and young of the species are delicious. We also were rewarded by a dead whale cast ashore about 4 miles distant. Its blubber lasted until we left the island, and when we sailed away several barrels remained behind. I took measurements of the beast as best I could and wrote a description of it, but most of the carcass had become buried in the sand and inaccessible.

The appearance of the lone adult male fur seal was a harbinger of others to follow, although the location of our camp would not be one of the *lyeshbitche* (rookeries). I had confirmed Ivanov's observation that fur seals in immense numbers were about to inundate the southwestern beaches, just a 12 mile hike from camp, and I intended to study them in detail.

Breaking apart the *St. Peter* commenced 21 April, and the men attacked her tired flanks enthusiastically. Morale had never been higher. We were now bound by a common task culminating in a common goal. The men were healthy, the weather warming, and food anticipated to become more plentiful. Everyone was active. Grindstones and tools were cleaned and put in working order. Charcoal was prepared and a smithy built for manufacture of tools and iron accessories such as nails. As raw material, iron parts of the *St. Peter* were carefully set aside and recycled in the forges.

During this period my natural history investigations began in earnest. Flocks of new birds arrived with the spring; plants sprang from the land, replacing the snow and ice. All around, life awaited the naturalist's keen eye and ready pen. Fortunately, I had hoarded sufficient ink and paper through the winter. Quills were in short supply until I discovered that the flight feathers of young albatrosses make perfectly suitable pens. I cleaned, sharpened, and sorted the dissecting equipment while Lepekhin put the guns in top working order to shoot game for us to eat and acquire specimens for the Academy. Plenisner readied his brushes and paints to illustrate the many new findings I anticipated. Thus equipped and with camping gear packed we set out to describe the natural wonders of this strange and fascinating island.

Collections until now had been minimal. Over the winter Lepekhin had shot several specimens of an undescribed eider, a kind of sea duck. This new species is colorful and variegated. Enormous flotillas drifted offshore throughout the winter and early spring, occasionally coming closer and knifing through the breakers or waddling ashore and standing idly about on the beach. I prepared the skins for eventual shipment to the Academy.

More impressive was a monstrous cormorant. It was the size of a goose, unafraid of humans and easily approached. What we first thought was loss of the capacity to fly turned out to be laziness. The birds could fly clumsily, certainly well enough to escape, but seemed disinclined to do so even when facing imminent death. They were present in large numbers along rocky parts of the shore and could be approached and clubbed without even trying to escape. Just one specimen could feed three men. We welcomed it into our larders despite the fishy flavor, mostly because ptarmigans, our principal feathered prey, had by now abandoned the tundra and dispersed into the mountains. This giant cormorant was a wonderful find for science, and the skins I prepared would astonish all Europe when discovery of the species was announced at some future time by the Academy.

The food supply was still tenuous. Although spring brought more game, our relentless hunting had made the wildlife nervous. Birds took wing before our hunters came within range; sea otters and seals had also become more alert and slipped quickly into the sea at the sight of men. In addition, we had depleted many of the mammals and birds in the vicinity. Less game and the heightened wariness of what remained forced the hunters to travel farther.

With spring, housing also became a concern. Melting snow augmented by heavy rains flooded the subterranean dwellings, diverting everyone from his assigned tasks to help build above-ground shelters. If there was a positive side to this change in conditions it was the sudden appearance of huge amounts of driftwood previously inaccessible underneath the deep snow. Collecting wood for charcoal production and cooking fires became far more convenient.

35

JUST OFFSHORE LAZED THE biggest larder of all, the sea cows gathered in drifting herds. I watched them daily as they floated and dozed beyond the surf after stuffing themselves with giant kelp that grew in dense forests in the shallows. I estimated that the largest specimens were 30 feet long and weighed several tons. Just one of these creatures would feed us for weeks. A successful capture could divert those assigned to hunting detail for work on the new ship. This meant finishing the job faster and permitting us to leave this wretched camp well before the end of summer, thus avoiding the autumn storms and headwinds. To say we were motivated would vastly understate the situation.

When we eventually killed a manatee and tasted its meat we were astonished. After a diet of barely edible sea otters, seals, sour groats, and, early in our isolation even foxes, this new meat was equivalent to the finest beef, probably because sea cows, like cattle, are vegetarian. When exposed to the sun the fat turns yellow like butter and tastes even better. Most startling, the meat does not rot when left exposed, nor does it emit an odor of decay even when riddled with fly maggots. Salted and aged in the barrel, sea cow flesh tastes like fine corned beef. On this new diet even the weakest among us were quickly restored to full health and eager to pursue their tasks.

Other known manatees are much smaller, and likely I was the first naturalist ever to observe this specific kind alive and swimming. We needed to devise a method of capturing them for food, but I also required a specimen to measure and describe. I had already spent several hours observing their activities from the entrance of our dwelling and from the high dunes and rocks and offer this synopsis of my more extensive written description:

> *Sea cows gather preferentially about the mouths of streams where these flow into the sea, and also in shallow, sandy places near the shore. Adults keep the young protected on all sides. They generally travel in families of two adults and two calves, one older and the other young, indicating the young stay with their parents for a time after weaning. The families gather and move together in loose, un-organized herds. Sexually mature adults mate primarily in spring and give birth in all seasons, but mostly autumn. Gestation is one year. Adults are probably monogamous. During courtship the male slowly follows the female, who eludes his amorous overtures by twist-ing away and swimming in meandering paths. Finally she relents and the two embrace like humans in mutual passion. One calf is born at a time, which I deduce from the presence of only two teats, never having seen a female with more than one calf, and dissections revealing short* uterine cornua. *Sea cows display no innate fear of humans. Many times I got close enough to prod them with a long stick and even stroke their backs with my hands. The skin is rough, thick, and resembles tree bark in relief and texture. Sea cows are grazing animals and feed almost continuously, dipping their heads underwater to rip kelp fronds from the rocks oblivious to activities around and above them. Not even the appearance of the longboat alters this fixated behavior. Every five minutes or so an individual rises for air after exhaling with a horsey snort. While grazing they move slowly forward, first one foot then the other in a half-swim, half-walk along the shallow bottom. Gulls frequently rest on their backs picking sea lice from folds in their skin. They feed on many kinds of sea kelp, including the species with wrinkled fronds resem-bling Savoy cabbage and another that is latticed. They leave floating mats of stems and holdfasts in the wake of their gluttony. When satiated they roll onto their backs to sleep. In winter they become unthrifty, losing mass and looking emaciated, at which time their ribs and backbones are visible. Occasionally one is crushed in the*

*ice and cast ashore dead, or moves too close to shore and is dashed
against the rocks by storm surge.*

Through trial and error we devised an effective means of capture by
forging a large fishing hook resembling half an anchor—in nautical language a shank with a single arm and fluke. The other end of the shank
terminated in a thick ring. One end of a long, stout rope was tied through
the ring; 30 men standing on the shore gripped the other end. The longboat carrying a half-dozen men was launched. One operated the rudder
while four rowed quietly toward the herd. When close to a sea cow the
harpooner standing in the bow struck, sinking the fluke as deep as he
could while those on the beach took up the slack and began pulling in the
rope. Meanwhile, the boatmen weakened the stricken animal by stabbing
it repeatedly with knives and bayonets as it sighed and hyperventilated
before spurting fountains of blood and eventually succumbing. During
the struggle its relatives and comrades sometimes gathered around pressing down on the rope, trying to overturn the boat by lifting it onto their
backs, even attempting to rip out the hook by striking it with their tails.
In this last endeavor they were sometimes successful.

The conjugal affinity of this species is undeniable. On one occasion
when a female was hooked her mate refused to leave her side despite
being beaten with clubs. Even after she was dead he followed in her
wake as she was pulled to shore. We tethered her body near the rocks
overnight, and the next morning when we went to butcher the carcass
he was by her side. And he was still there the morning after when I
went alone to the makeshift abattoir to examine the intestines.

36

Until the first sea cow was secured we existed on fur seal meat. The lone male that had come ashore and been killed in April was an anomaly. We soon learned that all the rookeries were on the south-western shore facing west, where we presumed Kamchatka lay. This was the destination fur hunters had searched decades to find. It was a gold mine waiting to be tapped.

The seals were easy to kill with clubs, and they were present in the many thousands, but the meat then had to be packed over the mountains to our side of the island. The flesh, heart, and tongue of the females and pups are delicious.

Although the northern fur seal, or "sea bear" as some call it, was a familiar animal to the Cossacks and Itelmen of Kamchatka, its behavior and biology had never been described. On 28 May I measured and dissected a large *sikatch*, taking 32 measurements and describing both the external and internal appearance and anatomy in detail. At this time the only fur seals on the rookeries were these adult males, which arrive early in the breeding season and partition the shoreline into patches they defend vigorously against competing males. Smaller *kholyustiaki* ("bachelor" males), sexually mature perhaps but not big enough to battle for space with a *sikatch*, arrive simultaneously and gather in herds on the tundra behind the beaches.

I wondered what sensory apparatus the males were using to assess their surroundings. As a test my Cossack and I blinded one of them using clubs, beating him on the face until his eyes were destroyed. We could then walk slowly into his defended space without him noticing, but any grunting or bellowing from a neighboring male sent him shuffling swiftly toward the sound to check his perimeters for possible encroachment, prepared to attack intruders even if they were invisible to him.

Beginning around 10 June the mature females, or *matki* (mothers), began coming ashore, moving into the spaces defended by the large breeding males, which had spent their time waiting for the females, bellowing at their neighbors on all sides and occasionally battling them, dozing, and inspecting the perimeters of their stations but not daring to leave and feed at sea for fear of losing their places. Many were already bloody or displayed healed wounds from skirmishes during previous summers. Soon after arriving each mature female gives birth to a single pup with thin black hair and afterward stays to nurse its young and mate with the resident male.

Breeding activity nears its peak by mid-June. The pungent odor arising from countless seals crowded into such a relatively small area became nearly intolerable, making me feel nauseous at times. It was a blend of shit and urine, decaying flesh from dead seals and placentas, and a pungent smell given off by the seals themselves, seemingly from their fur. The rookery was a cacophony audible for miles. The bulls bellowed like foghorns, and the monotonous bleating of the females and pups was reminiscent of countless frenzied ewes and lambs. Screaming gulls and yipping foxes prowled through the maelstrom feeding on afterbirths and carcasses, adding their voices to this deafening choir. All around the cycle of birth and death was on spectacular display.

Bodies of the dead lay rotting among the boulders or stirred lazily in the swash—old bulls terminally weakened by their struggles to hold spaces and mate, females killed by enraged males or dying in parturition, stillborn pups, females and pups crushed to death by infuriated males intent on repelling invading neighbors. How this last happens is easily discerned on seeing the size disparity between the sexes: a breeding male weighs 450 pounds, an adult female 80-100 pounds, a pup is 12-15 pounds. Females and their young are at an obvious disadvantage if a male attacks, steps on them, or merely rolls onto them in his sleep. I often witnessed males grasping females in their jaws then hurling them several feet, ripping huge gashes in their hides.

A few are killed instantly; others limp away probably to die later of their wounds. Dead pups I examined often had broken bones, a result of heavy trauma. Other pups were emaciated, either from disease or because their mothers died before weaning them. A female might leave the rookery to feed and succumb at sea leaving her pup ashore to starve.

My travels back and forth for the 12 miles in each direction had become distracting. I was missing interesting observations and the opportunity to record some behaviors sequentially. Plus, it became increasingly clear that the breeding season lasts only a couple of months. I decided to stay and built a blind in the middle of the rookery I had been observing, remaining in it 6 days and recording the comings and goings, the fighting, interactions of the pups and their first attempts to swim, maternal care, mating and parturition, causes of mortality. . . . Everything witnessed was transcribed in exact detail. I noted that the females went to sea periodically, I assumed to feed, but each miraculously recognized her pup from among thousands of others seemingly identical and bleating impatiently to nurse. I noticed that the males became leaner, their skins hanging ever more loosely as summer progressed. Specific individuals I monitored hadn't eaten since coming ashore, and I saw how on warm days when the sky wasn't overcast and drizzling the seals sat around waving their hind flippers, evidently a mechanism for cooling the blood. I counted the females in a *gynaecum* (harem), noting numbers ranging from a few to 50 or so and wondered how they selected the males with which to breed. Clearly the males did not select them because they never left their stations, waiting instead for the females to decide. During later trips to the rookeries I recorded how as summer slipped into autumn the pups molt their thin black birth coats and grow thick replacement pelts of silver.

Sea lions interspersed through the rookery in fewer numbers were also breeding. I took notes of their activities, made measurements and dissections, and recorded everything I saw and discovered.

37

IN SUMMER THE TUNDRA explodes in an artist's palette of colors represented by the pink primula, yellow Siberian rhododendron and Siberian buttercup, white narcissus anemone, purple beachhead iris, and maroon sarana lily betraying its edible bulb. I collected specimens wherever I went, writing descriptions of unfamiliar plants and pressing examples of them for eventual shipment to the Academy's herbarium. Plenisner illustrated as many as he could. Conditions had become pleasant. The temperature sometimes rose to 60° Fahrenheit during the day and rarely fell below freezing at night. The men building the new ship stripped to the waist, thanking God for the extended daylight and respite from worry of frostbite. More commonly the weather was foggy and drizzly, but sometimes we saw the sun. We had several such days in July, permitting Yushin to take a celestial reading of our position and determine the compass variation.

12 July 1742 was a high point of my career as a naturalist. On this day I dissected a sea cow. The lax discipline precluded conscripting men to assist. Their gratitude for my having saved them from the scurvy did not extend to helping with messy dissections and the handling of putrefying organs. To my eternal gratitude Assistant Surgeon Betge, Surgeon Apprentice Konavalov, and my illustrator Plenisner pitched in. All contributed useful skills and experience. At the last minute I was able to coerce four crew members to help for a single hour by bribing them with tobacco.

The specimen was an adult female killed and beached a few days before. I estimated the carcass to weigh 8,000 pounds; the heart weighed an actual 36.25 pounds. In all, I took 47 measurements of various features of its external and internal anatomy. Its length from the upper lip to the fork in the tail measured 296 inches (24.7 feet); abdominal circumference was 244 inches (20.3 feet), and breadth of the caudal fin at its two extremes was 78 inches (6.5 feet). My recollection was that all other manatees and the closely related dugong have rounded tails shaped like paddles, very different from this species. We measured the stomach at 6 feet long and 5 feet wide, dimensions nothing short of astonishing. My notes state that it was *so stuffed with. . .seaweed that four strong men, with a rope attached could scarcely move it from its place and with great effort drag it out.*

Some have claimed that sea cows come ashore to graze on terrestrial plants, but this is impossible. The animal we examined is entirely aquatic, as shown clearly by its anatomy. The hide, as mentioned, is more like the bark of a tree than the skin of a living animal. It is about an inch thick, wrinkled, black, hairless, and nearly tough enough to turn an axe. A detailed description of the animal's exterior and interior anatomy can be found in my monograph *De bestiis marinis*, which I hope to see published eventually by the Academy. This work also includes descriptions of the northern fur seal (sea bear), sea lion, and sea otter. For lack of time and materials my draft manuscript containing descriptions of all four species prepared here on the island will be sent to the Academy for later revision, assuming it survives the voyage to Kamchatka.

Working conditions this momentous day were deplorable. Adding to the cold and rain were the recalcitrant tides, which forced a long pause on the flood when our makeshift dissecting theater was mostly underwater. The foxes worked their mischief continuously, tearing away at tissues and organs we were trying to examine, sometimes plucking samples directly from our hands. They stole my paper and books, even ripping at paper on which I was trying to write, and carried off my inkstand. Add to these major nuisances the indifferent boredom of the hired men, who carelessly tore holes in tissues I was trying to remove intact for examination and measurement. On balance, the damage they caused outweighed any benefit of their presence. Plenisner's contribution was immense. Under these trying circumstances he made accurate drawings and paintings of our findings. Sadly, only his sketch of the whole sea cow reached the Academy.

38

WHILE I WAS CONSUMED by my natural history projects Captain Waxell was experiencing crises of his own. For starters, all three ship's carpenters had died of the scurvy, but among the remaining men was a Cossack named Sava Starodubstsov who once worked for Spangberg as a laborer in the shipyard at Okhotsk Ostrog. He approached Waxell and agreed to build the ship if Waxell would direct his efforts. He had never built a vessel before; in fact, he had never even been employed as a carpenter, although he had seen carpenters at their tasks. This wasn't encouraging, but Starodubstsov was Waxell's only option. Then there was Waxell himself, a sailor, not a shipwright. As an officer he had overseen shipyards, although never participated in the design and construction of ships. It was all very aleatory.

Real work had begun 6 May in the face of three other impediments. First, many of the men were still recovering from the scurvy and had little energy or enthusiasm. Second, the weather was damp, foggy, and generally disagreeable. Third, the chain of command was now broken, and decisions had to be arrived at by vote, a slow and often contentious process.

Camaraderie got better as the men regained health and the weather improved, and cracking the whip became unnecessary. Everyone recognized that the only way to avoid staying another winter was by building the ship quickly. Sea cow meat was now supplemented by salmon, which flooded the rivers to spawn and could be caught by the hundreds. Waxell led the men by kindness and encouragement instead of driving them like donkeys, and they responded positively, happy to work for a leader who appreciated their efforts and listened attentively to their suggestions, which were often valuable contributions.

Starodubstsov proved himself dogged and reliable, although I had doubts at first. I wondered how a man who outwardly seemed so stupid could have such intelligent hands. His half-dazed expression never changed. It was the look of an idiot, yet the hands moved with genius, fingers manipulating his rough tools like musical instruments, objects of precision emerging from shapeless blocks of wood while their creator drooled absently, his mind seemingly elsewhere, or nowhere.

The new ship was a one-masted hooker 40 feet long, 13 feet wide, and drew 6.5 feet, roughly half the size of the original packet boat. She was christened the *St. Peter* in honor of her progenitor that, like Adam, had donated a rib to assist in the creation of Eve. The keel was fashioned from the original *St. Peter*'s mainmast sawed off 3 feet above the deck. Its stump became the new ship's prow, and from a capstan the men made a stern-post. Other parts of the old ship were scavenged as necessary, and she became skeletal before our eyes as her replacement took form and gained mass.

She was caulked by the end of July. A sliding bilge-block then had to be constructed to launch her. This consumed some time because she had been built high on the beach in the event of unusually severe storm tides, making it necessary to put together a block 25 fathoms long.

On 10 August she was launched, and immediately Waxell began to worry. This was the lagoon that had been the first *St. Peter*'s demise. It was unprotected from wind and storm surge on all sides, and we could only hope God would withhold heavy weather until we could be underway. Waxell had given Ivanov a deserved field promotion from boatswain's mate to sub-lieutenant and assigned him to hurriedly supervise installing rigging, bending on the sails, and hanging the rudder. Ballast consisted of cannons, cannonballs, and miscellaneous iron parts from the old ship. Stores comprised 10 casks of water, five casks of salted sea cow meat, 11 sacks of flour, and some biscuits baked ashore using the remaining barely edible flour.

Finally, the baggage was brought aboard. Sind had been made responsible for checking the weight each man was allowed. Room also had been allotted for the pelts collected. Each man submitted his request, the total not to exceed 3.5 tons. My baggage was fixed at 10 poods, or 360 pounds, half of Waxell's allotment and less than Khitrov's.

My collections were admittedly large, but also extremely valuable. I had labored tirelessly. In addition to dozens of pressed plants, skeletons, and miscellaneous other objects I had skinned a young sea cow and stuffed it with grass to hold the shape. I did the same with a sea otter, sea lion, and fur seal. I was stunned and dismayed when told there wasn't room for them and they must be left on the island. I stormed about cursing and yelling at Waxell, who stood before me stoically, not even blinking.

"Dr. Steller," he said calmly, "Please be sensible. I realize all these artifacts are important to you and to the Academy, but my foremost concerns as chief naval officer must be for the safety of the men and ship. We simply don't have space."

"Goddammit, Captain, you *must* make room! What I've collected is invaluable to science, the sea cow especially. No naturalist except me has ever seen one, much less described it!" I know my face had turned red and the other men were watching curiously. I must have resembled a whale about to spout.

"And I commend the effort you've put into making these objects both presentable and portable, but there isn't room," Waxell repeated in that calm voice.

"Never mind the effort," I said. "Effort is part of everything, and my efforts weren't greater than anyone else's. It's that. . . ." I paused and glanced around, not able to look at Waxell any longer for fear of assaulting him and being marooned alone on the island while the rest sailed off.

"As to your being the only naturalist to visit this place, surely others will follow after learning it's where the fur seals come to breed." Waxell examined his pipe in a gesture of displacement activity. We had been using albatross quills as pipe stems since I discovered they had uses other than as writing quills.

"Well, fuck you," I said, and stalked away. There was nothing I could do. Returning at some future time to retrieve my collections would be fruitless. No doubt the foxes would have destroyed them within a day.

All I ended up taking were my manuscripts, some dried seeds, and a pair of palatal plates from the jaws of a sea cow that serve in place of teeth. And the plants? I had listed and collected 211 species. Now everything was left to the mischief of the foxes and whims of the wind, rain, and tides.

We departed late in the afternoon of 10 August 1742, warping the vessel through the reef to 9 fathoms, then taking to the sweeps and rowing offshore about 9 miles before coming on a fair north wind and hoisting the sails. God had shown mercy so far, leaving us becalmed while rigging the vessel and keeping her anchorage safe and on firm bottom. She sailed reasonably well, but we were terribly cramped, literally forced to lie atop and crawl over one another.

On 15 August we hit a strong headwind. Simultaneously, we noticed a leak and started one of the bilge pumps. The leak worsened and the second pump was activated. To augment the pumps Ivanov ordered a bucket brigade: a man standing in water in the hold filled a bucket and handed it to a shipmate on the stairs, who passed it up the chain until it reached topside. After exchanging hands a few more times it was emptied over the gunwale. To raise the ship's waterline we tossed cannons and cannonballs overboard, plus pillows, blankets, and much of our luggage. It was some small comfort to realize that my specimens, even had they made it aboard, would have been among the first objects jettisoned. With the hold sufficiently cleared the leak was found quickly, stuffed with rags and caulked, and boards nailed over the opening.

On 17 August we sighted land lying west-northwest of Avatcha Bay, but because of contrary winds it wasn't until the 26th that we reached the harbor entrance and the next day arrived at Petropavlovsk, 13 days after leaving the place that would later be called Bering Island, part of the Komandorski (Commander) archipelago, also named in Captain Commander Bering's honor. Our joy on stepping ashore can't be described, but the feeling was soon supplanted by irony: thinking us dead, our companions ashore had disposed of our belongings. We arrived with little more than the rags on our backs only to find nothing with which to exchange them.

39

I WON'T DESCRIBE THE events of Captain Tchirikov's voyage because I know only the rudiments, and these indirectly. Suffice to say, Tchirikov and his crew also discovered America, and like us suffered ravages of the scurvy. In addition, several of Tchirikov's men were murdered by Americans at one of his stops. Details of this tragedy will never be known because Tchirikov himself could never learn exactly what happened. The *St. Paul* returned in autumn 1741, wintered at Petropavlovsk, and left in early spring of the current year, 1742, to search for us, finally deciding the effort was futile and putting into harbor at Okhotsk Ostrog.

De la Croyère's fate is relevant because he was one of three professors sent to Siberia by the Academy to participate in the Second Kamchatka Expedition, the others being Gmelin and Müller, neither of whom reached Kamchatka or even boarded a ship.

Bering had assigned de la Croyère to the *St. Paul's* roster as geodesist and astronomer, although he failed in his duties because of incompetence and having contracted the scurvy. He apparently relied minimally on the *St. Paul's* buoyancy, keeping his person afloat throughout the voyage atop a small ocean of *raka*. He tried convincing himself and everyone else that drink is a curative for this disease, but his shipmates knew that it only serves as a painkiller. De la Croyère died the morning of 10 October 1741 as the *St. Paul* entered Avatcha Bay. He had dressed to go ashore and was royally drunk when he toppled over dead. His remains lie buried on a hillside north of Petropavlovsk. Tchirikov was near death from the scurvy and had to be carried to land, but recovered and survived.

The men under my command were at Bolsheretskoi Ostrog. I

stashed my few belongings at Petropavlovsk, and my Cossack and I left 27 August 1742 to hike west across the Kamchatka Peninsula, a straight-line distance of about 87 miles. At this time of year the surface of the tundra has thawed, and the ground is marshy. Progress was slow. Many rivers and streams had to be forded, and the journey took a week.

I had been out of touch with events in Russia since embarking from Okhotsk Ostrog in autumn 1740. Much had happened. Empress Anna had died that October, about the time we departed. Her niece's son Ivan Antonovitch, age 2 months, succeeded her. Too young to rule, he was placed under the auspices of Ernest Biron, who became regent. In a palace revolt Ivan's mother, also named Anna, usurped Biron and exiled him to Siberia. The second Anna's plan was to then overthrow her son, but Peter the Great's daughter Elizabeth anticipated this. She and her followers arrested and imprisoned the whole royal family, and Elizabeth captured the throne for herself. We poor castaways from the two ships named *St. Peter* had, without knowing it, served three rulers and a regent, one not yet potty-trained, while assuming the whole time we were laboring in deference to the first Anna.

Matters at Bolsheretskoi Ostrog were in reasonably good shape despite not benefiting from my supervision. Krasheninnikov had gone to Okhotsk Ostrog in June 1741, as were his orders, and I learned Gmelin finally had been recalled to St. Petersburg, a relief to us both and him especially. Berckhan had generated many illustrations, and Gorlanov completed the trip I'd assigned him. I was disturbed, however, to discover that he had written to Gmelin and Müller behind my back complaining about certain disadvantages he was suffering, the most serious seeming to be a shortage of vodka. My Cossack hunters had not been idle, having made good collections and even killing a walrus at Cape Lopatka, an animal rarely seen that far south. It would make an excellent addition to the Academy's collections.

Only Danilov had been remiss. I had left him as my trusted replacement in charge of affairs at Bolsheretskoi Ostrog. Thinking me dead, he had disposed of some of my valuable possessions. But what truly drove me to a fit of fury had not been Danilov's fault. That selfish bastard Spangberg, without either permission or authorization, had conscripted Danilov for his second Japan expedition, leaving my unit adrift and leaderless.

As I fumed over these matters long out of my control a message from Plenisner in Petropavlovsk arrived saying he would be coming to Bolsheretskoi Ostrog to spend the winter. His companionship would naturally be welcomed. I anticipated regaling each other in German and tipping the bottle, but Plenisner is a grand *fur temporis* (thief of time), and I was buried under deadlines. There was correspondence to send out, including a letter to Birgitta-Helena, whom I was starting to miss a little more each day. I also wrote Gmelin giving him a synopsis of my findings on the island. I told him that despite the great suffering, *I would not exchange the knowledge of nature which I gained on this rotten voyage for great wealth.* And I meant it truly.

I needed to continue expanding my treatise *Beschreibung des Landes Kamchatka* (*Description of the Land of Kamchatka*). In this document I have put forth my original theory that America was settled by migrants from Asia. Eventually, someone else will come to the same conclusion and receive credit for its formulation, unless I set down my thoughts first. Considering the closeness of these land masses and the numerous stepping-stone islands between them the human link I propose seems eminently logical. Following considerable reflection I now consider pre-Adamism, as postulated by the Frenchman Isaac La Peyère, to be preposterous, along with all other fanciful notions about how Earth was populated by humans. In fact, I no longer think about this in a theological manner, but simply lay out the evidence for examination, presuming not everyone has been rendered blind and stupid from reading the Old Testament literally.

I've noted that the Koryaks, Tchuktchis, and Americans build and make use of identical skin *baidaras* and kayaks. Their languages and appearance are similar, including dress, stature, and voice inflections. So are their tools and uses of raw materials like grasses and animal skins. The Americans manufacture waterproof shirts from whale in-testines, and so do the Tchuktchis. The Tchuktchis have told me that Americans living inland away from the sea herd reindeer and rely far less on marine resources, similar to inland Koryaks of northeastern

Siberia. I could go on, but the information at hand already makes a strong case. Naturally, my positing of a migration theory has been ridiculed and discredited by many, even learned confreres who ought to know better than dismiss tangible evidence and continue favoring unverified—and unverifiable—myths.

Several reports were long overdue, including one to the Senate in which I intended to castigate Bering and the other naval officers for ignoring my advice on certain nautical matters while at sea, failing to allow me sufficient opportunities to explore lands we found in America, and several additional shortcomings of leadership I found annoying, disruptive of my work, and had put us all in danger. In addition, my journal of the voyage with Bering, the time marooned, and the journey back to Kamchatka needed updating.

There were species descriptions I'd scribbled in rough form while marooned that had to be finished, plus other incomplete descriptions left behind at Bolsheretskoi Ostrog. The collections made by our Cossack hunters in my absence needed to be sorted, labeled, and packed for shipment to the Academy. Most important, the treatise *De bestiis marinis* lacked a preface and required minor editorial changes before being sent off, the manuscript having been composed in near-final form while on the island. And, of course, the illustrators were always behind. Plenisner would help them catch up. Some of his drawings and paintings executed during our time as castaways were complete or nearly so, and he and Berckhan worked well together. And thus I spent the last months of 1742 mostly confined indoors with pen in hand.

40

DURING WINTER 1741-1742, WHEN I was on that island and out of touch with events at Bolsheretskoi Ostrog, Spangberg had wintered there preparing for his second expedition to Japan. This bully and my nemesis, whose second voyage ultimately cost much and produced little, had issued a divisive and puzzling directive to all Kamchatka. I never actually saw a copy, but whatever it said reinforced a fear in every regional garrison officer and *voyevoda* that the Kamchadal uprising of 1731 was about to be reprised. As a result of Spangberg's thoughtless action and the unwarranted paranoia of everyone else, 17 Itelmen were declared rebels and herded 467 miles by four Cossacks to Bolsheretskoi Ostrog for my interrogation. This was early in the year 1743. *Me*, I asked the Cossacks incredulously? You've brought them to the wrong person. I'm a naturalist, not a magistrate. I don't have either military or civil authority. They told us to bring these rebels to you, Steller, the Cossacks replied.

The entire scene was ridiculous. When I questioned these unfortunates they told me that Cossacks everywhere on the peninsula had been ordered by Spangberg's directive to exterminate all Itelmen. Even if true, the Itelmen standing before me explained, how could it apply to them, baptized Christians? Hadn't we pledged our souls to Jesus and our loyalty to Her Imperial Majesty, Ruler Brilliant as the Sun? The Cossacks were surely wrong. We would rather be slaughtered on the spot than accused of sinning against The Lord and disobedience to Her Majesty.

These people obviously weren't rebellious. In fact, their love of God and loyalty to the empress exceeded that of most Cossacks, who regularly blaspheme the Holy Trinity and would instantly swap their Siberian citizenship for a bottle of vodka. Few Itelmen I'd met matched the rectitude of the poor souls I was questioning. Most are happy idolaters unconcerned about the Afterlife. In contrast, these people seemed like saints with Mongolian features.

I released the prisoners immediately, explaining to their captors how they evidently misunderstood the instructions. Not even Spangberg would openly advocate the annihilation of an entire people. Furthermore, I repeated, why bring them to me at Bolsheretskoi Ostrog? I wasn't *voyevoda* of this dung heap with powers over administrative matters. Even if I had been I didn't have provisions to sustain their abductees. Their Cossack captors had not shown me any written charges against them or orders to retain them, and there was no jail in which to put them. The event, stupid as it was, had considerable repercussions, as I later show.

I promptly put the matter behind me and went off with my Cossack and Berckhan to explore the Cape Lopatka region of southern Kamchatka and the northern Kuril Islands, where during late spring and early summer 1743 we collected many unusual fishes and marine invertebrates from the coastal waters. Berckhan made drawings of a sea otter and several unknown birds and plants. Another objective completed was to observe and record how people of the Kurils hunt sea otters. By 20 June we were back at the mouth of the Bolshaya River.

In his travels through western Siberia, Messerschmidt reportedly found a frozen mammoth, long thought by some to be the Behemoth mentioned in the Old Testament Book of Job and which supposedly drowned in the Great Flood, a notion immediately debunked after Johann Duvernoy assembled a nearly complete skeleton at the Academy museum and proved it to be an extinct elephant. Nonetheless, I was enchanted by the idea of finding a whole mammoth preserved in the permafrost and being first to describe its soft anatomy, but the search would entail a trek north to the Icy Sea where bones and teeth had been recovered near the mouth of the Kolyma River. The mammoth's existence was well known in northern Siberia, as indicated by the brisk trade in fossil ivory.

Before I could go anywhere I needed money. We Academy alumni of the two *St. Peter*s were broke because the chancelleries at Okhotsk Ostrog and Irkutsk, thinking us dead, had stopped our salaries. Fortuitously, Krasilnikov was in Okhotsk Ostrog, and on hearing I was alive immediately notified the chancellery there to send my back pay to Bolsheretskoi Ostrog on the next vessel, saving me considerable time and trouble. Krasilnikov's refusal to go to America as de la Croyère's student assistant had worked out well for him. With de la Croyère dead he was now the Academy's senior geodesist in Siberia with influence at the chancelleries, especially the one at Okhotsk Ostrog. On 8 July 1743 I received what was owed me: 1,927 rubles and 64 kopeks. I could now put my manuscripts and illustrations for transshipment to St. Petersburg aboard the vessel just arrived. I decided to keep the collections with me for fear of them being lost in transit. Nonetheless, the consignment I relinquished was not received at the Academy until 12 February 1746, and when it was opened some items were missing.

I was also beneficiary of another source of revenue. Of the nearly 900 sea otter pelts taken aboard the second *St. Peter*, a third were given to me by my shipmates in gratitude for saving their lives. Because the Chinese pay the highest prices I later sold them in the market at Irkutsk, and the sale brought me much additional capital.

Now I could afford to explore northern Kamchatka. Lepekhin and I left Bolsheretskoi Ostrog for Verkhne-Kamtchatsk on 27 July, following the Bolshaya River inland. I estimated the distance at 162 miles. Our destination beyond Verkhne-Kamtchatsk was Nizhnekamtchatsk, another 310 miles. Lepekhin was familiar with the route because Nizhnekamtchatsk, located 20 miles inland from the Kamchatka River estuary, was his place of origin, and I figured he would look forward to visiting family and old acquaintances. We left on foot, our only means of transportation.

The going was slow, both the weather and terrain holding us back. We were always wet from the frequent rain and near-constant drizzle, from sloshing across the thawed tundra and through swamps and marshes, and from fording rivers and streams and hacking through soggy thickets of alder and willow. If we made 13 miles in a long day, that was good progress. And stopping for the night when deep in the wilderness meant having to build a shelter, in itself time-consuming.

Both Lepekhin and I were carrying heavy packs, mostly collecting and dissecting gear, paper for pressing plants, and my journals. Otherwise, we carried only clothes for the coming winter, some tea, plugs of tobacco, and a little bread. We had been saving the last by living off the land. The rivers were filled with salmon, the forests and meadows with berries and edible plants, so finding something to eat was not an issue. We grazed as we traveled, picking fruit and munching sarana lily bulbs along the way. I wrote in my journal that I would never fear starving in Siberia, at least not in the warm months, *after having learned here of the many things with which an idle stomach may be kept amused.*

We passed near Apatcha, a small Itelmen village, without stopping. It was my intention to explore this area for new plants and animals, then cross the divide between coastal Kamchatka and the mighty valley formed by the Kamchatka River and continue northward. But just outside Apatcha I slipped and fell on algae-covered stones while fording a stream, badly spraining an ankle.

Within the hour it swelled to grotesque size. No bones had been broken, but I was unable to put pressure on that leg. With one arm around Lepekhin's neck and leaning on a stout stick with the other we limped like conjoined twins into Apatcha, greeted by a discordant choir of village dogs. I told Lepekhin that the season was getting late, and if my ankle mended soon we would continue; otherwise, there was no choice except to stay through at least part of the winter, a prospect unappealing to us both.

On the bright side, one of my objectives had been to study Itelmen culture and traditions and prepare an ethnographic description of these fascinating people. In my following writings about them, extracted from a larger monograph in preparation, I use the terms *Itelmen* and *Kamchadal* interchangeably and apologize for any inconvenience to the reader. It was simply an inconsistency arising from entering daily journal observations without first reading previous notations. In my defense I had neither time nor suitable facilities for properly organizing my thoughts before scribbling them down, and paper is too precious to waste in rewrites. Both terms encompass the majority of native peoples inhabiting Kamchatka, except in the north where Koryaks, Tchuktchis, and several lesser groups are considered separate tribes with their own cultures and languages, although similar to those of the Itelmen.

41

THE VILLAGERS GREETED US in a friendly and welcoming manner, and Lepekhin and I quickly made living arrangements with different families. Mine's household included a beautiful daughter of marriageable age named Aphaka. Her mother was Itelmen, but her father had been a transient Cossack who disappeared before Aphaka was born. The infusion of Russian blood had given her long, straight legs, unlike the short bowed legs of Itelmen men and women, and her skin was fair as a German milkmaid's. The widely spaced almond-shaped eyes with their light-brown irises showed a perfect blend of both races. She was also tall, a few inches above 5 feet, whereas most Kamchadal women are under 5 feet.

The man of the house and the mother's second husband was an Itelmen named Pikankur. He was small, cloying, and obsequious. Itelmen wives often dominate their husbands, so I paid little attention to their relationship until noticing how Aphaka and her mother teamed up to intimidate him. They also worked in concert to protect Aphaka's younger half-brother, who limped badly on a crooked leg that had been broken but not pulled, straightened, and splinted at the time of the break. As a young boy he had fallen from the sea cliffs at the mouth of the river while gathering bird eggs and fledglings. Many men and boys take part in this dangerous undertaking every summer, and not a few are injured or killed. Pikankur beat the boy regularly with a stick because his disability left him unable to work.

My ankle healed slowly, and we ended up staying through autumn and into the new year, at which time I proceeded north while Lepekhin remained behind, as I explain later.

I begin my observations and impressions of the Kamchadals by defining some common terms in their language. An *ambar* is a structure raised on poles used to cache food. A large family might build several near its two dwellings, a summer and a winter house. A *balagan* is an Itelmen summer house raised on poles and accessible by ladder. When abandoned in autumn it serves as extra storage space for household goods and an auxiliary *ambar* for caching food. A *kisutsh*, or *yurt*, is an Itelmen winter house, partly subterranean and accessible through a smoke hole at or near the center of the roof above the fireplace. A draft hole facing the river at floor level provides draw for the fire when open; when closed it helps retain heat after the fire burns out. Occupants and guests enter from the roof and descend to the interior by ladder via the smoke hole.

To build a *kisutsh*, soil is excavated 3-5 feet deep in a rectangle 8-12 feet square, depending on the size of the family that will occupy it. The dirt is piled 2 feet back from the edge of the opening. Closely spaced willow sticks 5-6 feet long are driven into the ground between the edge of the pit and the earthen mound to form a vertical wall. The space between stakes and earthen barrier is stuffed with dried grass to prevent dirt from seeping in. Corner supports are thick posts sunk into the earth. Roof and rafters are constructed from smaller posts secured to the vertical supports and each other by leather thongs. Closely spaced sticks are then lain over the rafters and covered with grass and earth.

The Itelmen move into their winter houses in early November and remain through March, after which time melting snow starts to fill them with water. For the rest of the year they live in their pyramid-shaped summer houses. These simple dwellings, which require neither illumination nor heat, consist of a platform raised on poles with access through one of two doors by ladder. The walls meet at the apex like a teepee and consist of dried grass. A cluster of *balagans* is often connected at the platform level by an intricate arrangement of catwalks, allowing neighbors to visit without needing to use the ladders. *Ambars* and *balagans* are raised to discourage foxes and keep supplies from being continuously wet during the warm months. Still, an occasional village dog inevitably learns to climb the ladders and gain access. This is discouraged by catching the dog and tying a stout stick around its neck perpendicular to its body so it can't enter the door. That children are sometimes killed, crippled, or suffer broken bones after falling from *balagans* is simply shrugged off as part of life.

Temporary huts made of sticks and covered with grass are built wherever fish are being dried or someone must spend the night tending to a task like turning over the fish so they dry evenly, boiling seawater to make salt, or rendering fish fat. The Cossacks call these structures *barabaras*. Little thought or effort goes into their construction, and after a few months in the near-constant rain nearly all are derelict and must be rebuilt the following season.

Apatcha, like nearly all Itelmen villages, is located along a river (in this case the Bolshaya River) for convenience of travel and obtaining fish, the principal food. Most of these places have 10-20 adult male inhabitants. Because a village like this consists of both summer and winter houses it looks superficially to be more populated, but seasonal occupancy of the dwellings only makes it appear so.

At first, Lepekhin and I lived in the summer houses with our adopted families. Being unable to hike and collect specimens, I filled the hours by diligently working on manuscripts and journals, trying to ignore the crawling babies and careless idolaters who sat or walked on my pages as if they were leaves scattered on a forest floor instead of priceless new knowledge acquired through unspeakable hardship. Not even the time on Bering Island coexisting with nine adult men in an even smaller space proved as trying. We at least had been deferential to each other's duties.

This situation worsened in the winter house, when in addition to crawling babies and general indifference to my belongings my manuscript pages became susceptible to flying embers, the occasional hungry dog that crawled through the draft hole, the jostle at loud social gatherings, and puking residents and guests. Then there was the smoke. Itelmen, being lazy, cut only as much willow and alder wood as can be burned in the course of a day and a night, and because most of it is green and wet the result is more smoke than fire. The idea of cutting a year's worth and letting it season under cover has never occurred to anyone. Therefore, my work had to be accomplished quickly and efficiently so I could periodically escape the confinement where my eyes stung and dripped tears continuously.

I wasn't the only one affected. Many Kamchadals are blind or nearly so, some still young enough to be productive were it not for one or another visual affliction. Among those with barely adequate sight are sufferers of cataracts and rheumy eyes causing blurred vision. Others lose their sight because of the syphilis. Even young children have chronically inflamed eyelids, which they rub frequently with their grimy hands. A native remedy against eye inflammation is to paint the lids with a decoction prepared from *sühsu* grass. The efficacy of this treatment is difficult to assess because both treated and untreated persons continue living in the same smoke-filled habitations. Sexually active girls and women—essentially, any female nearing or past her first menses—sometimes apply this same preparation to give the pudenda a pleasant odor. To treat my own eyes, those of other sufferers of the household, and anyone else requesting my aid I made a tincture of meadowsweet flowers steeped in hot water, then let it cool. A drop into each inflamed eye cures the itching and instantly clears vision, and because the plant blooms well into autumn I prepared enough to last several months after cold weather arrived and we were increasingly confined indoors.

Spring sunlight reflected off snow causes extreme sunburn and snow-blindness that in severe cases can be permanent. During March, April, and May when the sun reflects brightly off the snow, both Cossacks and Itelmen who take the trouble can prevent becoming snow blind by using goggles made of cloth, leather, or bark. Itelmen women find dark skin unattractive and go a step beyond goggles. To prevent sunburn and tanning they stretch bear intestines across their faces.

42

BUT APHAKA WAS MY main distraction. From the start her good-natured teasing and shameless flirting aroused in my heart and loins animal instincts lurking in all healthy males of our species. They sorely tested the chaste lifestyle I had adopted since leaving my wife behind, not to mention my devotion to God in Heaven, who had seen me through such perilous times. I could only hope that in the end, when I've breathed my last, He casts down His benevolence and forgives my sins. Although this was my fervent hope, it would be more than I deserved. How so? Because within a week I fell shamelessly into carnal sin.

As time passed I tried to curb my baser instincts by praying, which was effective only until Aphaka came to where I knelt and started kissing my ear or nibbling my shoulder, at which point any consideration for God vanished abruptly, replaced by the mindless drive of a rutting goat. I was fully in her power. I rationalized during intervals when we weren't fucking that it was all part of my ethnographic research. Because skeptics will undoubtedly read this journal and doubt that Aphaka's embraces left no time to record anything of value, here are some discoveries I've set down about Kamchadal practices and traditions.

Itelmen eat all animals from the land and sea except rodents, lizards, and dogs. Dogs are consumed in times of famine and in desperate situations like being buried in snow along the trail, but dogs on this part of the peninsula are bred and kept mostly to pull sleds in winter and for their skins. It's important to note that in my time the dog was the only domestic animal anywhere on Kamchatka. The Itelmen do not raise chickens, ducks, or geese, although all would do well. Nor do they own cattle, sheep, or goats, of which goats would fare best. The country is generally too boggy for sheep, and feeding livestock of any kind would be difficult during winter when vegetable food even for humans is scarce or inaccessible underneath the snow.

Trained sled dogs are highly valued by their Kamchadal owners, and a typical team of four with sled, traces, and harnesses can cost 60-80 rubles. In appearance they resemble the pariah dogs seen throughout Siberia. Most are of medium size and stocky build, long-haired and black, white, or mottled black and white. Some are gray tinged with brown, resembling the color of forest wolves.

Sled dogs are strong and have considerable stamina. A team of four can easily pull a sled carrying three adults plus nearly 60 pounds of cargo. If the musher doesn't ride atop the sled his dogs can pull 5 poods, or nearly 200 pounds.

The distance traveled in a day depends on snow conditions, weather, and terrain. In mountains, over rough terrain, or when traveling through willow or alder thickets, a good day might be 10 or 12 miles. When pulling a light load over moderately easy terrain a day's run can extend to 25 miles; atop frozen spring snow (March and April), more than 90 miles. This last feat far surpasses the capacity of horses, which sink belly-deep into even the hardest snow.

In summer, when released by their owners to fend for themselves, the dogs forage on rodents, berries, and fish captured in the rivers. Starting in October each Kamchadal family rounds up its dogs, ties them underneath the *balagans*, and starves them until they shed summer fat and once again become lean and fit for pulling sleds. When feeding commences they are fed only fish, but in two forms. The first is rotten fish thrown in summer and autumn into large pits covered with leaves and earth and allowed to "sour." When uncovered the stench emanating from them is worse than the stinkiest shitfield and sufficient to sicken anyone not Itelmen or Cossack, even in the middle of winter when the ground is frozen.

This *kislaia ryba* (sour fish) is a principal winter food for dogs and humans alike. Kamchadals and Cossacks sometimes eat *kislaia ryba* by cooking it in wooden troughs filled with water and heated with stones from the fire. The second form of fish used as dog food comprises the moldiest of the *iukola* (dried fish) prepared during the summer and autumn salmon runs. A third food, which the dogs obtain serendipitously, particularly while on the trail, is human feces.

It's important to realize that Kamchadal dogs are not pets. They steal from their masters at every opportunity and regularly disobey commands while pulling sleds, to the point of trying to escape their harnesses. Neither party is faithful to the other or displays interspecies friendship of any sort. Consequently, the dogs are shy of humans, wary of being beaten. Their owners are often treated in kind and bitten when a dog is suddenly grabbed and restrained, or resists being strapped into its harness.

When becoming too old and tired to pull sleds the dogs are killed for their skins, which make superior outer garments, more durable and warm than any cut from reindeer skins, which might not last a single winter before losing hair. Well-crafted clothing fashioned from dog skins lasts up to 4 years under the harshest conditions. Usually four reindeer or six dog pelts are required for an adult garment.

The Itelmen exist almost exclusively on fish, salmon in particular, which invade Kamchatka's rivers to spawn in numbers that defy belief. They migrate inland from the seas in such great masses as to displace the water, causing rivers and streams to overflow their banks and stranding fish by the thousands to rot in the flood zones when the water recedes. During these migrations the wolves, bears, and dogs enjoy a seasonal feast of fresh fish, and the Itelmen join them.

But summer is also when the fish must be netted or speared and then split and dried for winter in sufficient quantity to feed the villagers and their dogs. It's a time when everyone works. Much of the bounty is lost to inclement weather and scavengers. Constant rain and high humidity hinder desiccation, and part of the catch inevitably spoils and becomes riddled with maggots, eventually to be stored and eaten anyway. Rotten food is better than no food when the people must then subsist until spring on tree bark and whatever else they can scavenge. Crows, ravens, and magpies are common all over Kamchatka, especially near human habitations. They rob much of the catch before it can dry and become *iukola*, but the Itelmen tolerate them thinking they keep away the cold. Kamchatka is rife with blowflies, and their maggots inevitably infest the fish as it cures. They fall to the ground by the thousands, forming carpets of squirming yellow mush underneath the drying racks. The Itelmen ignore them too.

Itelmen generally have fine white teeth, Aphaka included. Toothaches are rare. So are loose teeth because the scurvy is seldom observed. This good health comes from eating mostly cold food, in particular fresh and frozen fish, and most importantly from incorporating greens into the diet. Healthy teeth and gums are attractive features of the women. Aphaka's teeth were brighter, straighter, and more closely set than any European woman's I had ever seen. Remarkably, Kamchadals keep their teeth into old age, ordinarily dying with a complete set.

I know this and other medical facts about their hard tissues from examining many Itelmen skeletons. These people don't bury their dead. They simply drag them onto the tundra or into the forest where the bodies are quickly dismembered and eaten by bears, foxes, vultures, crows, magpies, ravens, and their own dogs let loose in summer to scavenge. Soon nothing remains but picked bones scattered over the landscape like broken pottery. The bones eventually acquire gnaw marks and fenestrations. Minerals are sometimes scarce at inland locations, and any small mammal coming across bones finds a welcome source.

Cursory examination of the remains shows how little care is afforded victims of accidents, in particular arms, legs, and phalanges of both children and adults, which are rarely pulled and straightened but left instead to heal crookedly or not at all. Evidence of arthritis and beatings is not uncommon. Cossacks are a major cause of adult mortality among Itelmen. As I recorded in my journal (perhaps too flippantly), *Most of these were delivered from toothaches at the hands of the Cossacks.*

Suicide is common and accepted in Itelmen society. If depressed or seriously ill or injured it's best to kill yourself or assign the task to a friend or relative. If a man is ill and asks his son to kill him, the deed is done quickly and without remorse. Many persons ask to be strangled or hanged. Others, if physically able, walk onto the tundra or into the forest where they lie down and die of exposure or starvation. Itelmen never learn to swim, so still others wade into a river or the surf and drown themselves.

Drowning intentionally is a straightforward act, simply another method of suicide. However, falling into the water accidentally in the company of others and either surviving or not drowning immediately and trying to save yourself present interesting exceptions. Someone who survives as a result of his own effort might be considered dead by fellow villagers, shunned and forced to suicide or moving away. If a person falls into a river or from a *baidara* and tries to save himself his comrades might refuse aid, reasoning he was meant to drown and they shouldn't interfere. They might go so far as to push him back again and again until he tires, gives up, and drowns.

If the suicide urge strikes in autumn when the dogs are tied and left starving underneath the *balagans*, a willing victim might be thrown to them to be torn apart and eaten alive. Alternatively, the dogs might be confined in an open pit with walls too steep to climb. Eventually, they become ravenous, occasionally killing and eating one another. Someone contemplating suicide might ask to be thrown alive into the pit, or simply jump in. An Itelmen's best death is to be eaten alive by good-looking dogs because they and their pelts will belong to him in the afterlife.

Murder in many circumstances is acceptable. Giving birth during a severe storm is considered bad luck, and the child might be left outside to die. Children are also aborted when the woman asks to be punched in the belly until the appendages or vital organs of the fetus have been broken or otherwise damaged enough to induce abortion. If twins are born, one is immediately killed. More commonly, a woman tries birth control by drinking a decoction of angelica, or less effectively by shamanizing over leather thongs tied in knots. Insulting someone can get you killed without consequences for the murderer.

Typically, Itelmen are good-natured and happy, seeking only sensual pleasures and seldom planning for the future. They live without interest in accumulating wealth, and if they accrue a few rubles they "sell" them at the first opportunity to acquire something actually useful like tobacco, brandy, or a knife. In this sense they are correct: if money is not for gaining utility or comfort, what good is it? Stealing, although common among Cossacks, is rarely encountered in Itelmen societies with exception of women and dogs, which are often stolen because both are highly valued for their usefulness.

Despite the social nature and generally sunny disposition of the Kamchadals, feuds arise on occasion, usually because of a theft, at which time they fight using bows and arrows, bone-tipped spears, and clubs. A favorite war club is a seasoned penis bone from a walrus, the hardness and durability of which exceeds most woods.

Poisons are useful in hunting and also to deploy against enemies. Itelmen dig the bulbs of monkshood, a ubiquitous tundra plant in Siberia, dry them, and beat them into powder. Arrowheads smeared with this substance are deadly. The wound turns blue, then the area around it swells, and within 2 days even whales and other large animals die in agony. Arrowheads are glued to the shafts with a concoction that includes powdered monkshood roots. If blood is not sucked from the wound of a human victim at once, death inevitably follows. The faces of those who suck the blood often swell grotesquely for a time.

The Itelmen labor as little as possible, and in winter when they should carefully manage their food supplies to last until spring they waste what they've stored in socializing and feasting, either depleting their own resources or someone else's during frequent visits up and down the frozen rivers. Every Itelmen considers every other to be a relative with whom sharing food, drink, and sex is an obligation. Hosts commonly stuff guests and themselves to the point at which everyone pukes on the floor and after recovering falls onto the sleeping mats to have sex. This is how good times are defined and memories made among the Kamchadals. Such a gathering is thought to have been insufficiently sociable if everyone did not vomit three or four times, leaving the earthen floors ankle deep in partly digested food and drink. Considering such profligate practices I find it unsurprising that Itelmen villages are often on the brink of starvation by late winter. Not even baptism, recounting Biblical parables, and instruction in the ways of a just God can teach them thrift.

43

WHICH BRINGS ME TO religious practices, such as they are. As to their idolatry, Kutka is sometimes the Itelmen's supreme god, creator of Heaven and Earth, and other times the first inhabitant of Kamchatka. Despite possessing mantic powers the Itelmen consider him a dimwit for the haphazard way he conducts business. Were these people Christians we would label them blasphemers. Just look around, they tell you. Would any sensible deity have placed such high mountains in our path, so many rapids to be circumvented? Why would he put fish in the rivers then make us bend down to catch them? And the rain and snow? Kutka is clearly a very thoughtless and stupid god. We could have done a lot better with someone else watching over us.

Kutka and his wife Chachy settled the rivers one at a time, hunting and having children, then moving to another location, stopping eventually on the Ozernaya River at Lake Kuril where Kutka tipped over his boats against some rocks and became invisible. Chachy isn't much to look at, but she's smart and sometimes able to divert Kutcha's attention before he can make obvious mistakes, and she nags him constantly so he doesn't make more subtle ones.

Kutka is easily outsmarted by the animals he encounters. Even the tundra mice manage to fool him repeatedly. Confusing it for a beautiful woman, he once fell in love with a lump of his own shit and attempted to marry it over Chachy's objections, this turd, this *excremental bride* as I refer to her in my journal.

Kutka is undoubtedly daft and horny, once castrating himself accidentally when a clam he was raping closed its shells on his genitals. Not surprisingly, his own children often beat him and even try to kill him. And once when Chachy became weary of his debauchery she changed her pudendum into a duck, which then praised Kutka, the ultimate narcissist, so highly that he kissed it. When it instantaneously resumed its original shape the message Kutka took from the experience is that fucking his own wife could never be effected as passionately as performing the act with someone (or some*thing*) strange and forbidden.

Kanna is an Itelmen devil, clever and much given to prevarication. He can live anywhere, even inside certain trees. Tull is the maker of earthquakes. He rides a sled pulled by his dog Koseia. They travel together under the earth zooming through subterranean caverns, and when Koseia shakes to rid himself of fleas and snow he causes the earth to quake in resonance.

When I try explaining to Kamchadals about Heaven and the prospect of eternal happiness if they put their faith in God, many express uncertainty and others outright rejection. The Cossacks have accepted God, they reason, and therefore Heaven is already filled with Cossacks who on Earth beat, enslave, and cheat Kamchadals, and give us the French pox. They would be waiting in the clouds to inflict Heavenly suffering no different from what Itelmen presently experience on Earth. Everything considered, Heaven is best avoided. No thanks, we'll take our chances down here. Others flatly deny any possibility of a Cossack entering Heaven. Have you ever seen one yawn, they ask? No Cossack ever covers his mouth. Devils of all sorts can enter the bodies of Cossacks this way and toy with their souls. It's doubtful any uncontaminated Cossacks even exist, much less inhabit Heaven, but because I can't be certain I'm not going there. As the Cossacks say, *nu naher* (fuck it, I don't care).

The Itelmen have many strange beliefs and superstitions. They believe that when the mice disappear (their populations are cyclical) they sail in conch shells across the sea to hunt. The *malma* is a freshwater trout. Because it occurs in high mountain lakes with no evident access to lower rivers, Kamchadals claim that the *malma* originates as a ptarmigan, turning into a fish when flying over high-altitude waters and falling from the sky. A species of gull found along the rivers lays two eggs. According to the Itelmen, one develops into a flounder, the other into a gull. Kamchatka has no frogs, toads, or snakes, although lizards are widespread. Itelmen view them as spies dispatched from the underworld to announce their deaths. When seeing one an Itelmen immediately chops it to pieces so it can't return and report his activities. If the lizard escapes the person becomes depressed, convinced death is stalking him.

It's considered taboo to go barefoot in the snow (brings storm wind); enter hot springs (the spirits cook there); cook meat of land and sea animals together (induces abscesses); sharpen tools while on the trail (generates storms); call to the first wagtail in spring (scabs will grow on your ass); step in bear tracks (the skin of your feet peels away); eat the roots of oysterleaf (causes lice); give birth to twins (the wolves must be upset); have intercourse while lying atop or underneath your partner (salmon fuck sideways, so you should too). Itelmen venerate many animals, but in particular the bear, wolf, and *kosatka* (killer whale), the last because they claim it drowns them by overturning their *baidaras*. These animals are never called by name when encountered. The Itelmen instead exclaim *sipang*! (oh shit!).

Now to man-woman relationships. Unless a man has a wife, an unmarried lover, or an adulterous arrangement with another's wife he has no one to wash and mend his clothes, dry the fish he catches to make *iukola*, collect the bulbs of sarana lilies and other vegetables from the wild, or perform any uxorial obligations at all in his behalf. In return, a wife or lover expects repayment in sex, and any man not taking proper care of his woman can reasonably expect to be replaced by someone more attentive. It's common knowledge that Itelmen women who have the most lovers are happiest. And things are much the same in Cossack villages. Women there, whether married or single, commonly have several lovers, and men in turn pursue women indiscriminately. As I've written in my journals, in their sexual sins the Kamchadals and Cossacks can hardly be distinguished from the Sodomites and Quakers. All will stand on that fateful day of reckoning and confess their sins before God.

In summer, Itelmen villages cut entire fields of wild cow parsnip to make *raka* and to use in various dishes. A cow parsnip harvest has the stimulating feeling of a festival. A man intent on getting laid simply goes to where a field is being cut and there finds willing women and girls offering to set aside their sickles for a quick roll in the cow parsnip. As mementos they like to leave bundles of cut stalks on the ground where they were penetrated, and alert naturalists (myself included) can quickly gain an estimate of sexual activity by counting these bundles.

Itelmen culture holds that wet dreams and dreaming of sex bring a man good hunting. Either is also a cause of considerable promiscuity. A man who fancies a certain girl merely mentions that he dreamed wetly about her the previous night. This makes her both flattered and afraid, the latter because refusing or ignoring his request to have sex (which this is considered to be) would be sinful and she might die.

The Itelmen's knowledge of plants is astounding, and it extends impressively to their medicinal uses. Throughout Siberia the native peoples successfully treat and prevent the scurvy by eating raw fish (both fresh and frozen) and a variety of fresh vegetable matter, or imbibing decoctions derived from plants. *Importantly, they recognize the cause-effect relationship between the scurvy and uncooked foods, including antiscorbutic plants.* The Kamchadals and other indigenous peoples of Siberia know more about preventing and treating the scurvy than the learned men of any modern seafaring nation. Only by studying the dietary practices of mainland tribes prior to arriving at Kamchatka was I able to save my shipmates and myself while we were marooned.

One scurvy remedy used by Itelmen is prepared from leaves, inner bark, or buds of scrub pines, birches, and alders; another from wild celery, and still another from Kamchatkan gentian. Wild garlic, scurvy berries, and crowberries are also recognized antiscorbutics and eaten raw. Cloudberries (also called yellow scurvy berries) are collected in huge numbers and used throughout the winter as a preventive. Lingonberries (also called lowbush cranberries) are a valued food and antiscorbutic. Bearberries and dogwood berries are eaten too, but their flavor is inferior. All this is common knowledge among Kamchadals, making the scurvy rare among them.

To addle the mind and see things that aren't there, Itelmen value the poisonous fly amanita mushroom, which they call *ghugakop*. These are dried and swallowed whole with cold water. Hallucinations begin within a half-hour. Those too impoverished to trade for them with the Cossacks achieve the same effect from drinking the urine of those who have, and the effects hold equally well through the urine of a fourth and sometimes even a fifth stoned participant. Reindeer also like these mushrooms. Itelmen have told me of finding stoned reindeer staggering about on the tundra or fast asleep in the snow oblivious to any danger around them.

As to clothing, a *kuklianka* is an ankle-length skin coat similar to a Russian greatcoat except that it must be pulled on like a sweater because there is no opening in front. It also has a hood that drops down in back when not in use but can be raised over the head and secured in inclement weather. The hood's rim is lined with fur to keep the face from freezing. A flap made from a dog's hind foot commonly hangs down in front. This is flipped over the face at night to warm the nose, similar to how dogs, wolves, and foxes use their tails for this purpose when curled up asleep. The women's *kuklianka* has, in addition, a pendulous piece of skin dangling from the bottom back edge, but it's function is purely decorative. Summer parkas are made from marmot skins, which are lighter and obtained in trade with the Cossacks, who get them from Koryaks in the north.

ON ONE OCCASION I learned about Itelmen sexual practices without having to ask. I had just climbed down the ladder into the *kisutch* after taking a break outside from the smoke and to enjoy my pipe. My eyes, as usual, were tearing and swollen, and I had also needed to piss. When I returned I found Lepekhin sitting on the floor with his boots off trimming his toenails with a knife. His toes resembled fat hairy sausages. Although we lived practically next door we rarely interacted unless I sent him on an errand. He was enjoying considerable female company and wasn't lonely, so he had obviously dropped in to whine about something.

"Steller, you must help me," he said, still focused on his toes. The odor from his boots was overpowering. "I think I have the French pox."

"Stand up and pull down your trousers," I said. "And bend over so I can look at your asshole." Lepekhin did as he was told.

Just then Aphaka appeared at the foot of the ladder. "What are you doing?" she asked.

"Lepekhin says he's ill, and I'm performing my doctor's duty of examining him." I pulled Lepekhin's butt cheeks apart and tried to focus my smoke-filled eyes. "Hold the lamp above my hands," I said to Aphaka. In the improved light I saw the tell-tale chancres. "Pull up your trousers, sit down, and open your mouth wide." Aphaka held the lamp above Lepekhin's head so I could see. "Your mouth also has lesions," I said. "And your cock is no doubt filled with pus, am I right?"

"Yes, and it hurts when I shoot the male fluid or even piss. Can you cure me?"

"There's no cure I know," I said. "You'll have to live with it. Don't go around fucking every woman you see and spread it through the whole village."

"They gave it to me," he said. "I've heard the French pox can be cured by crushing sea urchin spines and drinking the liquid."

"It won't cure you," I said. "Nothing will. Not even the so-called local treatment made from a decoction of what the Itelmen call *katanagtsh* and to a botanist is leatherleaf."

"But I feel weak and feverish. Maybe you could bleed me."

"That won't help either. Go rest and pray the fever passes, and while on your knees plead with God that your dick doesn't fall off and you become blind and demented." I rummaged around in my belongings and found a small bag of dried fruit called *kutkunu* by the Kamchadals. I handed it to Lepekhin. "Eat one of these before you go to bed at night. It's soporific and will help you sleep. Now I must get to work."

"What's with this work?" Lepekhin said crossly. "It looks to me like useless scratching by a bird's feather making mouse tracks on paper. No sensible man would call it work. Does doing this produce food or firewood or brandy? Can you eat it or fuck it? No. And when finished you put these mouse tracks in a box along with dead animals and plants, even bones, as if such a package contained a beautiful woman and you're afraid of bruising her. Then you ship the box guarded by two armed soldiers all the way to St. Petersburg so other foreigners can wonder and gape at its contents, items a normal person would discard as trash. For this I'm forced to stay in these god-forsaken villages and scavenge on barren islands as your servant or else be knouted and go to prison for desertion." He shook his head and vanished up the ladder into the smoke.

Aphaka set down the lamp. "I was surprised when I saw you looking up Lepekhin's *mudak*. I thought you and he had become lovers, men who defile each other, who dress as women and live among them mending stockings, cooking, and making clothes. Then I remembered you'd both been baptized, and your god frowns on this practice, which in the Itelmen language we call *koiach*. Sometimes a man takes another as a wife and keeps him along with his female wife. The women don't mind. Male wives help with the housework and raising the children.

Often these strange men are very feminine and pretty, to such an extent that even a Cossack man might keep one to dress him, make and mend his boots and clothes, prepare his food, and provide sex."

Aphaka went on to tell me that women often have female lovers, each stimulating the other's *netshich* (clitoris). A Cossack man, she said, might keep several Itelmen slave girls with whom he has sex. He commonly takes them to the tavern and uses them as gambling collateral, losing some and perhaps winning others to replace them. The winners usually fuck their new possessions promptly on the tavern floor, and a girl might be lost and won several times over the course of a night, each new owner fucking her. The girls don't mind, and in fact insist on being provided regularly with sex. When a Cossack master declines to fuck one his girls she might become despondent and run off to the forest or tundra to die.

I heard a few stories of women having intercourse with male dogs, but this seems unlikely: Itelmen dogs are too unfriendly and wary of humans to ever have sex with them. Such ostentatious lechery and the consistent venery by both races—Itelmen and Cossack—can be explained in part by diet. In western medicine it's well established that excessive consumption of fish eggs and wild bulbs causes promiscuity.

Aphaka also told me that Itelmen people are hot-blooded in the literal sense as well, seldom feeling cold or shivering even in the most inclement weather. While waiting out a blizzard on the trail an Itelmen strips to his boots and drapes his *kuklianka* around his shoulders. He then squats with forearms resting on knees and falls into a peaceful sleep, gradually disappearing under the falling snow like a cemetery statue and awaking several hours later fully refreshed. During sleep his skin is hot to the touch, and steam can be seen rising from it in windless weather. I was about to witness proof of this.

45

It was late December when Pikankur said he must visit a Cossack *ostrog* to obtain a supply of leather he could trade with other villagers who wanted to make pants, which the Itelmen call *kuaeh* and are worn by both men and women. All he would say about this Cossack trader is that he was a *kotanakum*, or fat-ass. Skins of both reindeer and dogs are tanned into leather and used to make these garments, the latter being more durable. Pikankur also was to deliver a young Itelmen woman from our household to this same Cossack, who wanted her back. Whether she was his wife, lover, or slave I found impossible to determine, and how Pikankur decided now was the time to make the trip was equally mysterious. I questioned him as to why leave now when we would only sink into soft snow. Wouldn't it be better, I asked, to wait until early spring when sleds can run atop the frozen snow? For replies I got only mumblings and shrugs.

In any case, this unnamed Cossack valued his woman enough to pay in tanned reindeer leather for her return. Evidently Pikankur considered the exchange agreeable. I asked but never learned how she came to be in his village and his house specifically and how long she had been there, nor did I ever hear her addressed by name. She was demure and mousy, never looking directly at anyone, and slept on a mat in one of the corners of the room. Aside from Pikankur, who fucked her occasionally, she interacted only minimally with the rest of us, and never with visitors. She participated in household duties with the other girls and women and was always busy at some task, but seemed out of place.

When I asked Aphaka if this woman was related to a family member or anyone else in the village she laughed and told me I could have sex with her if I liked and she wouldn't be jealous, so long as I didn't give her gifts. She added that I wouldn't enjoy the experience because the woman had an old-style vagina. The vaginas of Itelmen females tend toward large *labia minora*, sometimes hanging an inch or more past the vulva. They are considered unattractive, even disgraceful, and these days are clipped off like a Schnauzer's ears when the girls are young. Aphaka had once proudly shown me her cropped inner labia, holding up a lamp so I could examine them closely.

I pointed to my documents and asked Pikankur if this Cossack might have paper to trade. My supply was running low. I had enough to complete my reports and journals but would need considerably more for pressing plants come spring. Finding a source was becoming urgent.

Pikankur gave assurance that he had watched this Cossack making marks with a bird feather on thin sheets of paper no different from mine. He might trade some for kopeks, considering the material I needed (I'd used the Russian word *bumaga* for paper) was no less useless than money, except to strange bearded men like me who showed up to eat the winter food stored by poor Kamchadal men. That and to fuck their wives and daughters, offering in exchange only a handful of kopeks and the French pox. He said this last with an impish smile. Lepekhin, whom I'd asked over to assess his health, was not amused and grumpily declined when asked if he wanted to come along.

Pikankur figured on returning with perhaps 2 poods of leather, or around 70 pounds. Pikankur's sled and runners seemed in good condition, as were his dogs. He and I agreed that a standard team of four dogs was adequate, provided they had run together before and were mutually familiar. Teams of up to 10 had been used to transport goods from Bolsheretskoi Ostrog to Avatcha Bay in preparation for the America expedition, but the terrain there is rougher and the loads had to be heavier. Still, the difficulty of training that many dogs to run together had been a frustrating experience for those responsible. Placing just two inexperienced dogs in harnesses with an established team is asking for trouble, even discounting the inevitable fighting. Confused by the new arrangement, each dog tries to escape in a different direction resulting in chaos and snarled traces. Also to be considered were the bites we would receive in attempting to untangle and separate them. I pointed out too that the sled would be carrying leather on the return trip but not the woman, who probably weighed 90 pounds. The load would therefore be less, the weight of any paper I acquired, doubtfully no more than a pood or so. Although our food supply would be reduced by half, there would be only two of us to share it instead of three, and if necessary we could feed the excess to the dogs to keep them strong.

Few Itelmen can count beyond 20, the sum of their fingers and toes, making them incapable of calculating distance. The trip would take 2 or 3 days each way, depending on contingencies like blizzards or the dogs slipping their harnesses, running away, and stranding us. The surrounding terrain was moderately difficult for sledding, and the ground was now frozen solid, traveling conditions placing the *ostrog* perhaps 75 miles distant, assuming Pikankur's estimate of transit time to be reasonably accurate.

Pikankur and the woman to accompany us retrieved enough frozen dried fish from the *ambar* to feed us and the dogs for a week. They packed it in several baskets of woven grass and secured everything on the sled with leather thongs. This *iukola* would be our only food while on the trail. We had no bedding to carry, the clothes on our backs being sufficient. Winter travel requires a parka over roomy reindeer hide or dogskin pants (*kuaeh*), both parka and *kuaeh* worn with no additional clothing underneath. Bearskin travel pants are pulled over the *kuaeh* and worn fur-side out. The legs of these extend past the boot tops and are tied firmly around the ankles to keep out snow. To provide insulation, many stuff their boots with the combed heads of cypersedge before inserting their feet. Covering all this is the trusty *kuklianka*. Mittens sewn from whatever animal skins are available complete the outfit.

So attired, the next morning before dawn we wrestled Pikankur's reluctant dogs into their harnesses, hitched them to the sled, and started north along the river at a dead run. I had not carried a thermometer during my entire time in Russia, their expense and delicacy being prohibitive and impractical. The only temperatures I've recorded have been in the towns and larger *ostrogs* where permanent thermometers are kept and carefully curated. As to the temperature on this day I can say only that before departing I took a piss and noted that my urine froze into yellowish crystals immediately after pooling in the snow.

The dogs had been tied under the *balagan*. Inactive now for several weeks, they were eager for exercise. Sledding by dog team in Kamchatka is tiring, the mushers forced to lope long distances alongside the dogs in an effort to keep the sled upright on its runners. When you do ride you sit the sled sideways, always prepared to abandon it quickly when the dogs inevitably disobey a command and dump you over. At such times you pray not to be near a cliff edge or an unfrozen stream.

I had earlier inspected the harnesses for signs of mold, decay, and tooth marks, finding them sturdy and in traveling condition. Sled traces and harnesses, like the winter's supply of dried fish and other perishable items, are stored in the *ambar* away from dogs, foxes, mice, and other creatures that could damage them. Sled dogs are strong, and their constant pulling and jerking eventually parts weakened leather.

A dog that breaks free along the trail seldom returns, wandering around living off the land until coming to an Itelmen village or Cossack *ostrog* and there takes up residence, resuming life in another location identical to the one it sought so eagerly to escape. As I've mentioned, Itelmen dogs are borderline feral and only tenuously domesticated. They live without loyalty to their owners or each other, unmotivated except by food and sex; in other words, very like the Kamchadals and Cossacks.

Late the first day we were forced to stop in a blizzard. The wind was rising, and visibility in the rushing darkness dropped to the distance of a man's height. We gnawed frozen chunks of *iukola* and threw some to the dogs, which swallowed them whole. Pikankur tied the sled to a nearby tree so the dogs could not run away with it in the night. He predicted the snow would stop before morning and saw no reason to cut pine branches for a shelter. I lay down wearing everything I wore. Pikankur and the woman removed both sets of pants and tossed their parkas aside, leaving them, as Aphaka had described, naked except for boots. With *kukliankas* draped across their shoulders they squatted in place, forearms on knees, and fell instantly asleep, becoming the dim silhouettes of hunched gargoyles as snow gradually covered them.

At mid-morning of the third day we arrived at the *ostrog*, and I use the term in its most inclusive sense. If the place had a name, I never heard it. Most of the palisades had collapsed and lay buried under the snow. Some had been removed, probably for firewood. I counted eight dwellings made of wood in the Russian Cossack style and constructed nearly at ground level with two low steps up to a small porch and then the door. Pikankur stopped the team in front of the largest house and tied the traces to a sort of hitching rail evidently designed and built for this purpose. The sky was black, hinting at a storm, but for now the air was clear and crisp. Ravens squawked and quarreled on the rooftops. The three of us went to the door and knocked. From inside a man's voice called out in Russian to come in. We kicked the snow from our boots and entered.

The burly man behind the voice sat staring straight at us and puffing a pipe, his oversized nose a sunburst of gin blossoms. Everything about him was slovenly and unhealthy, from his rheumy eyes with their yellowed sclera to the cirrhotic liver bulging from his abdomen. He was indeed a *kotanakum*, although a fat ass was the least regrettable result of his bibulous habits. Not surprisingly, on the table beside him was a large cup of *raka*. He made a motion with one hand, not breaking his gaze, and an Itelmen woman with a bruised face shuffled from the shadows carrying two cups and a bottle. She filled the cups and handed them to Pikankur and me, ignoring the woman we had brought.

We lifted the cups to our lips, as did our host. Then he motioned to our female companion to come closer. She obeyed, reluctantly. When within reach he smashed her across the face with the back of his big meaty hand, crushing her nose and sending her sprawling to the floor in a spatter of blood. She sat up with eyes smarting from the pain, whimpering and dabbing gingerly at her nostrils.

Pikankur drained his cup and held it out to the Itelmen woman to be refilled. He drained it again, then another, and was drunk. He started stumbling around the room shouting in the Kamchadal language, "I'm drunk! I'm now a Russian, a real Russian!"

The Cossack did indeed have a supply of paper, which I bought at a reasonable price. The Kamchadal woman and the woman we delivered disappeared into a back room, each emerging with a sizeable stack. It was more than I expected, and I was elated, although careful not to show any emotion. From the dust it had evidently been stored many months. I was doubtless the first passerby to express interest. This, of course, wasn't news to the Cossack, but he acted indifferent about selling, hinting I was just one of several interested parties. We bartered about 2 hours until finally compromising on a price and sealing the deal with cups of brandy.

Pikankur was by then passed out on the floor. The Itelmen women brought two sleeping mats and rolled them out. Our traveling companion, apparently a former member of the Cossack's household, knew her duties without being told. I rolled out my mat and for the first time in months lay down on a wooden surface instead of a dirt floor. Our host ordered more sticks tossed into the stove and poured himself another drink. When I awoke at dawn he was gone, evidently to his bed somewhere in the back of the house.

In the morning Pikankur fought gamely through his hangover after the Cossack abruptly upended their deal. The woman, he said, was insufficient payment. After looking her over he concluded she was no longer worth the original number of reindeer hides. For all he cared we could take her back. Either that or renegotiate the terms. Pikankur bargained as best he could, but he was no match for the wily Cossack. In the end Pikankur got what he wanted, although now he was in debt for part of the consignment. In such arrangements Cossack traders invariably come out on top, Kamchadals having no conception of material value.

Pikankur accepted and I declined our host's offer of a morning cup of *raka*. He and I each ate a piece of frozen *iukola*, then fed some to the dogs, loaded our newly acquired treasures onto the sled, and left without saying goodbye to the woman whose name I never knew.

46

APHAKA WAS SITTING ON the dirt floor of the *kisutch*. She looked up at me. "I have a roll of *laftaki* skin, which I've spent many days softening in my hands. There's enough to make you boots and also trousers. If you prefer I can use reindeer hide for the boot tops and the trousers and make boot soles from the *laftaki* hide. They will be very durable. I have sufficient reindeer sinew for sewing, so tell me what you want."

I knew *laftaki* skins had value. They were obtained from the gigantic bearded seals harpooned from *baidaras* in the Penzhine Sea. A new skin (more commonly a piece of one) is rolled up wet and stored in a warm corner of the *kisutch* near the fire to hasten depilation. Afterward, it's stretched, dried, and sometimes dyed using a decoction of alder bark. If the purpose is to make clothing the hide is squeezed and pounded with a club until pliable, then softened further by prolonged squeezing with the hands. The seamstress later cuts it into appropriate patterns. What Aphaka was proposing would take considerable investment of her time.

While I was standing beside her in thought she tugged on my trouser leg and said coyly, "Of course, you must have sex with me often or I'll lose interest and let the clothes and boots you're wearing fall apart. You don't seem to care about your appearance or comfort anyway."

She kept tugging until I sat down. We started kissing and a moment later stumbled and half-crawled to our sleeping mat and wriggled out of our clothing. She was now naked, prone, and facing me, lithe and pale in the smoky shadows, her teeth white as the finest porcelain. She pulled me to her. I smelled her breath made sweet by chewing stone fern, what in Itelmen is called *segöltsch*. The women also prepare a decoction of this herb and drink it hoping to become fertile. And she had rubbed her cheeks and lips with a red algal extract blended in fish oil to make them rosy. She apparently was sparing no effort to please me. Here lay my wife, if I so wanted her to be. Birgitta-Helena and St. Petersburg were far away, as distant as the stars. Did Aphaka love me? Itelmen women are promiscuous by nature. Talk and gestures are always amatory in some way. A westerner can never be sure of their fidelity. The captain commander had aptly described the Itelmen in the report of his first voyage, which I had now read in its entirety: *They are known for their dirt and bad passions*. Certainly, his words contain some truth because the Kamchadals don't bathe or even wash their faces, and routine hygienic practices are unknown.

Did I love her? I didn't know. Did it matter? What I knew was the taste of her lips and her hand gently guiding my cock toward her vagina.

Suddenly there were voices, familiar and not. My host and hostess were descending the ladder accompanied by guests. Unfamiliar children ran shrieking around us, one bumping against my foot. I too had become a prisoner of the mindless lust I'd so railed against during my student days at Wittenberg when I preached on Sundays to the congregations, representing myself as God's messenger and bringing down metaphorical fire and damnation on their quivering heads. The poor souls who had come to hear pious words of wisdom received instead puerile drivel from a man barely out of boyhood. I reveled in the exhilarating power of the pulpit, but I was merely an inexperienced poseur unable to foresee his future incarnation as a hypocrite and sinner.

I heard Aphaka's mother preparing fireweed tea a few feet away, discussing with her female guests how the fishing would go when spring arrives and the ice has disappeared. From another part of the room Pikankur laughed while dipping cups of *raka* from the covered bucket to entertain his male guests. Soon he would move to the fire and start cooking *selaga*, further polluting the room's air. This special Kamchadal treat is prepared by throwing together sarana lily bulbs, pine nuts, fireweed, cow parsnip, and any available berries, kneading everything together with unwashed hands, then cooking the concoction in oil derived from seals, whales, or fishes. The finished dish tastes as disgusting as it sounds, which I know from experience. As I wrote in my journal, *Even though I am not squeamish, I could not force myself to eat more than a pinch of this soap-like mishmash, and I only took it as medicine against an irrepressible attack of curiosity.*

I also know from witnessing previous soirées that clothes had already been shed, and everyone was bare-ass naked. Through all this Aphaka and I fornicated in plain view, gasping and moaning and thrashing about in our passion, both of us deaf to her animal screams. But I didn't care. I'd lost all shame that moment weeks before when we had sniffed each other like dogs, oblivious to everything but the other's scent and touch. This time, when we finally lay spent and huffing, she whispered, "I also like sucking your manhood, Steller, but the male juice is starting to taste like an Itelmen's." It must be the strict fish diet, I thought.

Female visitors had arrived dressed in their finest. I could tell without looking from the strong odor suddenly permeating the room. A Kamchadal woman plaits her hair in long strands. To look fashionable she ties the ends together atop her head and thickens the braids by stuffing tufts of hair into them cut from her husband's head and the heads of friends and relatives. The result is a composite wig comprising her own hair and that of others. The appearance is of a grotesque, outsized fur cap. She then pours fish oil over the arrangement to make it shiny. This final touch imparted by a clutch of women in a poorly vented, smoky space is what I was smelling.

Genuflections to style aside, these hairdos are partly alive, and not merely because they contain the owner's own hair. They also provide exceptionally comfortable living quarters for fleas and lice. Unable to scratch their scalps the women suffer greatly. At times when a woman disentangles her braids she can easily collect an entire handful of these vermin with a single pass of a tight-toothed comb. I pitied them, although lice and fleas are the age-old companions of humans everywhere. To this menagerie of delights we can add bedbugs delivered to Siberia from European Russia courtesy of the two Great Northern Expeditions. Bedbugs don't inhabit human bodies because heat repels them; they merely hitch rides on our possessions and torment us in the night. A decoction prepared from stavesacre seeds would surely have alleviated some of the pain and annoyance caused by lice and fleas. European physicians routinely apply it to the scalp for this purpose, and the effectiveness is well demonstrated. The plant is a member of the delphinium group and common throughout Europe and the Mediterranean region, but I have yet to encounter it in Siberia. And so we continue suffering and scratching.

Christian protocol demands that the hair be sheared away at baptism, and many women procrastinate turning over their lives to Jesus for just this reason. When they finally submit it's with much shrieking and weeping, and no amount of consoling by their husbands and lovers seems to help. Beauty and fashion rule, no matter the culture.

When Aphaka became too much of a pest by interrupting my writing I threatened to drag her off to the mountains, dangerous places to Itelmen. Peaks emitting smoke or fire are especially to be avoided. Spirits called *gamuli* dwell there, and anyone going near their mountain haunts usually dies instantly of fear, or soon after if initially surviving the encounter. The spirits inhabit these places because of the constant fierce heat, which they find convenient for cooking whales. At night the *gamuli* descend the slopes to the sea where each catches up to 10 whales. Then they return to the their mountaintops, a whale dangling from each finger, and roast them over the internal fires. The mountainsides are said to be littered with whale bones gnawed clean by the *gamuli*, but no one has ever been brave enough to climb up and see for himself.

In a nearby mountain range lives a spirit called Billutshei, who sometimes rides on the backs of partridges or in a sled pulled by them; at other times he travels in a sled drawn by black foxes. He wears only the finest wolverine *kukliankas*. He too is to be avoided, although the reason is unclear. Billutshei is responsible for lightning and thunder, and a rainbow is the colorful hem of his *kuklianka* as he flashes across the heavens.

No animal skin is more dear than the wolverine's. "Do you love me, Steller?" Aphaka said one day.

"Of course."

"Then you'll buy me a piece of wolverine fur to line the bottom of the new parka I'm making for myself. It will be the most beautiful parka anyone has ever seen. All the women will envy me, especially..."

. I won't tell you her name because then the two of you will have sex, but she's making herself a parka of white skins from young reindeer and edging them in sea otter fur. It will be very beautiful but still won't match mine, if only you'll help. I can get a suitable length of wolverine the width of a hand for 20 rubles, which is half the usual price. I'll give you much, much sex in return and even let you get on top in that strange way Russians like to fuck."

"*Twenty rubles!* That's a fortune. I'm paying Pikankur only a few kopeks for room and board to stay here with you, and when spring arrives I'll be leaving." She was requesting a tenth of the amount I'd allotted to Birgitta-Helena in St. Petersburg for an entire year. It occurred to me that both women were clueless about money, having eyes only for spending it. But it was also true that Aphaka was more a wife than Birgitta-Helena had ever been, and for this she deserved consideration. I dug around in my belongings and handed her 20 rubles, which she accepted without thanks.

"Are you taking me with you?"

"I can't," I said, knowing that even if I offered she would never leave this village. Everything she had known was here, everything she could ever want or need.

She pouted a moment then smiled and said, "The wolverine skin will be a gift I'll never forget. Each time I put on my parka I'll think of you, Steller, and wherever you are you can think of me wearing it."

I envisioned Aphaka on the sleeping mat with another man, facing each other on their sides in the Itelmen way and humping belly to belly like salmon spawning in a gravel redd, hips cushioned from the hard ground by her fancy new parka. The image gave me a fleeting pain where I knew my heart lay, and I wondered if such a response might be physical evidence of jealousy or love. Could they be separated? I was too inexperienced to know. Personal loyalty wasn't a moral quality held in high regard among the Itelmen, and sexual loyalty wasn't even a vague consideration. Having sex was something everyone did, like eating and sleeping, a part of life's daily rhythms.

47

WE WERE SITTING NAKED on the floor of the *kisutch* in front of the fire. Aphaka was picking lice from my torso and cracking them between her teeth, a form of Itelmen grooming common throughout the peninsula. "Your body is very hairy, Steller," she said, intently inspecting my shoulder for vermin. "Hairy as a bear's." She glanced at me and smiled, showing those spectacular teeth that looked polished. "In fact, maybe I'll call you my hairy bear. Would you like that, my hairy bear? Even your face looks like a bear's with that curly brown hair growing on it, and the hair of your head falling to your shoulders. Your head is a tangle. Someday I'll comb it, but first I should cut off some and add it to my braids. It will make the other women jealous because it's so pale. Would you mind?'

"Go ahead, I don't care." Aphaka jumped to her feet and went to fetch a knife. I had actually forgotten about my appearance, my face in particular. I had not seen it looking back at me from a mirror in months.

Aphaka returned and started slicing off strands and placing them in a basket. "The women already envy me because I have a man with blue eyes. No one here had ever seen eyes the color of the sky until you came. They're very beautiful. Will our children have eyes like that? I hope so. I've been eating spiders before intercourse, which my mother says is a sure way to get pregnant."

I didn't answer and instead prayed silently for sterility. Maybe I also needed to prowl the dwelling and declare war on spiders. Birgitta-Helena had not become pregnant during our time together, so there was hope. But Aphaka wasn't about to drop the subject. She set down the basket and knife and said, "Will you marry me, Steller? The year of winter is starting, but before long the year of summer will come around."

"I've told you, I must go away soon. My work calls, and it would be necessary for you to leave this village too and never come back. You might not see your people again. Also, I refuse to go through the Itelmen custom of marriage, plus I have a wife in Europe."

"You could have a wife here too," she said. "An Itelmen man can have several wives, provided his first wife approves."

"My wife is far away in St. Petersburg, and she would never approve."

"Then we should marry and tell her later. She can live here with us if she likes. And about the courtship tradition, you shouldn't worry. Pikankur is only my stepfather. He's been trying to have sex with me since before my first menses, and even though custom allows it I've refused him."

The marriage tradition in Kamchadal culture is an ordeal, one I had no intention of following even in the unlikely event that Aphaka and I did marry. Before a father consents to give away his daughter the suiter must become his servant. Having picked out a marriageable girl, a man moves into her father's dwelling. He does this without saying a word to anyone, including his intended bride and prospective father-in-law.

Once there he works diligently attempting to prove he can be a good provider. If the girl's father wants to cool his drink the suiter trudges off to the snow fields and brings back ice or snow. He gathers firewood, hunts and fishes with the father, maintains the dwellings, and assumes all tasks men perform to provide for their families. At night he sleeps as close to the girl as he can without touching her. If she doesn't like him she tells her father, who relays the message and the suiter must leave the village. If she likes him she offers encouragement by flirting. After at least a full year of servitude, but no more than 4 years, the father says to him, "She's now yours if you can catch and overpower her."

But a Kamchadal girl being courted is wily. She ties the tops of her pants tightly and wraps her waist and thighs in fish netting. On finding themselves alone the suiter grabs her and tries to cut away the netting and trouser cord while the girl screams and struggles, ostensibly defending her virginity even if that *baidara* has long since left the shore.

Men hearing the ruckus come running and beat up the suiter, who by custom is not allowed to defend himself. Eventually, if the girl wants him to literally get into her pants, he does. Having loosened her waist cord (typically with her assistance) he removes his neck pendant and shoves it inside her pants. Then he sticks his finger in her vagina. As I've written in my history of Kamchatka, *This constitutes the courtship, wedding, and consummation.* . . .

As often as not the bride has already experienced several lovers, and many couples commence having sex early in courtship, keeping up the game merely for appearances. Nobody is fooled, of course, considering that fornication is a pastime open to any and all spectators. To declare Aphaka my wife would require a public statement and nothing more. I lacked a pendant to shove down her pants, but I'd already stuck more than just my finger into her vagina.

Even early in winter Kamchatka retains an undercurrent of impending spring, no matter how distant it might feel in the midst of a snowstorm. I was anxious to be in the field collecting. I was sitting on the floor of the *kisutch* scribbling in my journal when Aphaka sat down beside me. "What are you doing?"

"I'm writing about the Itelmen people."

"Are you writing about me?"

"Yes. I want to know everything. I've seen how you live and the foods you eat. Now I want to know about your gods, your myths and legends."

"I don't understand."

"I want you to tell me an Itelmen story. Can you do this?"

"Of course. We know many stories. I'll tell you one about a good wife, then maybe you'll marry me and stay here in our village. I could be like her and make you happy. The story takes place in the north where the people herd reindeer, and marriage customs are a little different." This is the story Aphaka told.

According to legend, dogs and Kamchadal people once spoke the same language, and men pulled their own sleds. But one day when the god Kutka's descendants were drifting downriver in kayaks some dogs on the bank called out asking whose people they were and what was their origin. The arrogant travelers declined to answer and floated past without a word. This angered the dogs, and they agreed from then on to speak among themselves in a way humans could not understand. And this is why dogs bark at strangers and guests, always asking in their own language, "Who are you? Where do you come from?"

But many years prior even to this event was a time in Kamchatka when dogs and Itelmen were indistinguishable to each other and looked different only to Cossacks and other outsiders. Not only did they speak the same language, they had the same customs and traditions, and both accepted Kutka as the one who created them. In fact, during this very early time when Kutka lived only with his wife and they had not yet produced any descendants to populate Kamchatka, humans and all the other animals were equal. Kutka's wife Chachy eventually saw the disadvantage of humans sharing their authority. Chachy, as everyone knows, is a woman of average appearance but superior intelligence, and she advised Kutka to intercede and make humans dominant over the animals. But Kutka is a stupid, fickle god.

He eventually accepted Chachy's advice, but took many years completing the task because not only is Kutka dumb, he's scatterbrained. After demoting one animal from the universal kingdom, a field mouse, say, or a mosquito, he either forgot his mission or lost interest and wandered off to examine another distraction, often an enticing woman. So it is with someone having the concentration of a gnat, even though he's a god.

This story takes place during that hazy interval before Kutka had gotten around to lowering the status of dogs. As I said, it was in the time when people and dogs were the same and neither dogs nor Kamchadals could distinguish between them, only outsiders, whose opinions matter little.

If you are a young man (or a young dog) needing a wife and your village offers no marriageable girls, what do you do? The answer is obvious: you travel to another village and seek a wife there. So one day a young dog—or young man, they look and speak the same—left his home village in a swirling blizzard and walked many miles upriver on the ice. Eventually, he came upon a scattering of winter houses. No one was about, so he went to the outer-most *kisutch* where he got down on hands and knees and peered through the draft hole. Inside he saw many dogs (or people, if you prefer), including several females who from their appearance seemed of marriageable age.

A child (or was it a pup?) crawling on the floor looked out through the draft hole and seeing the stranger began to point and babble, drawing the attention of the other occupants. Soon an old man climbed out through the smoke hole in the roof and asked, "Who are you? Where are you from? Why did you come here and look into the draft hole of our *kisutch*?"

"I come seeking a wife," said the strange young dog (let's call him that).

"Well, you found the right place," said the old man (or old dog). "This is your lucky day because I have four daughters seeking husbands. Come inside and let's talk." With that he returned through the smoke hole in his roof and down the ladder inside. The stranger waited a respectable time until he was sure the old man (or dog) was now on solid ground below, then followed.

As soon as the strange dog descended to the room and his eyes had adjusted in the dim light the father said, "What do you think, girls? This young dog has come in search of a wife."

The youngest daughter said, "I'll take him and be his wife. He looks like a decent provider."

That night he ate with the family. Afterward, the father dipped two cups into his bucket of brandy, and they each drank. At bedtime the youngest daughter stood on her sleeping mat and undressed, then beckoned over the stranger. After he undressed they knelt on the mat and fucked doggie style. Everyone witnessed the act, and thus they were married.

The next morning the mother fed them breakfast and gave them food for the trip back to the young dog's village where they would live. Among the items of food were some reindeer sausages she had made. Before they climbed the ladder to leave the mother told them, "If you encounter any sick or dead dogs along the way, give them these sausages." Then she said goodbye to her daughter.

They walked several miles downriver on the ice until coming to a place on the shore that looked like any other, but the young dog, now a husband, said to his new wife, "My ancestors are buried here." She didn't say anything and kept walking.

When they reached his village they went straight to the *kisutch* of her new husband's extended family, where they would live. Outside they were greeted by three filthy pups covered in dirt and losing hair from mange.

The new wife asked him, "Are these scroungy creatures your relatives?" And she ordered them to stay away from her.

On hearing this the pups began yipping and crying. They ran across the roof, through the smoke hole and down the ladder, and told their mother that Older Brother had come home with a wife who seemed very cruel.

Before they could enter the house an old female dog, an aunt perhaps, approached the new wife with a piece of smoldering kindling in her mouth. The new wife shooed her away, saying, "Don't come near me! You'll burn my fur and whiskers, which I've just combed and made shiny with fish oil to impress my husband's family!" These words caused the old dog to slink sadly away.

Then the husband's relatives waiting outside to greet the newlyweds said in unison, "Come into the *kisutch* with your eyes closed." She refused, and entered with eyes open. They told her to go to the nearby *ambar*, their storehouse raised on poles, and fetch reindeer meat, then go to the ice hole in the creek and fetch water, not opening her eyes until she reached each destination. She went open-eyed and returned saying, "I couldn't find either an *ambar* raised on poles or an ice hole in the creek. All I found near the creek were dog claws."

When night came the husband said to his wife, "Lie down and sleep, and don't go out unless you hear the same noise twice." Again she ignored the instructions and went outside after hearing every noise. The next day the husband took her back to her father and renounced the marriage.

But he still needed a wife, so this time instead of traveling upriver he went downriver. Again he came to a village of several winter houses and as before was welcomed by an old dog with four marriageable daughters. And as happened previously the youngest daughter agreed to take him as a husband, and their marriage was consummated in the traditional way.

The next morning the mother fed the newlyweds breakfast and packed them food for the trip, including reindeer sausages she had made. And as she handed them the package of food and said goodbye she advised her daughter to give the sausages to any sick or dead dogs they encountered.

They walked several miles upriver until coming to a place on the shore that looked like any other, and the husband said, "My ancestors are buried here." He was prepared to continue when his wife said, "Please don't hurry. I want to treat your ancestors to my mother's reindeer sausages." Although the husband's relatives were actually buried upriver from the village, which they had not yet reached, he was pleased to have a wife so respectful of his ancestors, and after leaving sausages at this place on the shore they went on.

When they came near his family's *kisutch* several filthy, mangy pups tumbled out from underneath some bushes to greet them. The new wife patted them on their heads and gave each a piece of reindeer meat with a bone. They ran home and reported to their mother that Older Brother had returned with a very fine, compassionate wife.

When an old female dog approached them with a smoldering stick of kindling in her mouth the new wife said to her, "You are old and infirm and likely to burn your fur and singe your whiskers. Please let me carry that."

The old dog said, "But then you will dirty your fur and singe your own whiskers, both of which you've taken such care to comb and oil to present yourself to us."

The new wife said, "It doesn't matter. My fur can be combed and oiled again, and my singed whiskers will grow back."

When told to enter the *kisutch* with her eyes closed, she did. And when advised to go to the nearby *ambar* on poles to fetch reindeer meat and to the ice hole in the creek to fetch water, again without opening her eyes until reaching each destination, she did. Inside the *ambar* she opened her eyes, as was permissible, and saw many kinds of lovely bronze utensils for cooking and serving, and she knew they were hers to share. Then she closed her eyes and went to the ice hole in the creek and on opening them saw clear, pure drinking water burbling inside. And so she returned to the house of her new relatives carrying meat and water.

The new husband said, "Now we sleep. Go outside only after hearing the same noise four times." She subsequently ignored all sounds, but on hearing the same sound four times she climbed the ladder and upon setting foot on the snowy roof saw her husband on the ground below, transformed as if by magic into the most handsome young dog in all Kamchatka. Beside him frolicked three pups with thick, clean coats. The rest of his family members stood there too, everyone dressed in beautiful parkas trimmed exquisitely in sea otter fur, new trousers sewn from soft white reindeer hides, and shod in sealskin boots with whaleskin soles, the kind that never wear out. Surrounding them were a hundred reindeer so fat and healthy they could barely walk, such immobility leaving them no choice except to urinate on their own feet. They were so numerous that no one in this household would have to hunt or go hungry ever again, even during winter's deepest fury.

The first wife upriver heard of the second wife's good fortune and envied her. She complained loudly to everyone that the second wife had usurped her place and was undeserving of it, but there was nothing she could do. What is done can't be undone, and Kutka becomes displeased when one of his dogs mistreats another. That is all.

49

THE TIME HAD COME to leave. Seeing me pack, Aphaka had been clinging to me more than usual. Lepekhin was in a typical foul mood. "Hundreds of people, even the wealthiest *boyars*, are exiled to Siberia every year when they piss off someone in power. These unfortunates call this place 'the misery.' Those of us born here don't know a better place. We only know here and its many forms of pain and suffering, yet you choose to come of your own will. Are you crazy? You surely have met some of these poor souls traveling the roads from St. Petersburg or Moskva on their way east into exile. Look around at all the Swedes sent to Siberia by Peter the Great after his wars. They'd give anything to return home." He shook his head. "You are a very strange man, Steller."

"You should be packing, Lepekhin," I said. "We're leaving for Nizhnekamtchatsk, your home town. I thought you were looking forward to it."

"Not so much. I left Nizhnekamtchatsk because I owe money. If I return I'll be arrested and knouted and thrown in jail. So to improve my lot I went to Bolsheretskoi Ostrog where no one knew me thinking I'd find happy times along the Bolshaya River. I no sooner arrived than Krasheninnikov conscripted me into service for your accursed Russia Academy. Later I found myself marooned on a wretched island and nearly died. Now I follow you through these wilds when we could be living in a town with taverns and music and real beds. My life is the shits. Since being in your service I've nearly died of drowning, starvation, exposure, and only by the grace of God avoided the scurvy. Now I have the French pox. What else could go wrong?"

Lepekhin was sitting on the floor beside Aphaka, who was looking equally morose. "Well, Lepekhin," I said. "What do you want?"

"I want to stay here. I've found a woman I like."

"Among the savages?" I said sarcastically. "But where are the taverns and soft beds? Where's the music?"

"Yes," he said glumly. "Among the savages. But I'm bound to you by the law, so I have no choice except to go where you go."

"No, you have a choice," I said. "If I release you from service you couldn't be conscripted again. However, neither will you have any money. Until now I've paid your expenses. I've given you money for food and drink when we stayed in towns, paid for your soft beds and firewood and lamp oil, even bought your clothes, tools, and camping gear. Working for me hasn't cost you anything, and you aren't in anyone's debt."

"You'd let me go?"

"That's what I said. I'll write a letter releasing you from service to the Academy. If a *boyar*, military officer, or anyone else in power tries to conscript you, simply show the letter. And pray that unlike you he knows how to read."

"Thank you, Steller. Your offer is very kind."

"I'll write the letter tonight."

My last bit of haggling was with Pikankur. Over cups of *raka* he agreed to sell me his best dog team and sled for 60 rubles, a fair price and a fortune to him. Included were the harnesses and traces, an oiled reindeer skin to cover and protect my papers and other belongings, and a couple of poods of *iukola*. I needed to leave soon so I could travel on the frozen rivers and buy food as necessary from Itelmen villages along the way. If I waited until spring thaw I would be forced to abandon the rivers along with the dogs and sled and trek inland, which would slow progress and lengthen the trip considerably.

The next morning following a tender hour with Aphaka I dressed and gathered my things. She was crying. "You're not really going, are you?"

"I invited you to join me earlier, but you said you had to stay."

"Yes, I can't leave my village. I want you to stay with me. We can be happy here."

I said goodbye and climbed the ladder where Pikankur was waiting. The dog team had been fed and harnessed. The dogs were whining and eager to be off. The load was light. I could ride the sled and let the dogs run until they expended the initial burst of energy and settled into a steady pace.

Pikankur and I led the team to the river. He handed me the traces, and I climbed aboard the sled. It was then I noticed Aphaka standing on the roof of the *kisutch*. "*Balach dolem*, Steller!" she shouted as the team and I pulled away. "Fuck you!" This was followed by "*Kuutschang kailuk!*" ("Eat shit with your fish eggs!")

50

My intention had been to travel north on the frozen rivers as far as possible in the direction of the Icy Sea to search for carcasses of mammoths preserved in the permafrost, but I was now alone, and the futility of this dream soon became apparent considering the great distance. I still had Nizhnekamtchatsk ahead of me, and from there to Anadirsk was another 754 miles. I spent the remainder of winter along the Olyutora River with the Olyutortsis, an irascible tribe noted for murdering travelers and harassing Russian tax collectors. While enjoying their hospitality I wrote a detailed account of how they trap beluga whales near the river mouth using nets of smoke-strengthened walrus hide. Their traditions and dwellings are similar to those of the Itelmen, one difference being the use of dogs for food. I had to intervene more than once to save my team of four from the skewers. Nothing else of particular interest happened. I found a few unfamiliar plants, but my journal pages throughout this period are mostly blank.

I decided to cancel the excursion north and started south toward Petropavlovsk early in the year 1744 while the ground was still frozen, eventually coming even with Karaga, a large island inhabited by a small colony of Koryaks and separated from the eastern Kamchatkan coast by a channel perhaps 17 miles wide. No naturalist, to my knowledge, had yet examined this place, so I decided to be first.

I had barely started across the channel, the mainland still visible behind, when suddenly the ice began to crack. I tried to turn the team, but the dogs resisted. I stopped and carefully unloaded my journals and writing materials just as the dogs and sled fell through. I survived by stepping and jumping across ice floes until reaching land, arriving safe and dry but with only a few chunks of *iukola* in my satchel to eat and no means of transportation. Fortunately, the snowshoes had been strapped to my back, and on these I eventually made it to Nizhnekamtchatsk, obtaining food and taking shelter in native villages along the way and on occasion bedding down in the snow. At Nizhnekamtchatsk I was able to resupply myself, buy another dog team and sled, and eventually reach Avatcha Bay. I continued on after a few days of rest and visiting old acquaintances at Petropavlovsk. The snow having now melted, I abandoned the dogs and sled at the settlement and hiked west across the peninsula to Bolsheretskoi Ostrog.

On 23 September 1743 the Senate had issued a *ukase* officially ending the Second Kamchatka Expedition and ordering its members still in the field back to St. Petersburg. As I state again later, we heard rumors of this in August the next year while preparing to leave Bolsheretskoi Ostrog for Okhotsk Ostrog, having independently decided it was time to return to St. Petersburg despite not receiving official orders granting permission. As I shall describe, word of the *ukase* eventually reached me along with a list of tasks Gmelin asked I accomplish on the return trip.

As I was to learn, Johann Georg Siegesbeck, who arrived in St. Petersburg from Germany shortly after I disembarked from Danzig, had been named director of the Academy's botanical garden, which he was expanding well beyond its earlier limited function as a place where medicinal plants were grown. Siegesbeck and Gmelin proposed to jointly prepare a catalog of plants I was to collect on the way home for both the garden and herbarium. Each wrote his "wish list" separately, and on 5 December 1743 they met to compare them.

After eliminating redundancies and superfluous additions it was agreed that Gmelin would prepare a final revised list. However, on seeing it Siegesbeck accused Gmelin of purposely omitting some of the plants he had originally requested. This led them to not speaking or making eye contact, an awkward situation considering they worked in the same building. Instead, their feud was conducted through the St. Petersburg mail system in a series of letters in which each accused the other of skulduggery and incompetence. Siegesbeck, for example, denounced Gmelin as a poor plant collector, writing that I, Steller, had left for Siberia already a more accomplished field botanist than he would ever be. Gmelin naturally issued an equally acrimonious response.

This epistolary pissing contest continued up and down the Academy's hallways and into the new year, each anticipating in cold fury the next letter from the other. Not until 31 January 1744 was the official notice of my recall to St. Petersburg with the list of plants and other specimens I was to collect finally signed and mailed. I should add that Siegesbeck was a waspish individual, incapable of being anyone's friend. Even Linnaeus in distant Sweden was put off by his inflated self-esteem. This attitude and way of dealing with colleagues eventually got Siegesbeck expelled from the Academy.

I had arrived back at Bolsheretskoi Ostrog after my long trek north to find matters in chaos, its authorities having changed several times in my absence. There was no longer a senior naval officer, Waxell, Spangberg, and Tchirikov all having left Kamchatka. Eventually, Maksim Gurvitch Lebedev, a civilian who had married de la Croyère's alcoholic widow, was placed in charge.

But Visilij Andreyevitch Khmetevski, a midshipman and now senior naval officer, arrived after completing a coastal survey assigned him by Spangberg. Khmetevski had an unpleasant and quarrelsome nature, and he and I were soon at odds. We accused each other of usurping authority, and I dashed off a letter to the Senate citing evidence that Khmetevski was mistreating the Kamchadals. Not content to let this pass, Khmetevski wrote his own letter to the Senate accusing me of having acquitted a group of Kamchadal rebels without grounds or authority. These were the 17 poor souls I described earlier, all devout Russian Orthodox Christians, dragged nearly 500 miles to Bolsheretskoi Ostrog the year before by four Cossacks acting on dubious authority.

Both letters reached the Senate, although only Khmetevski's had any effect. Always fearful of a native uprising the Senate ordered the chancellery at Irkutsk to investigate the accusation against me. And there was more. Quartermaster Larion Byelyayev accused me of assuming unauthorized authority over men in the Academy's arm of the Expedition stationed at Bolsheretskoi Ostrog. He told them they could disobey my orders effective immediately and, if they wished, begin treating me like the lowest *slushiv*. They disregarded him, but were Byelyayev and Khmetevski acting alone, or colluding to denounce me? Was Krasheninnikov working behind the scenes, perhaps with help from Gmelin and Müller, to get revenge for what he perceived to have been my mistreatment of him? I never found out. I only knew that trouble was coming.

As if matters could not worsen, Khmetevski and Ivan Turtchaninov, a shady individual exiled to Siberia by Peter the Great, did openly collude by submitting a list of false charges against me to the chancellery at Irkutsk. Turtchaninov's involvement in these plots is puzzling, especially after I helped obtain a reprieve allowing him permission to leave Siberia and return to St. Petersburg. I can only hope he gained something of value by denouncing me when I had shown him friendship and respect.

51

I HAD NOW BEEN in Siberia 7 years and discharged my duties to the Academy and Russia. I was ready to return to St. Petersburg. Berckhan and Gorlanov had left there as students 11 years before, barely out of boyhood. They were desperately homesick.

After spending years in mainland Siberia I had gone to Kamchatka where I traveled its length and crisscrossed its width, studied the customs and languages of its peoples, examined its plants, animals, and minerals, investigated its coastal seas, and ventured to America and the northern Kurils. In the process I could claim many original observations and contributions and the debunking of several myths. One of these is the belief that unlike Kamchadals, Russian peasants quickly starve to death without bread. It was nonsense. Soon after arriving at Kamchatka I relinquished bread for 4 weeks, living exclusively on a *slushiv* diet without ill effects. And the fact that 46 of us survived as castaways for 10 months without bread is further refutation of the theory.

The annual supply ship from Okhotsk Ostrog would arrive soon with supplies and mail. I advised the men to pack and prepare to leave, that orders for our return might be among the letters. The mail did not include any correspondence for us, but we agreed to go to Okhotsk Ostrog and start for St. Petersburg anyway, thinking we would intercept our orders along the way. We went aboard for the return trip loaded with manuscripts and boxes of specimens on 3 August 1744 and arrived at Okhotsk Ostrog the 19th. There I met Plenisner. We tipped the bottle and reprised old times.

Social life in Siberia is crude by any standard, and years of living here coarsened me considerably. I can't deny it. I considered myself a pious and stalwart Christian soldier on leaving Germany, but the years had compromised both my beliefs and behavior. I had proven regrettably weak, drinking and cursing like the lowest, most ignorant sailor, losing my temper and uselessly raging at events beyond my control, verbally assaulting colleagues and anyone I felt had demeaned or dishonored me for any reason, no matter how trivial. I engaged in premarital sex with Birgitta-Helena, committed adultery with Aphaka, and frequently held lustful thoughts about other women I'd met, both Russian and Kamchadal.

Although I accept responsibility for these sins, the stimulus for my weakness is attributable to this unruly country and its permissive and unholy populace. The distinction between cultured Europe and primitive Siberia is most glaring in winter when the cold climate, frequent blizzards, short days, and long nights combine to foster lethargy, indolence, and drunkenness. When not sleeping or eating, most of the citizens are drinking and fucking, hardly surprising in a place where sobriety and resistance to lust aren't virtues, and drinking and unbridled sex are not sins.

Everywhere across the vast mountains and plains inebriation and appalling manners have always defined Russia's benighted peoples, a pattern simultaneously baffling and astonishing to visiting Europeans. At banquets the food is presented haphazardly, and *boyars* and guests reach for it at will. Russian customs at table prevail, and to the disgust of European guests arguments often devolve into food fights that Peter the Great, during the height of his reign, seemed not to notice, and few of his countrymen since have either. Of course, Russia's apotheosis of manhood is this very tsar, whose social exploits are legendary.

During Peter's youth his retinue of adventurers, often 200 strong, traveled the countryside temporarily invading and debauching at the estates of noblemen. They called themselves the Jolly Company and usually ate, smoked, drank, and womanized themselves into oblivion wherever they stopped, puking on the banquet tables and each other before passing out only to awaken later and start again. They fucked the maids and serving girls on their host's furniture and floors and even pursued his wife and daughters with immoral intent. Orchestras played around the clock, providing background noise for the dancing, singing, and target shooting; for the masquerades, fireworks, speeches and toasts, drinking contests, spontaneous brawls, even duels in which wounds were rare because the combatants were usually too intoxicated to stand. The host *boyar*, whether willing volunteer or conscripted hostage, footed expenses without a word. These excursions, typically organized by Peter's best friend Francis Lefort, a Swiss, sometimes continued for days. At one point Lefort graciously relinquished his German mistress Anna Mons because Peter admired her, and she became Peter's companion for the next 12 years.

I heard stories about Peter that even if unembellished give credence to his reputation for crudity and delight in the strange and danger-ous. In September 1712 during one of his trips abroad he stopped in Berlin and dined with King Friedrich the First of Prussia and his son Prince Friedrich Wilhelm. Peter's reputation for coarseness was widely known in Europe, but his manners that night exceeded expectations. He extended to the queen his hand encased in a mostly clean glove, and a witness wrote that he later entranced the diners by not belching, farting, or picking his teeth.

Peter did much to yank Russia out of the Middle Ages, but he wasn't particularly religious, apparently content with leaving manners and morals as they had always been. But his legacy of social and moral laxness is not entirely to blame for the present situation. The Russian Orthodox Church and its tenets are equally guilty.

The piety of the Orthodox population I found on arriving in Russia put to shame our Lutheran practices in Franconia, but only if sincerity is replaced with mindless rituals for which Catholics are also famous. With few exceptions each day of the Julian calendar is assigned to feast or fast or dedicated to a saint. No icon or image, however modestly placed or hung in poverty, can be passed without genuflection and making the sign of the cross, as I learned from living with Birgit-ta-Helena. These people with their idolatry immediately struck me as only a small step above the Catholics and pagans, and their ridiculous practices extend even to the bedroom: before sex the parties remove the crucifixes from around their necks and drape a cloth over any religious objects in the room. Only then is the situation safe to disrobe and wallow in animal sin.

52

I was in Yakutsk on 13 March 1745 when the winter mail delivered our official orders to return to St. Petersburg, along with the list of plants from Gmelin and Siegesbeck to be collected on the way back. The documents had taken more than a year to reach me. In addition, there was a letter from Augustin telling me our father had died at age 79 and our sister Maria Louise had married in 1744. There was also a letter from Birgitta-Helena complaining she hadn't been paid by the Academy because word had yet to reach all the chancelleries between St. Petersburg and Yakutsk confirming I was still among the living. The collections list would involve several detours. Berckhan needed brushes and paints, and our entire contingent required provisions.

My plan was to go to Irkutsk as soon as ice broke on the Lena River and the spring flood had subsided sufficiently for boat travel, and from there proceed on the late winter road to Tomsk. In spring and summer 1746 we would collect in the Ustkamenogorsk region, as directed, and take the early winter road to Tobolsk. With luck we could enter European Russia from the Siberian frontier in early 1747 and continue directly to St. Petersburg. This itinerary was wildly optimistic, as we shall see.

The Lena became ice-free in May. After waiting for the spring flood to subside we proceeded slowly upriver, arriving at Irkutsk just as the water was starting to freeze again in late autumn. The city now boasted a population of about 8,000, and Laventij Lange, a native Swede and former favorite of Peter the Great, had been appointed the new vice-governor. His name is important in this narrative only because he was an unfortunate participant in one of my more embarrassing and dangerous faux pas.

To reiterate, Khmetevski had lodged charges against me with the Senate for releasing 17 innocent Kamchadal prisoners accused of treason. The Senate's reply had reached Irkutsk ordering Lange to start an investigation. Added to this, Turtchaninov had arrived in Irkutsk where he personally handed Lange his and Khmetevski's joint complaints against me before promptly departing for St. Petersburg. No sooner did I appear in town than Lange summoned me to meet with him. Lange was a reasonable, cultured man with extensive experience in administration and diplomacy. He also had maintained a lengthy and warm relationship with the Academy and returned from his many missions as envoy to China with books and specimens for its library and *kunstkammer*.

He quickly saw the absurdity of the charges, weighed the evidence of two disgruntled troublemakers against my background and experience, and exonerated me unconditionally on the spot. Needless to say this came as a great relief, and we immediately went to his residence to celebrate. As should be evident by now, getting drunk, brawling, puking, and wenching are normal, honorable activities in Siberia, so no one was surprised or insulted when I got stinking drunk, which anywhere in Russia is hardly disgraceful. It was what came out of my mouth that stunned Lange and his compatriots.

In 1649 Tsar Aleksej Mikhailovitch, Peter the Great's father, passed the denunciation law *slovo i dielo*, a *lèse-majesté* covering any crime against the ruler or the state, notably treason. To implement it he formed the *Tainaya Kantselyariya* in Moskva (since moved to St. Petersburg), the dreaded Secret Tribunal. With passing years the Tribunal's authority has expanded, culminating in severe abuses of power. People across the land, including faraway Siberia, live in terror of its shadow. Even criticizing a tsar, empress, or the government is enough to initiate inquiries. Grounds for charges have grown increasingly arbitrary and opaque, punishments more unpredictable and harsh. These days a public denouncement against a government agent of any rank can trigger an investigation leading to a smorgasbord of punishments including sanctions of all sorts, forfeiture of property, stripping of rank, knouting, branding, imprisonment, exile, and execution. The victim is entirely at the Tribunal's mercy because Russia's unbalanced legal structure is without appellate courts with which to lodge appeals. The Tribunal is both jury and judge.

Everyone anywhere in Russia can shout *slovo i dielo* at someone, whereupon others present are required to arrest and immediately imprison both accused and accuser. The parties are then transported under armed guard to St. Petersburg to stand before the Tribunal, no matter the distance. Conviction and sentencing are hardly unbiased. The accused can be declared guilty even if his accuser fails to provide proof of the crime, and sometimes even after refusing the alternative of proof by the knout. If the accuser still won't renounce his charge the accused might be condemned to death and his property confiscated and given to his denouncer. Only in rare instances is the accused declared innocent, in which case his accuser is only knouted. Clearly, someone having no fear of the knout often has more to gain than lose.

So it happened that while enjoying the vice-governor's splendid hospitality at his private residence, and drunk as a Jesuit priest, I shouted *slovo i dielo* in his face—I accuse you of *lèse-majesté* in word and deed! Why did I say this awful thing? I don't recall, but the man had just acquitted me of false accusations and invited me to be a guest in his home and celebrate with his friends and associates. He was treating me in a fair, friendly, and courteous way. Everyone present was apparently shocked and promptly hustled me off to bed. On awaking the next morning to the terrible news I immediately went to Lange and apologized profusely. Lang was a gentleman about the episode and forgave me, doubtless because he too had no wish to be dragged on a long, hazardous journey to St. Petersburg under armed guard and made to testify before the Tribunal, after first being tossed into jail in the very city under his jurisdiction. His other guests, not wanting to see either of us in trouble, agreed to stay quiet.

For whatever reason—the Christmas holidays, perhaps—Lange did not send the report of his inquiry concerning my tangles with Khmetevski and Turtchaninov until 30 January 1746, 5 weeks after I left. News of his decision to exonerate me unconditionally didn't arrive at Senate offices in St. Petersburg until that August. The delay was to cause me considerable anguish and inconvenience.

Immediately following my apology to Lange I rounded up Berckhan, Gorlanov, Danilov, and the others in our entourage, loaded our belongings, and got the hell out of Irkutsk, skipping the holiday festivities and departing Christmas Eve west along the winter road for Tomsk. On 15 January 1746 we came to Krasnoyarsk, having traveled 584 miles.

I was happy to have Danilov once again in my service. He had disappeared from Bolsheretskoi Ostrog, but I came across him at Irkutsk where he had been assigned guard and courier duties. I demanded to know why he disposed of my belongings and deserted his post after I left for America, assigning him responsibilities to be carried out in my absence. He then told me of having been conscripted by Spangberg and forced to accompany him to Japan. As to my possessions, he thought I had died during the voyage. These reasons suited me, and I had asked Lange to release Danilov back into my service, which he graciously did.

Our entourage, traveling in several sleds pulled by *troikas*, reached Tomsk, capital of Siberia, at the end of January. I was on schedule to explore the upper Yenisei and Irtysh rivers, but these instructions were beginning to look unreasonable because of the great distances and slowness of summer travel. Therefore, after a brief rest we continued on to Tobolsk, 866 miles farther, arriving in early March.

Here I appealed for provisions and was denied. It was also here that I petitioned the recently appointed governor of western Siberia, Major General Aleksej Mikhailovitch Sukharev, to release my salary, some of which was still being withheld because news of my reappearance among the walking and breathing had still not filtered down to every pay station along the route from St. Petersburg.

Then another problem arose. Tobolsk is headquarters of the region's chief of customs, and officials under him were refusing to let us pass, implementing delays in hope of obtaining bribes. Anger got the best of me with this bureaucrat, whose name I forget and is undoubtedly forgettable. I threatened to bring him up on charges when I reached St. Petersburg. Whether this helped I can't say, but our luggage and specimens were eventually released, and no bureaucrat's pocket gained weight from the lightening of mine. The major general lost his temper when I did, and we ended up shouting at each other. He dismissed my demand to be paid what I was owed and later did me an even greater disservice by purposely delaying the forwarding of Lange's report of my exoneration.

On 25 March we arrived at Verkhoturye, the westernmost city in Siberia with a customs station before entering European Russia. Thanks to the evasive tactics used by my predecessors in the Second Kamchatka Expedition, customs officials were ready for us, but we had little of taxable value and passed through with only minor inconvenience to our schedule.

53

OUR FIRST DESTINATION WAS Solikamsk in Perm and the home of Grigorij Akinfeievitch Demidov, a wealthy *boyar*, landowner, and amateur botanist. Demidov maintained extensive gardens at his estate and several glasshouses where he grew citrus, pineapples, bananas, and other exotic tropical plants the year around. He was acquainted with my work, having previously entertained Gmelin and Müller, and welcomed us enthusiastically, glad to have a visiting naturalist. Demidov offered to botanize with us in the Perm region and show off his family's mines and salt works, the sources of their wealth, but we only stayed a few days and reluctantly embarked 16 May 1746 on the first of a series of riverboats that would take us to Moskva.

Then a sudden eagerness to botanize in Perm won out over the desire to return to St. Petersburg. I sent all personnel and my collections, manuscripts, and most of my baggage ahead by boat. Even the excitement of seeing Birgitta-Helena had largely dissipated, replaced by fear of rejection and disappointment. I had been away more than 9 years; she and I would be strangers, her daughter no longer a girl I'd barely known but now a young woman. I was also ruminating about the current situation in St. Petersburg, which considering the present political climate was sounding less enticing.

Demidov, who kept in touch with acquaintances at the Academy, described an institution in disarray. Russia was entering a new period of nationalism with Elizabeth on the throne. She was welcoming back the old aristocracy and encouraging its dislike of all things "German." In addition, she openly backed the Orthodox Church, which had become increasingly paranoid about encroaching Protestant influence. Foreigners, so important in her father's campaign to modernize the country, were becoming second-class citizens everywhere, and the Academy's ranks were not excluded. According to Demidov, several of my colleagues had already returned to Europe; those who remained were finding life difficult. Conversely, prospects for Russian nationals on the staff were growing ever rosier. Krasheninnikov, for example, had risen from student to adjunct, the same rank as mine but without a fraction of my education, and he and Gmelin were now at odds. Count Kirila Razumovski, inexperienced and all of 22, had just been appointed head of the Academy.

On meeting Demidov my first request had been permission to plant my live collection of about 80 specimens in his gardens and glasshouses to strengthen their roots before shipping them along to St. Petersburg where Gmelin could assume responsibility for their care in the Academy's botanical garden. I had brought some of them thousands of miles from such locations as Irkutsk, Lake Baikal, and the Lena River. A full spring and summer with roots in the soil would greatly increase their chances of surviving the rest of the journey.

Unknown to me, officials I met enroute had been noting my locations and passing along my itinerary until word eventually reached the Senate in July 1746 that I had entered European Russia. Having not yet received Lange's report, the Senate assumed I had avoided the inquiry at Irkutsk and become a fugitive, a ridiculous notion. For a traveler to be ahead of a letter or report in the national mail system is nothing unusual. Besides the normal delays between Siberian outposts and St. Petersburg, Lange had been late in initially posting his report, and Major General Sukharev in Tobolsk had delayed it further, a cowardly way of punishing me for disrespecting him and his rank and office. The assumption of guilt without evidence is inexcusable, but this is Russia.

My last known presence had been Verkhoturye in March and it was now mid-July. For all the Senate knew I was already secretly sequestered in Moskva or hiding out somewhere else. By a *ukase* issued 17 July 1746 a Senate courier named Aakhar Lupandin had been ordered to find me and deliver me to Moskva to face charges of ignoring Lange's inquiry.

Lupandin went to Moskva first. Not encountering me there he continued to Kazan. There he found my retinue, who told him I was in Solikamsk at Demidov's residence. Lupandin now received revised orders directing him to take me to Irkutsk, where presumably Lange could properly interrogate me. Every *voyevoda* along the way was instructed to provide transportation and other support as Lupandin requested. On 16 August, a day after Demidov and I returned from a strenuous botanizing trek in the surrounding countryside, Lupandin showed up at the door, *ukase* in hand. I was given a day, *a single day*, to put my affairs in order, finish reports due the Academy, post manuscripts and notebooks, complete labeling specimens and packing them for shipment, and myriad other details that required weeks of focused activity. I tried explaining this to Lupandin, but he could only shrug sympathetically. He was merely a courier. The matter was out of his hands, and there was nothing he could do. Everything I owned had been sent ahead. I had only my wagon, a thin coat, and 60 rubles.

Fortunately, Professor Johann Eberhard Fischer and his family were also staying with Demidov. Fischer had been part of the Second Kamchatka Expedition and was returning to St. Petersburg too. He agreed to assume responsibility for my most valuable manuscripts and journals and see them safely back to the Academy. I barely had time to write a brief letter to officials there explaining my untenable predicament and the hurried arrangements to protect what I could and dated it 18 August 1746.

54

As my time in Siberia dragged on I was becoming vaguely aware of a change in mood, or perhaps I should say a change in the elevations of mood. I seemed to be exultant or melancholy, either up or down, but seldom steady as a ship sailing on an even keel. The ups had become more extreme. When elated, I ran around like a madman working on several tasks simultaneously, fretting, talking to myself in German, Latin, Russian, even Kamchadal. If I learned anything it's that Latin is the poorest of these languages for expressing feelings. When downs came on me the troughs seemed deeper each time. I then sat apathetically with pen in hand, unmotivated to push it across the paper, too lethargic to reason, barely able to converse. In recent months the latter mood had begun to dominate until I entered extended periods when I felt like a pebble wobbling slowly downward into a black abyss.

At such times I turned philosophical, questioning my life's work and the very utility of existence. Have I wasted my time on Earth chasing the illusion of objects? Do they even exist? Do I? The world comprises change—events—not things. Every object is transient, on the way to becoming different. And without context every object is just that, an object. Like an isolated sentence plucked from a complex narrative it explains nothing, teaches nothing, contains no intrinsic value of its own. The features of a fruit I hold in my hand change perceptibly as I write a description of its properties and Berckhan sketches the outlines and details of its three-dimensional form. It isn't the same by the time we finish our tasks. We see the shifting changes in morphology most clearly with delicate plants and marine animals that must be described and sketched quickly before they wilt and deform before our eyes, their distinguishing characters collapsing into themselves and losing what makes them distinctive. But it's also the naturalist's duty to elucidate how the living things he describes interact and influence one another, how each fits into nature's great mosaic. Without this knowledge we're left simply with inventories.

Does God already know the names of these objects He places in my path? Or is He merely toying with me, allowing me in my ignorance to think I've named something that has never before had a name until I held it, measured it, weighed it, and wrote a description of its physical properties? The Kamchadals named it centuries ago, a name in the Itelmen language, not Latin. Why should their word be disregarded and replaced? And what of the term God uses? He never says. Perhaps He considers such matters irrelevant. According to Genesis 2:19, He delegated to Adam the task of naming Earth's biota: *And out of the ground the Lord God formed every beast of the field, and every fowl of the air: and brought them unto Adam to see what he would call them: and whatsoever Adam called every living creature that* was *the name thereof.* This is why we humans have names too. Without them God could not find us.

I was experiencing intermittent bouts of self-doubt and bursts of intense anger at small inconveniences and unintended slights. Several times I had become involved in tavern brawls. I was drinking more and frequently blacking out, although not passing out and becoming immobile, which would have been preferable. My unsociable behavior and incoherent babbling puzzled those nearby. I recall someone saying, "What are you doing, Steller? You're drunk, and like a wolf you howl at the moon, and also like a wolf you await an answer that never comes." Maybe there is no answer. Our eyes are clouded by cataracts of self-involvement; the passing of time deludes our static intellects. Nothing is real or unreal.

It was during one of these occasions that I had yelled *slovo i dielo* at Lange, unaware I had done so. And, truth be told, my present state was another reason why I dreaded facing Birgitta-Helena and her daughter. I was afraid I could not control whatever emotions attacked my head and heart. Would I erupt in a rage? Would I fall to the ground weeping

uncontrollably? Or would I merely stand before them feeling and saying nothing, allowing the air to stagnate between us undisturbed by
the vibration of voices.

So here I was with Lupandin, not a bad sort, just a man doing his
job, although with nothing to say, the two of us swatting bloodthirsty
mosquitoes and flies in the late-summer heat while squishing through
endless bogs. His orders were to push on as fast as possible, and so we
did, in silence, each with his thoughts contained. We stopped to rest at
the Cossack *ostrog* of Tara. Whiskey was cheap, the rye flour to distill
it costing only 5 kopeks a pood. We shortened the hours by getting
drunk with the *voyevoda*, a Tatar whose name I've forgotten. We were
a third of the way to Irkutsk and had been on the move 6 weeks.

We were traveling slowly, following the meandering Irtysh upstream,
but the rivers were freezing over, and it was time to switch to winter
travel. Bursts of anger sometimes overcame me, and I berated the startled Lupandin with insults. I ripped branches from trees in our path
and cursed God for having made me a prisoner and Lupandin my
idiot jailer. He didn't say anything during these episodes, but seemed
warier of me, perhaps afraid this insane German would murder him
in his sleep and vanish into the Siberian wilderness.

It was early October. We loafed at Tara longer than necessary, taking
in its pathetic amusements when a courier arrived in a sled pulled by
a *troika* and asked around if another courier and Steller had recently
come this way. He found us passing the bottle in a tavern and handed
Lupandin a revised *ukase* dated 20 August ordering my immediate
release from custody, Lange's report having been finally received by
the Senate. The *ukase* also allowed my command to leave Kazan, and
I presumed everyone was proceeding to St. Petersburg.

Nature's pharmacopeia contains cures for everything, if only we
could decipher it. Different herbs doubtless exist to stabilize the four
humors and heal aching brows, female hysteria, fleeting despondency, syphilis, hemorrhoids, the scrofula, angry wombs, peripatetic lust,
chronic melancholia, fevers, and the vapors. To redress life's myriad failures and celebrate its paltry victories, God took pity and at
least showed us the herbs useful for making alcohol. Following a few

celebratory drinks with the two couriers you can be sure I wasted little time. After taking a quick piss against the tavern wall I ordered a sled and post horses.

On arriving back in Tobolsk I celebrated excessively for 3 weeks, contracting a violent fever. I was once again anxious to continue to St. Petersburg and left despite the pleading of my friends to wait until completely recovered. I dismissed their concerns on grounds that as a physician I was fully qualified to monitor my own health. Besides, I was used to hardship. I had survived the climate, recriminations, and whims of this desolate land for 10 years. Nothing could stop me now. I intended to be back at the Academy in February 1747 and would tolerate no further delays.

The winter road was snow-covered, frozen solid, and in excellent condition. The distance to Tyuman, a town on the south bank of the Tura River, an affluent of the Tobol, was only 170 miles from Tobolsk. I was burning with fever, although wrapped warmly in heavy blankets, and I urged my Tatar driver not to spare the whip. As the horses flew over the frozen road I ripped pages from Bering's report of the First Kamchatka Expedition one at a time and loosed them into the wind, spreading his flawed legacy across the indifferent tundra.

55

I ARRIVED IN TYUMAN during the night of 12 November 1746 with a vague presentiment of impending death. By chance, two naval surgeons from the Second Kamchatka Expedition were also passing through on the way to St. Petersburg. I was well acquainted with Johan Theodor Lau and Heinrich Schäfer, Germans who had served aboard the *St. Paul* under Tchirikov's command during the voyage to America.

They are kind, touching me gently and saying words of sympathy, but what can they do? . . . . The fever's fury stokes the delirium, conflates and confuses my thoughts, but it will cool soon, driving away the jumbled dreams and delusions. . . . What makes me unique? Just that I can't feel anyone's pain but my own. . . . I wonder. . . . I wonder whether the wingbeats of angels can be heard above this fierce Siberian wind. . . . I wonder whether these same specters had come for Herr Krause on that Windsheim park bench and carried away his soul. Had he heard them or did they swoop down silently as feathered representamens of death? . . . . Or were they simply part of the universal harmony, one voice in the choir of nature's singing bones? For the first time ever I feel patient. I can retreat no further in time other than to where I've been. . . . I glimpse that sparkle of firelight in your eyes and breathe in the fragrance of your hair spread out across my chest, smelling like a fresh field. . . . . In a bursting fever dream I recall that *martyr* is Greek for witness, which has no relevance. . . . What color was Jesus? A faded tapestry hanging in my father's church shows Jesus with arms outstretched, his face beatific. His skin is fulvous. But what color was he really? . . . The night is transparent, showing off the crowded stars. .

. . A phosphorescent green curtain slides across them, retracts, returns and inundates them again. It moves fluidly, like the ebb and flow of a celestial tide or a vast, respiring presence in peaceful slumber. . . . The aurora borealis, God's supreme achievement. . . . Is that what Heaven will be like? Tomorrow's crystalline sky will flaunt sundogs, beckoning people to look up in awe. . . . And the tolling bells. . . . Why in Siberia is there no escaping the bells? These are telling me I must leave. . . . To where? . . . . Ah, that's the great mystery everyone learns but can never pass along to those who haven't yet stepped over death's threshold. . . . It's time. . . . I shall go now.

AFTERWORD

LIFE IN STELLER'S DAY was typically brutal and brief. Death at 37 wasn't unusual: people survived, on average, into their mid-30s, especially if they lived as hard and fast as he did. A man of 50 was already a geezer. Peter the Great died at 53 and Gmelin at 46, although Müller survived to the ancient age of 77.

Childhood mortality was 50% from birth through the first year, falling slightly with each successive year of survival. Plague took a huge toll, as did measles, typhus, malnutrition, malaria, smallpox and different forms of chronic diarrhea (the "flux"). Then there were the endless wars, regional skirmishes, and intermittent famines. That Steller and all his numerous siblings lived beyond childhood is remarkable. Yekaterina, Peter the Great's second wife, gave birth to 12 children, six sons and six daughters, although only Anna and Elizabeth survived to adulthood.

Steller was truly a brilliant naturalist, versed in botany, zoology, and medicine. He collected thousands of plants and described hundreds, including Alaska's spectacular salmonberry. His writings, descriptions, and specimens deposited at the Academy in St. Petersburg were mined by others for many years after his death, notably Gmelin and later Peter Simon Pallas.

Steller was the first European physician to discover the correlation between antiscorbutic plants and the prevention and cure of scurvy. He alone saved the remaining crew of the *St. Peter* when it crashed ashore on Bering Island in November 1741. In applying this medicinal palliative to European sailors he preceded the British naval surgeon

James Lind by several years. Lind is historically—and incorrectly—credited with being the first.

Steller provided lasting ethnographic descriptions of several groups of Siberian native peoples, including their hunting and fishing methods, diets, customs, medical practices, and languages, and his description of the Itelmen of Kamchatka is the only early work on this major ethnic group, which inhabited nearly the whole Kamchatka Peninsula. He was perhaps the first to propose that America was originally settled by migrants from Siberia, an idea later confirmed and accepted today.

Steller's classification and description on the northern sea cow (now Steller's sea cow) alone makes his name immortal in the natural sciences. While dissecting a specimen he correctly and presciently described its digestive system as similar to a horse's; that is, the sea "cow" is actually a hindgut fermenter, unlike cattle and other ruminants, which are foregut fermenters. Steller's sea cow, in other words, is not a cow at all, additional evidence of Steller's broad anatomical knowledge across species.

Most naturalists agree that Steller's crowning achievement is his monograph *De bestiis marinis*. The Latin edition, published posthumously in 1751, includes remarkably detailed descriptions of the biology and behavior of the northern fur seal and Steller's sea cow, plus notes and descriptions of the northern sea lion (today called Steller's sea lion) and sea otter. The text was composed in near-final form while Steller and his surviving shipmates from the *St. Peter* were castaways on Bering Island. While marooned there he also made notes on the near-flightless spectacled cormorant, common in his lifetime but now gone. When the last cormorant was killed and eaten by sealers who later swarmed the Commander Islands is unknown, but the sea cows had disappeared by 1768, within 27 years of their discovery. Of these two wondrous creatures we have only Steller's writings to tell us what they were like as living beings occupying their own places in the world.

De bestiis marinis remained unavailable in the Academy's archives for many years. The northern fur seal herds populating Alaska's Pribilof Islands, some 900 miles east of the Commanders at approximately the same latitude, were a primary reason justifying the purchase of Alaska from Russia in 1867. It was argued that the intense market for fur seal skins alone could eventually recoup the purchase price ($7.2 million), which proved to be true. In 1890, for example, income from the sale of fur seal skins poured $12 million into the U.S. treasury.

When American biologists and naturalists got around to investigating the species in the 1880s and discovered *De bestiis marinis* they were astonished to learn that Steller had scooped them more than a century earlier. In his *Report on the Seal Islands of Alaska*, published in 1884, Henry Wood Elliott tepidly acknowledged his German predecessor's earlier observations while making clear he considered them *absolutely valueless for the present hour*. In other words, either Steller was a callow naturalist or the species somehow had practiced a mysterious subterfuge over the intervening years, managing to substantially change both its biology and behavior and thus negating Steller's work.

Elliott's consigning of Steller's effort to the scientific trash bin is especially curious considering he admitted to reading *Journal of a Voyage with Bering* in which the man who penned it obviously had been in perfect health, easily capable of 24-mile, round-trip treks from the base camp to the fur seal rookeries on the opposite side of Bering Island. Steller eventually built a blind in the middle of one rookery and lived inside it for several days hidden from view so as not to disturb the animals and bias his observations. Nonetheless, Elliott wrote, *Steller, who, while suffering bodily tortures, the legacy of gangrene and scurvy. . .crept, with aching bones and watery eyes, over the bowlders* [sic] *and mossy flats of Bering Island, to catch glimpses of those strange animals. . . .* Strange animals? Steller knew exactly which species he was watching, having seen them at Kamchatka. And glimpses of them? He recorded life in the rookery for hours at a time from late spring into mid-summer, practically nose-to-nose with his subjects.

In addition to his other achievements, Steller was a superb marine biologist, describing many coastal invertebrates and fishes. He was first to decipher and explain the life-cycles of the several species of Pacific salmons inhabiting Kamchatka's coastal waters, reporting how they migrate up rivers and streams in summer and autumn to spawn, then die, and that after their eggs hatch in the gravel substrata (known as redds) the young return to sea to mature there and repeat the cycle.

These are the same salmonids that populate North American rivers and today pump millions of dollars into Alaska's economy.

The First Great Northern Expedition never should have been necessary, much less the Second. Yakutsk was an important regional administrative center in Steller's day, as it was earlier in 1655 when a Cossack named Semyon Ivanovich Dezhnyov handed a report to a government official there and asked that it be forwarded to Moscow. The actual author is unknown because Dezhnyov was probably illiterate, or at best semi-literate. He was a "service man" employed by the government to collect *yasak* (tribute) from the indigenous peoples of eastern Siberia. Dezhnyov's document recounts in some detail how in 1641, exactly a century prior to Bering's second voyage, he and two others, Mikhail Stadukhin and Yarilo Zyrian, hearing of riches in northeastern Siberia, sailed down the Indigirka River in open boats to the Icy Sea. From there the men continued east to the Kolyma River where in 1643 they built an *ostrog*, at the time the easternmost settlement in Siberia. The area was indeed rich in furs and other resources, but rumors told of even greater riches farther east where boundless furs, walrus ivory, and silver were there for the taking. To reach this place required rounding Asia's outermost point, the Tchuktchi Peninsula, and sailing abruptly south following the coast of the Siberian mainland.

On 30 June 1648 Dezhnyov joined a party comprising 100 or so adventurers who embarked on the Kolyma River (probably at Srednekolymsk) in seven *koches* (open boats propelled by oars and one or two sails). Their objective was to round the Tchuktchi Peninsula and see what was on the other side. An attempt by others the previous year had been turned back by heavy ice.

Two *koches* in the expedition were wrecked and the survivors killed by natives. Two other *koches* disappeared, their fates unknown. In late September the remaining three boats circumnavigated the peninsula where a fifth *koch* was wrecked, its survivors taken aboard the two vessels left afloat. In early October Fedot Alekseyev, the expedition's organizer, his Yakut wife, and their shipmates were lost in a storm. Only the Yakut woman was thought at the time to have survived. Thus, the sixth *koch* was lost. When Dezhnyov later rescued her from the

Koryaks she told him that her husband had also made it to shore but died of scurvy; the rest of their surviving shipmates had fled or been killed by Koryaks.

Dezhnyov's *koch*, the only vessel still afloat, was caught in the same storm and eventually wrecked south of the Anadyr River in eastern Siberia where it empties into what is now the Bering Sea. Initially there were 25 survivors. They walked north for 10 weeks, well into winter, eventually coming to the mouth of the Anadyr. Twelve men continued walking west upriver for 20 days before heading back; only three returned. The remaining 16 survivors, including Dezhnyov, then walked 320 miles or so up the Anadyr where they built winter quarters and began exacting *yasak* from the native Anauls.

The settlement they founded became Anadyrsk Ostrog, a trading post. A Tchuktchi in one of the *baidaras* that paddled out to trade with the *Gabriel* during the First Kamchatka Expedition told Bering's interpreters he had traded there with a Cossack, except that he and his companions had arrived by going inland riding reindeer, not by sea paddling *baidaras*.

Dezhnyov's adventure clearly proved that Asia and America are not joined. Specifically, some 80 years prior to Bering's first voyage and traveling in the reverse direction, Dezhnyov and his companions had sailed east in the Icy Sea, rounded Cape Tchuktchi at the tip of the peninsula, passed south through what is now the Bering Strait between Asia and America, and entered the Bering Sea before being shipwrecked on the Siberian mainland. The Tchuktchi man who had told Bering that a vessel like the *Gabriel* could reach the Big Land to the east in just a day or two had been correct. Bering ignored him. Instead of sailing east to America or choosing the other logical option of doubling Cape Tchuktchi and demonstrating conclusively that Asia and America are separated by water, he declared his work finished and turned south to Kamchatka.

Müller, remember, had been ordered to confiscate all archives he found in Siberia and send the contents by courier directly to the Academy in St. Petersburg. While examining the records housed at Yakutsk in 1736 he came across Dezhnyov's report, dutifully forwarded it to the

Academy, and Dezhnyov's tale later became generally known throughout Europe. Why the information never reached the Admiralty long before is curious. The clerk in Yakutsk evidently neglected to send it along to Moscow as Dezhnyov requested. This invaluable document containing the answer to Peter the Great's burning question instead collected dust in the Yakutsk archives for 70 years until discovered by Müller. Its contents would have made the First Great Northern Expedition superfluous. Almost as if to flaunt this fact the point of land originally named Cape Tchuktchi and later East Cape is today called Cape Dezhnev, and it separates the bodies of water now known as the Chuchki and Bering seas, the former, of course, being the easternmost section of the original Icy Sea (today's Arctic Ocean).

Steller died at Tyuman, where his Protestant faith prohibited burial in consecrated ground of the Orthodox Church. A shallow grave was chiseled in the permafrost on a bluff overlooking the Tura River. The resident Lutheran clergyman wrapped the corpse in his own red cloak, which was stolen when grave robbers dug up the body. Steller was promptly reburied, but spring floods washed the site away.

Birgitta-Helena remarried after learning of Steller's death. Whether she ever loved and mourned him or merely needed his salary to live the lifestyle she preferred in St. Petersburg will never be known. Her daughter, whose name I never learned, vanished into history.

ACKNOWLEDGMENTS

THE DESCRIPTION OF STELLER'S sea cow (chapter 35) was considerably condensed and modified from an English translation of Georg Wilhelm Steller's *De bestiis marinis*. The reference: Miller, W. and J. E. Miller. 1899. In *The Seals and Fur-seal Islands of the North Pacific Ocean, Part III: Special Papers Related to the Fur Seal and to the Natural History of the Pribilof Islands*, D. S. Jordan, L. Stejneger, F. A. Lucas, J. F. Moser, C. H. Townsend, G. A. Clark, and J. Murray (editors.). U.S. Government Printing Office, Washington, DC, pp. 182-201.

The myth that Aphaka told to Steller (chapter 48) has been re-imagined and expanded based on a brief story titled "The Dog and His Wife" and recounted in a compendium. The reference: Dolitsky, A. B. (editor) and H. N. Michael (translator). 1997. *Fairy Tales and Myths of the Bering Strait Chukchi*, Revised Edition. Alaska-Siberia Research Center, Juneau, AK, pp. 60-61. The basis of the tale is used with permission of Alexander B. Dolitsky.

Printed in Dunstable, United Kingdom